Christmas at the Borrow a Bookshop

Kiley Dunbar is Scottish and lives in England with her husband, two kids and Amos the Bedlington Terrier. She writes around her work at a University in the North of England where she lectures in English Literature and creative writing. She is proud to be a member of the Romantic Novelists' Association and a graduate of their New Writers' Scheme.

Also by Kiley Dunbar

Christmas at Frozen Falls

Kelsey Anderson

One Summer's Night
One Winter's Night

Port Willow Bay

Summer at the Highland Coral Beach
Matchmaking at Port Willow

The Borrow a Bookshop

The Borrow a Bookshop Holiday
Christmas at the Borrow a Bookshop

KILEY DUNBAR

Christmas
at the Borrow a
Bookshop

hera

First published in the United Kingdom in 2022 by

Hera Books
Unit 9 (Canelo), 5th Floor
Cargo Works, 1-2 Hatfields
London, SE1 9PG
United Kingdom

A CIP catalogue record for this book is available from the British Library.

Print ISBN 978 1 80436 003 3
Ebook ISBN 978 1 80436 902 9

Cover design by Diane Meacham

Look for more great books at www.herabooks.com

Printed and bound in Great Britain by Clays Ltd, Elcograf S.p.A.

1

This book is for Robin and Iris. I love you so much.

Advertisement: A Novel Holiday Idea

Borrow-A-Bookshop, Up-along, Clove Lore, Devon.

Borrow-A-Bookshop invites you to live out your dreams of running your very own bookshop in a historic Devonshire harbour village… for a fortnight.

Spend your days talking about books with customers in your own charming bookshop and serving up delicious cream teas in the cosy café nook. Get to know the friendly locals, always willing to offer a helping hand.

After shutting up shop, climb the spiral staircase to your double bedroom with picture window seat and settle down to admire the Atlantic views. When your holiday's over, simply hand the keys to the next holidaymaker-bookseller.

Request your booking early. Currently, there is a thirty-two-month waiting list.

Small, fully equipped private kitchen (self-catering) and shower room on site. All shop and café takings retained by the Borrow-A-Bookshop Community Charity. Treasurer: Ms Jude Crawley.

Apply by email.

£380 charge per let for 14 days.

Prologue

Some holidaymakers will think nothing of parting with four grand for a fortnight in a fully kitted-out villa on the Amalfi Coast, while devotees of the 'staycation' might invest as much as a third of their spare annual income to stay in a farm cottage in the countryside where the kids can feed goats, ride ponies and dodge the rain showers. And more power to them; no doubt they'll all have a wonderful time.

But there's still so much more to consider, what with lockdowns and cancellations always looming threateningly on the horizon like storm clouds, passport control lines as long as airport runways, the added taxes and insurance costs, all that faffery with roaming charges for your phone – and that's before you even consider the expense of meals out, the art of inoffensive tipping, or the fact that tariffs shoot up during the school holidays so you'd have to be Zuckerberg levels of rich to afford even a week during peak season at Center Parcs these days.

All reasons why there's a new kind of getaway growing in popularity, especially amongst a certain type of person, a person much like you, and it's called the bookselling holiday.

All over the place, bookshops are jumping on the holiday-let bandwagon and dusting off their storerooms, clearing basements and attics, and shipping in beds and IKEA kitchen cubbies, so that book nerds can live out their fantasies of living and working in their very own bookstore, even if it is only for a week or two.

The Borrow-A-Bookshop at Clove Lore, right on the coast in beautiful Devon, was one of the very first to open its doors to guests, and this year its fame had spread as far as the *Guardian* travel pages and one very tempting two-page feature in *The People's Friend*.

There's a lot to recommend a Clove Lore bookish break. Imagine shuffling around your own personal book-shop from sunrise till twilight, or what the locals call 'dimpsey light' making recommendations to customers (called 'hand-selling' to those in the know!), lovingly wrapping a customer's new book and sending them off with a smile on their face. Then, after hours, there's the village itself to explore.

Clove Lore consists of one zig-zagging steep street (known as Up-along when you're at the bottom, and Down-along when you're at the top) which leads from the visitor centre – where the tour buses pull up – with its concessions selling souvenirs and clotted cream fudge, and the donkey sanctuary next door, all the way down to the historic harbour, where Bella and Finan run their traditional English pub, the Siren's Tail, with its open fire and bar-restaurant, always cosy and welcoming on a winter's day.

In summer you can take a trip on one of the sea-life spotting boats, wander along the beach to marvel at the caves and listen to the music of the cliff waterfall, or simply soak up the atmosphere and chat with the locals on the sea wall.

You might even fall in love, if Jude and Elliot are anything to go by. They both came to the seaside for a break (lugging broken hearts with them) and left healing and happy. Actually, the leaving part's not quite true. Jude and Elliot met here last summer and look at them now, living, working – and in Jude's case studying – locally and every bit in love as they ever were.

Not that the village chooses to advertise itself as a top spot for romance. The dramatic seascapes are attraction enough and there's such a thing as *too many* visitors, according to Araminta Clove-Congreve, 'Minty' to her friends, the aristocratic owner of the Big House and estate gardens at the top of the village. She's slowly coming to terms with being skint and single since forever, up there in her grand old country pile, and trying to modernise, if a little reluctantly, to help turn the village into a *tastefully desirable* destination.

Sure, maybe there isn't *loads* to do in Clove Lore – very little in the way of water sports or nightlife – and the beach is pebbly, not ideal for sun-worshippers. Most are day-trippers, or weekenders enjoying dinner, bed and breakfast at the pub, but the bookshop holidays help bring guests in for two-week stays, long enough for them to feel a valued part of village life.

Plus, it's cheap.

With a bit of saving up, a bookshop vacation isn't really out of the reach of anyone, *if* you can get away from your own life for a while, and if you've been quick off the mark and secured yourself a spot on the waiting list, almost three years long now.

The most coveted of all bookshop borrowing spots is the fortnight including Christmas and New Year when Clove Lore is, when viewed from the sea, a sparkling winding ladder of Victorian street lamps and Christmas lights leading from the quay all the way Up-along. Not a single building is permitted to go undecorated, not if Minty has anything to do with it. It's been 'the way we do things' for as long as Minty can remember and traditions must be upheld.

This year, the December frosts have loaned the strings of lights and the Christmas wreathes on every cottage door an extra special silvery lustre.

Picture the dreamiest 'winter by the English seaside' Instagram post you've ever seen or the most nostalgic olde English jigsaw puzzle your granny ever completed and you'll be halfway to knowing how magical and idyllic the village looks this month, with smoke curling from each chimney pot, and the big twinkly Christmas tree by the harbour welcoming in the short, precious midwinter days.

Jowan de Marisco, the owner of the Borrow-A-Bookshop, wouldn't dream of taking advantage of the increased desire for a bookselling holiday at this time of year by raising the price, even if he does look every inch a pirate. Oh no, every holidaymaker slash bookseller pays exactly the same, whether it's for a slow and briskly cold February retreat or a bustling, blazing July when the cottage gardens of Clove Lore froth over with blooms and tourists arrive by the coachload.

Not only does everyone pay the same, everyone is welcomed with exactly the same spiel from Jowan too. Here's the new arrival now, making his way with Jowan down the steep cobbles from the visitor centre, ready for their Christmas holiday at the Borrow-A-Bookshop. Only, they don't look at all ready, or all that Christmassy either.

Chapter One

Magnús Sturluson and Jowan turned down the unassuming alleyway between cottages slap bang in the middle of the perilous path that descends to the harbour.

'Down-along's always been a no-car zone,' explained Jowan, while Magnús struggled with his suitcase over the cobbles. 'The village donkeys used to transport the luggage, not to mention fishes, coal and beer, up and down the incline. Now'days you have to do it yourself, though there's sleds at every doorway, you'll notice, to make it easier.'

Magnús only nodded and righted his case once more. Jowan's elderly Bedlington terrier, Aldous, trotted along between them, his skinny tail curled between his legs like a fallen question mark even though he was a perfectly happy creature.

Jowan, decidedly more weathered and sun-bleached than you'd expect for a sixty-something-year-old, yet still handsome and fine-featured beneath the sandy beard, persevered in spite of Magnús's silence, and as he spoke, his pearl-drop earring danced off his jaw.

'You'll have the volunteers on hand to offer assistance whenever they're needed. There's a whole band of 'em, you'll see. You'll have the running of not only the shop

8

but the little café too, as I'm sure you know. There's a kitchen and bathroom for your private use and, of course, there's only one bed, up at the top of the spiral stairs. It's what you might call cosy. But that won't be a problem for you,' Jowan assured Magnús. 'You'll have plenty space, bein' only one person.' He pronounced it 'perzon' with a lovely thickness in his voice like clotted cream.

'Correct,' Magnús assured him, his own voice deep and with a wonderfully musical Icelandic accent that had made everyone he'd encountered since the airport remark upon it.

It had been so long since he'd left his island that he wasn't at all used to this, and he especially hadn't enjoyed the taxi driver having a go at mimicking his speech patterns and getting it wildly wrong before asking if he'd ever met Björk.

Magnús had met her, as it happened, and she'd been absolutely charming, but he'd lied and said no, not wanting to confirm these people's belief that Iceland was some tiny backwater where everyone knew each other.

Magnús hadn't been at all aware that plenty of the women – and many of the men – he'd encountered during his brief time in England so far had in fact been smiling and staring in admiration, thinking him a rugged kind of attractive they weren't used to.

Back home, Magnús's height and breadth was pretty standard stuff, as was his shorn head and beard (easy to look after, he thought, but unintentionally really kind of attractive), but here in the south of England his piercing blue-grey irises and robust, impressive bearing provoked many people who saw him to draw the same salacious, thirsty conclusion: this was a fierce-eyed Viking invader.

That was not what Jowan was thinking as he handed over the keys. He was thinking the newcomer sullen, sad even, noting the way his broad shoulders slumped as he made his way up the shop's stone steps, his stare fixed on the peeling sky-blue paint on the door which back in the summer had been bright and glossy.

Jowan eyed the man, unsure what to do. Was he cross about the state of the place? He was only young, just shy of thirty maybe; he should be springing up those steps and excited for his holiday like the others usually were.

Jowan felt the need to defend his little bookish kingdom. 'Repaintin's a springtime job, for after the winter frosts have done their worst. No point even thinking about maintenance at the moment, 'specially not with storms predicted.'

The man seemed not to hear him so Jowan gave up and said the words he always said as he bade his guests goodbye and good luck.

'It's your bookshop to do as you like with. Remember, every guest changes the display on the table by the till on their last day to reflect their own readin' taste, and you must leave it for the next bookseller to keep in place during their fortnight – nice little tradition we have here, a legacy of your stay. You'll see Kim and Karamo, who were with us before you, liked home décor and lifestyle books, so that's what they've left for you. Otherwise, do as you please, same goes for the café.'

Still Magnús Sturluson wasn't smiling in the dazed, can-hardly-believe-my-luck kind of way that the other guests usually did. In fact, he was a bit sick-looking.

Even Aldous – who these days loved meeting new people – wasn't giving this guy the time of day. The little dog hadn't been offered so much as a scratch behind the ear. Everyone liked giving him a fuss now he'd had a makeover and a new lease of life at the hands of Elliot, the village's new vet.

Even when Magnús turned the key in the lock and the little bell over the door *ting-tinged* in the shop's papery stillness he failed to turn to Jowan and grin like all his dreams were coming true at once.

'She's all yours,' Jowan said again, as always feeling like he was bestowing the most wonderful gift in his possession.

Magnús only nodded, thanked Jowan and waited in silence on the threadbare doormat until the shop owner had accepted that this was all he was getting in the way of exuberance.

He and Aldous turned and plodded off towards the Siren's Tail where Bella and Finan were bringing their new Christmas ales on line and would be looking for a taste-tester.

'Right you are then,' Jowan called back. 'Number's by the till if you need uz.'

But the shop door was already shut.

Chapter Two

Alone at Sea

Alexandra Robinson had been at sea for seven days now and so far she'd managed to avoid all human contact, except for one brief stop at Penzance where she'd bought enough provisions to keep herself alive, if not exactly thriving. She'd been careful not to say a word to anyone during that brief shopping spree, trying to act inconspicuous as she scrabbled nervously in her purse for change at the Co-op's self-checkout.

She couldn't be one hundred per cent sure there wasn't a search party out looking for her and she couldn't face being recognised.

There'd been no mention over her radio of a runaway ferrywoman, so it was unlikely they'd launched the lifeboats. At least she hoped they hadn't.

Perhaps she should have put in a quick call to let someone know she was fine, but there was no one she wanted to talk to. Besides, that wasn't part of her plan to cut herself off entirely and get as far away as possible from Port Kernou.

What would they think if they could see her now, transformed by a week at sea? She knew her lips were cracked and her skin papery, and her hair hadn't had a proper wash since the day she'd run away. Quick, chilly dunks in salt water had turned her long, thick hair – still bleached from the summer sun – into crisp strands. No matter. Nobody could see her out here.

Everything was damp on board the *Dagalien*, Alex's twenty-seven-foot river cruiser, which, even though a relic of her father's from the 1980s, was perfectly adequate for her impromptu sea escapade. The rear cabin allowed her to sleep in relative comfort. There was a fresh water supply and a kettle for coffees and instant ramen (though she'd have given almost anything for a proper roast dinner about now), and even a porta-potty behind a folding door but still, the boat hadn't been designed for luxury, or to facilitate a heartbroken woman's mad dash to get the hell out of Cornwall.

Until now, it had barely deviated from its easy back and forth over the Fal estuary where Alex had operated her ferry service for tourists and locals for eight long years, having taken it over from her dad when he passed away just as she was fresh out of high school with a clutch of A-levels, finding herself orphaned at aged eighteen and with a house and ready-made business to run.

Running away, or rather, sailing away, had seemed the only rational thing to do last week and she hadn't been at sea long enough for the frenzied state to pass. She was still fizzing with anger and hurt, but there was a sneaking sense of shame and guilt emerging that she didn't like and was trying to ignore.

Coming home from a long day's ferrying to find your boyfriend hurriedly buttoning his shirt while your best friend cowers on the sofa will do that to a woman; make them inclined to bolt.

Alex hadn't stopped to think. She hadn't said a word. She'd turned on the heel of her flat boots (Ben was sensitive of his five feet seven inches in comparison to her six foot, so she'd been wearing flats for ages) and run all the way back to the jetty. Here, she'd drawn the wet weather canopy over the cockpit and clipped it into place before starting up the motor and gliding right out of the Roseland peninsula, where she'd lived for all of her twenty-six years, leaving Port Kernou far behind.

She'd consulted her charts and set a slow northerly course around the headland, hugging the land but trying not to draw attention to herself, a lone boatswoman in a vintage tub.

She had no idea where she was going or what she'd do when she got there, and all the while she shouted livid curses out into the waves, damning Eve, the woman she'd considered her best friend since she'd rocked up in Alex's village only a year ago to run the post office. She'd suspected Ben had fancied her from the start. Damn him as well, she told the dark water.

Eve had always seemed so sad and so put-upon. Alex would spend hours by the ferry mooring listening to her bemoaning her scruffy, inattentive, layabout husband who she supported with her wages. Their son spent a few hours a week at pre-school and Eve's husband Maxwell was proving to be an at-home daddy of the 'bare minimum effort' type. Alex had absorbed it all, and felt truly sorry for her friend.

Had Eve been slagging off lazy Maxwell to Ben as well? They'd obviously got to know each other much better than she'd been aware during their curry and quiz Friday nights at the Rising Sun. The very thought of them sneaking about behind her back made her stomach pinch painfully and her eyes burn.

The charts and weather-watching should have had her full attention as she sailed, but instead her brain wanted to replay the moment she'd discovered them, the cushions scattered everywhere and Ben fastening his shirt with shaky fingers.

'It's not how it looks,' Ben had dared to say. At least he'd had the decency to look immediately ashamed.

The betrayal was the worst bit. It was like something you'd read in the gossip mags.

Take a Break would love it. She could picture it now. The headline would read, *My Best Mate Stole My Man*, and there'd be a large picture of Alex looking all forlorn and stoic staring down the camera lens. She had zero plans to ring the magazines, though. For as long as she could remember she'd craved peace and privacy.

She had, nonetheless, considered phoning Ben's parents, just to let them know what he'd been up to. After all, she'd been part of the Thomas family for ages. How much had he told them, she wondered? Probably not enough to tarnish his apple-of-their-eye status. Soon, Eve would replace her in the Thomas family. This sent sadness blooming through her chest.

Actually, *that* hurt more than the betrayal. The affair, or whatever it was, had ousted Alex from her spot at their table. Now she had nobody.

Everyone in Port Kernou knew she had no parents of her own, no siblings or aunts and uncles, not even a spare grandparent or a second cousin of any kind, and the village had flocked around her back when her lovely dad died, but seeing how quickly she'd accepted her new line of work and how well she'd managed her independence, they'd soon left her to it. Then, after years going it alone, she'd met Ben and life seemed to begin again. She'd enjoyed being part of a family.

She'd even called Mr and Mrs Thomas 'Mum' and 'Dad' and while those words had never quite brought back the feeling of being with her own parents in her own family home, it had been the closest she was ever going to get, and she'd felt part of something happy and cosy. The Thomas family was massive, with cousins in every nearby village, and there was always someone around to have a cup of tea with when she popped in to Ben's parents' place. She wasn't at all ready to admit that she'd loved that family feeling a tiny bit more than she'd loved Ben.

Finding herself crying at the helm yet again she gave herself a sharp talking to about needing to keep her wits about her, out here all by herself. Everyone in Cornwall knew the dangers and there wasn't one of them untouched by a loss at sea at some point in their family history.

She kept her eyes on the horizon, avoiding the deeper water that she was afraid of, while navigating sandbars, rocks and wrecks, and dropping anchor to rest or to cry whenever she felt like it, always making sure the solar panels that helped power some of the dashboard instruments and the equipment in the tiny kitchenette were wiped clean.

There'd been a few hairy moments around Land's End where she'd been afraid to sail after sundown, but somewhere around day three she'd settled into a fine routine of sailing a little, turning in wide aimless circles just to slow her journey, stopping to watch the seals or racing the dolphins whenever they appeared alongside her, and drinking endless cups of black tea, huddled inside her father's long leather ferryman's coat from decades ago and still somehow smelling of him; Paco Rabanne, sea salt, tobacco, and pure love like only a good dad can give.

She tried not to think of what he'd have to say about all this, the absolute *talking to* he'd give her about needing to head straight for shore and a nice B&B with a bar stocked with brandy where she could get her head straight and have a long, hot bath.

That had been his cure for almost everything. 'You'll feel better after a nice long bath,' he'd tell her in those early days when she was desperately missing her mum and couldn't get to sleep, or when she had a tummy ache or a cold.

After she'd had a long soak he'd sing her fisherfolk songs and tell stories about mermaids and kelpies in his soft Cornish accent and, even when she was a young teen, he'd rock her in his arms like the *Dagalien* was rocking her now.

What was she doing? Maybe she should head for land? It was only a week until Christmas. Surely she couldn't spend it alone at sea?

She'd been looking forward to a family dinner round Ben's mum and dad's and a few days in front of the telly with the ferry moored up, but that had gone out the window along with her three-and-a-half-year-long relationship and a million promises that he'd move in to her dad's place with her one day. It was always maybe next year, or maybe once his car was paid off – or maybe never, with Ben.

All that was over now, along with her striving to be settled like a normal couple looking to the future and hoping that one day it would come back to her – that feeling of contented homeliness that she could just about remember from when she was little. She'd been willing to overlook how much hard work Ben was, and how – it was beginning to strike her now – indifferent he could be.

Her plans for a cosy, easy future with no more shocks and no more losses were shot to bits now. She'd lost Ben, his family, Eve, and now Christmas: all gone. Life had snatched every last bit of comfort away from her and she simply could not face her empty house reminding her of that fact, like a great big 'I told you so'.

The silence there would be hideous, especially at this time of year, and she'd have nothing to do but sit there thinking about how she'd let herself get comfy with Ben and the Thomases even when deep, deep down she'd worried she was on the wrong path with the wrong person. It was just that, when she was passing the veggies around his mum's dinner table or going to Thomas family weddings and parties, her vague misgivings about Ben were so very easy to ignore. She'd been as close to happy with him as she knew how to be since her dad died.

She knew too that if she hadn't got in her boat and bolted, if she'd stayed at home over the holidays, everyone would have come knocking at her door.

Eve would have been there, crying and apologetic – or maybe smug and triumphant? Either way, Alex couldn't bear the thought of seeing her. Mrs Thomas would *definitely* have been crying and saying how she didn't want the break-up to change things between them, even though nothing could possibly remain the same now.

Then there'd have been the whispers going round Port Kernou. It was that kind of place. She'd have given it to four o'clock the next day for the first of the lasagnes to arrive. Well-wishers and nosey parkers, the whiskery harbourside old timers and her school pals, they'd know all about it by now and it would be 'Poor Alex!' all over again, just like when her mum died; just like after Dad.

For months of her twenty-six years she'd lived off donated lasagnes and 'let me know if there's anything you need' (always said with the same pinch-browed concern). It was only people being kind, of course, but she couldn't help feeling bitter now. Everyone is always '*so* sorry' until they're spotted later that same day on Facebook grinning in selfies out and about, forgetting all about how 'heart-broken' they'd said they were on her doorstep.

Alex had had enough of that kind of attention, and Ben's cheating risked bringing it all back to her doorstep once more. There was no way she was sticking around to find out if she was at the eye of another pity storm.

She wanted solitude and to be where nobody knew her, and she wanted to be alone on her dad's boat, where she felt his presence the most. The feeling of going some-where in the *Dagalien* was certainly better than going home and facing December's brutal emptiness head on.

She'd have kept sailing too, if it hadn't been for that great tower of cumulonimbus just offshore.

When she set off from Port Kernou it had been a calm and misty winter's day; now the clouds claimed half the sky and reached up so far it hurt her neck to contemplate them; a mass of grey the likes of which she'd never seen before. It turned the water around her a deep, foreboding black like ink in a pot.

Perhaps she'd have made it all the way to Scotland, or Bergen, or Iceland maybe, if it hadn't been for the one-hundred-year storms intent on playing havoc with mellow old Clove Lore and her own little boat which today, on December the nineteenth, just so happened to be approaching the village's harbour mouth, where on brighter days the sunfish flap their fins over blue shallows. Alex had no idea her journey was about to end in Devon.

Meanwhile, in spite of the clouds gathering and the early weather warnings that foretold of storms expected to break over land in the coming days, nobody in Clove Lore yet knew how monumental, how life-altering, they would be. Everyone was simply going about their days, waiting in for Amazon deliveries, wrapping gifts, baking and buying, lighting hearth fires and getting ready to settle in for a well-earned holiday rest.

Chapter Three

The Siren's Tail

'The usual?' enquired Finan from behind the bar, where the ancient sound system was belting out some festive Mariah Carey and drowning out the swirling, icy winds outside.

The nautical knick-knackery that decorated the walls all year round had been draped with tinsel and plastic holly garlands. A fire blazed in the wide hearth and the lights on the pub's plastic tree flashed gaudily. Jude Crawley, who loved Christmas, thought it was gorgeous.

'Please,' she replied and the landlord, a true silver fox, set about making her Coke with ice and lemon.

Elliot was with Jude, as always. The pair were basically inseparable now that Elliot had put a tricky few months and a tangled, unhappy stretch of unemployment behind him, establishing himself at the veterinary surgery over the headland as the authority on domestic animals.

Jude was permanently to be seen lugging around a tote bag full of books for her postgrad course on book history and conservation. She was also never seen without a Tupperware carry-case of cakes and biscuits – the product of her small business which supplemented her studies and allowed her to follow in her Scottish baking family's footsteps. She'd drunk for free at the Siren ever since she started providing their weekly drop of almond biscotti and sultana scones.

Most of the tables were occupied with festive holiday-makers forced off the beach and cliff walks by the rising wind. Their chatter lifted the volume in the bar room to Christmas party levels.

'Fully booked for Christmas?' Elliot asked Finan as the landlord placed a long glass of milk in front of him. Elliot had decided not so long ago that if he was going to maintain the abs he'd worked so hard to attain while still helping Jude taste-test her new baking repertoire he'd have to switch something out, so it was goodbye Finan's draught IPAs and hello semi-skimmed for him.

'Yep,' Finan told him as his wife Bella joined him at the pumps. 'No room at the inn and two services for Christmas day lunch; noon and three o'clock. It's going to be a busy one.'

'Thank goodness,' Bella added in a tone that made Jude wonder if the Siren's Tail was still struggling after a sluggish autumn. She didn't say anything, only smiled and ordered some of the scampi bar snacks Finan had introduced for winter.

'One scampi tapas,' Bella called through to the kitchens.

'Aye aye, captain,' called back Monty Bickleigh, the pub's new chef. He'd been forced off the fishing boat he shared with his brother and into cooking for pub patrons by the financial impossibility of making enough money to get through another year. His brother, Tom, was out there on the water now in their late father's boat trying to make ends meet while Monty tipped the bag of frozen scampi, trawled from the north-east Atlantic on some lucky beggar's massive money-making boat, no doubt, into the fryer.

Just as Elliot was telling the bar about the recent rise in cases of kennel cough amongst his furry patients the pub door opened and Jowan and Aldous were almost blown inside. Jowan struggled a little to latch the door against the wind – nothing unusual for this time of year.

The pub was well used to having seafoam and salt hurled at it, having stood in its exposed position right out on the harbour wall for near on two hundred and fifty years, its stony shoulders huddled against the blast while its front door faced the calmer harbour shielded by the long concrete cobb that stretched its arms around the moored boats and stony beach in a big protective hug.

Bella was already pouring Jowan's half pint by the time he'd hung his coat by the door and Aldous had claimed his spot in front of the fire, since today there were no outsider dogs daring to make themselves at home on what he very much considered to be *his* hearth rug.

'New Borrowers arrived, then?' Finan never failed to be amused by his name for the bookshop holidaymakers. He smiled as he took Jowan's coins.

'That he has.' Jowan scratched at his grizzled chops with a tattooed hand (a faded blue anchor had stretched from his thumb to his wrist since he was a wayward teen), before taking a drink and declaring the latest guest ale, 'Not bad at all.'

'He's travelling by himself, isn't he?' Jude asked. 'I remember him emailing a while back to say he wouldn't be bringing someone with him after all.'

Jude and Elliot had recently helped update the shop's booking system from a paper ledger scrawled with Jowan's pencil marks to a spreadsheet. Now it was Jude's job to handle the email enquiries and any changes to the waiting list.

'S'right,' said Jowan. 'Magnús, his name is. His girl-friend was comin' with him once upon a time; now he's alone. And I'm not surprised, judging by the scowl he's got on 'im. You'd think he'd been sent to a prison island, not my pretty bookshop.'

Elliot and Jude's eyes met. Each knew what the other was thinking. Only Elliot said it aloud. 'Better not tell Mrs Crocombe he's single. She'll have him paired off with one of the local girls by lunchtime tomorrow.'

'What local girls?' put in Monty, emerging from the kitchen and setting down a bowl of golden scampi between Elliot and Jude. Two forks, two lemon wedges. He knew this pair and their cutesy ways. They shared everything. 'Last time I looked there weren't any.'

'You'll meet someone, Monty,' Jude told him, scanning the room. 'There's loads of people staying at the pub over Christmas.'

She adored a love story almost as much as Mrs Crocombe. Although the village matchmaker had ulterior motives, everyone knew. Mrs C.'s daughter was the head teacher at the local school and with their roll dwind-ling she wanted to encourage as many breeding pairs into Clove Lore captivity as possible in order to keep her daughter in a job. Local Authority cuts were always looming and the councillors would think nothing of bussing the few local kids off to schools forty minutes inland if it meant closing a half empty school and saving money.

'Christmas is for families, and couples,' Monty said, morosely, nodding at the inn guests swigging their coffees and ciders. 'Not singles' holidays by the sea. I'll have to wait for spring season to bring the hen dos and wedding parties back in.'

He seemed to get lost in memories of how well he and his charming brother did for long romantic summer nights with out-of-town women in bridesmaid dresses, until Bella reminded him that Jowan would be needing to be fed too, and he sloped back to the kitchen with his order – a prawn sandwich on granary bread with the inn's homemade pink mayo. Well worth the eight pounds eighty and delicious with a local beer.

Aldous only lifted an eyebrow at hearing his master ordering food, possibly wistfully remembering the days, pre doggie health kick, when he'd lived off the pub's cheese butties and chicken soup.

Elliot always seemed to understand the mutt and threw Aldous one of the biscuit bones from the jar by the pumps. It landed only an inch from Aldous's nose but he turned his head away from it, sulking. Nothing could replace his love of red Leicester on white bread.

The vet only nodded in acceptance and turned back to the group whose attentions had been taken by the news on the radio of the worsening weather.

'*Storm Minnie has been upgraded from a yellow to amber weather warning, wind gusts of up to 80 miles an hour are expected,*' the announcer said, and everyone in the bar glanced at one another. Not that the locals were too worried. This was coastal Devon, after all. High winds and rain were nothing they couldn't sit out.

Monty returned from the kitchen with Jowan's sandwich and stayed to prop up the bar. 'Someone should tell your Borrower about Storm Minnie,' he said.

'He's from Iceland,' Jowan reminded everyone. 'Surely he'll be used to worse than this.' Jowan took a bite, making

Marie Rose sauce and frilly lettuce ooze out between the bread.

'Hardy, Icelanders are, I imagine,' Finan added.

'Still, we should pop in and see him, shouldn't we?' Jude told Elliot, placing her fork down on their now empty plate. 'Make sure Magnús has everything he needs?'

'That'll be our cue to leave,' Elliot announced, lifting his long, athletic body off the bar stool as the pub door opened and everyone turned, expecting the mysterious, grumpy Icelander to step inside as though just talking about him had summoned him.

Instead a dripping hooded Barbour rustled through the door, and somewhere underneath it was Minty. Behind her, shaking a green golf umbrella, was Bovis, her red-faced estate manager.

Elliot threw Jude a look that begged her to hurry up with her coat and scarf. Now they definitely weren't hanging about.

Minty marched up to the bar, passing her coat to Bovis to deal with. Everything she did was brisk and clipped, as though she permanently had a debutante ball to attend in the next ten minutes and the whole thing would fall apart without her.

Bella set down a double gin and tonic for her without Minty having to ask. Bovis never drank anything on these visits. He leaned on the counter behind his employer, watching everyone talk. It was extremely disconcerting.

'Bally donkeys!' Minty said, smoothing her yellow-blonde bob before taking a long drink.

'Everything all right?' Jude asked, making Elliot wince. He'd thrown on his coat and was making for the door already. Any longer and he'd be inveigled in another of Minty's barmy local traditions and he'd had enough of them to last a lifetime, but Jude was forever interested in the local goings-on.

Minty continued. 'Do you think that raggedy old Moira will get out of her stall when the wind's up? No she will not!'

'*Umm?*' Jude was at a loss for how to respond to this.

'She needs to get to the chapel with the rest of the creatures,' Minty added.

Jude tipped her head to the side, hoping it would make sense any second now.

'For the donkey blessing? On Wednesday?' Minty threw in, before taking another long drink. She was always conspicuously exasperated at Jude's lack of understanding.

Jowan took over, thankfully. 'Long ago, the village donkeys were walked to the little chapel on Minty's estate for a Christmas blessing, a way of thanking them for their hard work dragging the shoals and the coal up and down the slope. Our Mint had the idea of bringing it back, since the donkeys are just as much a part of village life now that they're rescues up at the sanctuary. They're quite the tourist attraction.'

'Ah! OK, that sounds like a nice idea. So what's the problem?' Jude asked, and she was sure she heard Elliot exhaling sharply by the door. His hand had been almost on the latch.

'Well,' Minty said. 'It's all organised. The school children have been practising "Little Donkey" on the recorder all month long and the minister's had his orders about the service.'

Nobody seemed to hear Elliot mutter, 'I bet he has,' under his breath, except for Bovis who kept his narrowed eyes fixed on him.

Bovis was Minty's eyes and ears around the village. Any trouble, he'd spot it. He was in a state of permanent subservience and suspicion. It made Elliot shudder.

Minty talked on. 'Moira and a couple of the other donkeys don't like walking out in the bad weather, and you can't blame them, really. Mr Moke from the sanctuary's on leave to visit family for Christmas or else he'd help. I've got some of the estate men tending to their feeding and exercise, but they're no donkey-whisperers. How will they get to the chapel for my candlelit service to celebrate them when the brutes won't set hoof out of their stalls in a squall?'

With that she threw her head back and drained her gin as though it were water. When she clinked her glass back on the bar and straightened her green body warmer she seemed to have regained her usual poise. 'What's needed is an animal expert. Someone who can coax the donkeys out on a dark night.'

All eyes turned to see the back of Elliot's head and his broad shoulders in the door frame as they slumped in resignation.

Jude said, 'If that's all, I'm sure Elliot doesn't mind helping. He is the village vet, after all.'

With a thin smile of acceptance from him – met with Minty's triumphantly sparkling eyes – Elliot Desvaux found himself involved in Clove Lore estate's great Christmas donkey-blessing ceremony. Ticketed of course, and with all proceeds going to restore the estate chapel roof. The words 'not for profit' meant nothing to Minty.

'And there's a cocktail party,' she added to soothe the blow. 'Christmas drinks for a select few in the ballroom afterwards. You will all join us, won't you.' It wasn't a question.

Once outside and on the tramp up the cobbled slope to the visitor centre car park where Diane, Jude's trusty old van, was waiting, Jude tried to encourage Elliot to see the bright side.

'It'll be nice to experience another local tradition brought back to life, won't it? You don't get many donkey blessings in the Borders, so it'll be a first for me.'

'It's a new one on me too,' Elliot replied, placing an arm around Jude's back to help power her up the slope. 'But Minty's a liability, never happy unless she's getting her own way.'

'Och, she's not that bad, once you're used to her, and she's ever so lonely.'

'Is she?'

'Think about it. Massive house, all alone up there, nobody to talk to...'

'That's the problem,' snorted Elliot. 'She keeps coming up with hare-brained schemes and resurrecting mad old traditions when she could be kept out of trouble with a partner to do normal stuff with.'

'You sound like Mrs Crocombe,' Jude laughed.

'You take that back!' Elliot said with an exaggerated gasp, stopping Jude and threatening to kiss her – which, with a wicked smile, she surrendered herself to immediately.

Elliot's kiss was just as deep and delicious as the first one they'd shared when they were bookseller holidaymakers and getting to know one another back in the summer.

She pulled him closer, lifting onto her tiptoes to make up the height difference, and for a moment they forgot all about Minty and trying to figure out how on earth Elliot was going to encourage Moira – the smartest, most contrary donkey ever to have lived, and a terrible influence upon the younger ones in the stables – out of her warm bed on a winter's night to listen to tuneless carols played on recorders and the vicar droning on in the estate chapel.

'Let's get home,' Jude said eventually, dazed and breathless and remembering their warm bed waiting for them and Elliot's even warmer body.

'And quick, too,' Elliot agreed.

As they neared the turning for the bookshop, they wordlessly walked along the little passageway and into the square where the white shop sat beneath its conical roof, crooked like a witch's hat in a children's book.

It was almost completely in darkness, except for the fireside glow inside. Jude broke from the nook beneath Elliot's arm to ascend the steps and peered through the door, her hand raised as though she would knock. It was only six o'clock, after all, and the Icelander hadn't had much of a welcoming committee so far.

Yet the sight of Magnús, slumped motionless in the low armchair in front of the fire, staring into the flames, all the lights turned off, gave her pause. She could only see his face in profile but he looked solemn and set-jawed. Turning, she tiptoed back down the steps.

As she and Elliot left the new bookseller to his contemplation, she whispered, 'He'll take some work, that one. He doesn't know yet.'

Elliot didn't say a word, only dropping a kiss on the top of Jude's bobble hat, fully understanding her meaning. That bookseller didn't yet understand what a stint in Clove Lore could do for a lost and brooding man.

Magnús would have to find out in his own time, as Elliot had done, that Clove Lore was no ordinary

Devonshire village and that the shop, with its cramped bedroom, its window seat overlooking the Atlantic breakers in the distance, the café with its faded lace curtains, and the creaking shelves crammed to the rafters with a treasure-trove of books, *certainly* wasn't any ordinary old bookshop.

Passing beneath the strands of bright Christmas bulbs lighting their way up the hill, Jude smiled up at Elliot, thinking as she often did these days how lucky she was to live in this place, and the pair made their way home to their house out along the main road with its little Garden of Eden backyard and her gorgeous kitchen, where the couple fully intended to live out their lives together, weathering every storm life brought to them.

Chapter Four

First Night at the Bookshop

The thing about Magnús Sturluson's bookselling holiday was that it had been reserved almost twenty-four months ago as a bit of a joke.

You'd have to know Jón, Magnús's brother, and his dry, wicked sense of humour to understand why it seemed like a good idea to gift him a holiday doing his actual day job, only three thousand kilometres south and where he didn't know anybody.

The reservation of a spot on the waiting list had been made as a Christmas gift back when Magnús had worked in his very own bookshop, Reykjavík's Ash and the Crash.

He'd named his shop after the two things Iceland was most famous for overseas (apart from Vikings, whales, cracking Eurovision songs, and lovely knits): the great ash cloud that had sent news anchors everywhere into a sweaty panic as they tried to say *Eyjafjallajökull*, the name of the volcano that was grounding flights all over the world, and the financial crash of 2008 when the country was almost bankrupted by a handful of moneymen left unsupervised with the nation's economy.

The name had seemed good and droll and eminently suitable for a touristy street near the hop-on, hop-off bus stop in the centre of Reykjavík. Footfall, the letting agent had promised him, would be excellent.

Now that the shop had gone massively bust and Magnús had lost all his capital and almost all of his pride, the name didn't seem funny at all.

'You practically live in your bookshop,' his brother had joked. 'We can't get you out of the place. This way you take a holiday *and* sell books. Just the right thing for you and Anna.'

'I have three million króna of books to sell right here! Why would I sell an Englishman's books *and* have my brother pay for the privilege? Who will run my store while I'm gone, huh? You all have your own jobs.'

Nobody had seemed to mind that he was close to hyperventilating, scratching his fingertips inside his neat, sharp beard and running his hand over his dark-blond head as though this might somehow soothe him. Everyone had smiled knowingly as if to say, *This again! You worry too much.*

His father, often a little exasperated with his middle child who, according to family legend, had worn a tense and earnest expression since the day he was born, had patted him on the shoulder, saying '*Þetta reddast*; it will be fine,' and walked him to the dinner table where his mum was serving up the Christmas Eve *Hangikjöt* with *uppstúfur*.

Magnús had brooded all that evening while his family ate and exchanged books. His older sister's kids had been so excited for the *Jólabókaflóð* tradition that year. It meant that as soon as the hot chocolate was poured they'd all headed to bed to read glossy new books and dozed off dreaming of fairy tales and poetry until Christmas morning.

Anna had been there too, that night. Magnús had wondered at the time whether she had put Jón up to it. She'd resented the bookshop since it opened – or rather, she resented the way it took him away from her every weekend and late into the evenings. He'd be there at all hours – he was, after all, its only bookseller.

'You work like you're an android, and not a man,' she'd told him, pleading that he take some time off to rest, even if he only observed Sunday mornings when the whole of Reykjavík was closed, but still, he'd get out of bed and walk to his shop while the church bells tolled.

Eventually she'd had enough, and last Christmas – when the bookshop holiday gift was an old joke and half forgotten, even though Magnús was edging closer to the top of the waiting list – she'd dumped him.

He'd simply accepted it. Of course she wanted nothing more to do with him. She'd accused him of becoming a boring robot of a man, and deep down he recognised that every single time they managed to grab a bit of lunch together or take a walk, he'd spoil things by stopping to peer in the windows of the other, thriving, bookstores, racking his brains to figure out why his seemed to be the only one without any customers and he'd get lost in self-pity, forgetting he was supposed to be on a date.

At least he understood now why he'd lost Anna. He'd bored her right out of his life. The mystery of why his shop failed was, however, still unsolved. Was the window display too drab? The ambience too cool and unwelcoming? Had he bought the wrong stock?

A good bookseller must be a composite: half curator, half mystic. They must buy up enough of the classics and the popular stuff to keep up with demand, as well as trying to predict new trends and catch up when the market surprises everyone with a breakout bestseller by an unknown author. Magnús had done all that, alongside trying to recommend books based on his gut feeling about the customers who he'd weigh up as they browsed the shelves.

He'd even catered for the tourists, hoping to entice them in with translations of Icelandic folk tales, sagas and songs, but all he'd really shifted were maps of Reykjavík. He could have set up a kiosk outside Hallgrímskirkja for that, instead of sinking his last króna and all his hopes into his own bricks and mortar store.

Ash and the Crash Bookshop had been his dream since high school, and it was a source of pure joy and satisfaction for him at first. Then it became a millstone, and suddenly, before it had a chance to really get off the ground, it was over.

Nobody had rented out the empty unit yet, as far as he was aware. His parents might well know, but they hadn't mentioned it. He couldn't bring himself to pass by it any more, walking down side streets to avoid it.

His shop, he imagined grimly, was standing unoccupied, a white box that couldn't remember a thing about how beautiful it had been when stocked with books and with its doors flung open in summer. The indifferent tourists would still be rolling by on the red buses and never noticing it.

It was therefore understandable that tonight, while sitting in another man's bookshop, Magnús would be somewhat forlorn. Nothing could penetrate his gloom. Not even the rich, dusty, papery scent that mixed in the air with the dried summer flowers clustered in vases – a gift from Minty's estate gardens. Not even when the timer on the fairy lights ticked its way round to half past six and the window display had burst into a warm golden glow did he manage a smile. Even when Mrs Crocombe had bustled in a few hours ago with the gift of ice cream from her shop a little way Down-along and told him he'd better eat it up or it might freeze he hadn't laughed at her joke, only staring dopily at the proffered tub between them.

The truth was, he loved ice cream, could eat tubs of the stuff, but didn't know what to do with this kindness from a stranger. She'd shrugged and pushed past him, showing him how to light the fire in the little hearth near the shop counter. It had taken her a long time, longer than Magnús thought was needed – she really had made a meal of prepping the kindling and crumpling newspaper – and all the while she'd fired questions at him.

He hadn't understood or liked the gleam in her eyes when he'd told her he was single. 'I'm not interested in that kind of thing at the moment,' he'd said, but she only chuckled and struck at the match.

After she'd shuffled off, leaving him alone again, the fire had brought a drop of comfort, and the ice cream – something called 'rum and no raisin' (again, he didn't get it) – was really very tasty indeed, and quite, quite boozy for a dessert.

The shop itself was beautiful in its own way – nothing like the sleek, bright Ash and the Crash, of course, but mellow and aged. The place felt exceedingly *English* to Magnús. Once-white walls seemed tea-stained, the beamed ceilings eccentrically squint and oddly low, and the warped floorboards made him feel a little drunk whenever he tried to cross the room.

The shelves were reassuring, though. He knew where he stood with books. Even though he longed to be back in his own shop faced with row upon row of shiny new books by Icelandic authors printed in his own language, there was still the feeling of an abundance of choice, an embarrassment of riches when browsing the Borrow-A-Bookshop stacks.

He'd already put aside a copy of Heaney's *Beowulf* and a Works of Ezra Pound which he'd take home with him to Iceland. He knew he'd find plenty of other irresistible titles in the coming days that would end up in his suitcase, too.

Magnús loved the absorption and distraction that reading brought him. He'd been at his happiest when sitting behind the till of Ash and the Crash with his head buried in the latest Arnaldur Indriðason – having promised himself he'd only take a peek at the opening pages before being helplessly drawn in to the story. He was at his happiest, that is, until he realised the time between interruptions to his reading by customers entering his shop was growing wider with each day that passed.

Still, the comforting sense of being surrounded by opportunities to escape – all he had to do was open the door into any one of these books and he'd dissolve away entirely – helped his mood. Maybe there was hope of some good things, some solitude and solace, in this strange spot in the south west of England after all.

Having spent his childhood immersed in Norse legends, he'd always been drawn to mythic stories, so tonight he picked out a copy of *Mermaid Myths of Devon and Cornwall* from the shelves marked 'Folk Tales' and read until the fire had lost its warmth and the coals in the basket were running low. He closed his eyes and slept right there in the shop armchair.

That night he dreamt – though he'd never remember it – of a beautiful woman with long white hair fanning out like unpicked rope. He gazed at her from a rock while beneath dark waves she flicked her long legs together like a tail, watching him with wide, appealing eyes, her mouth moving as though she wanted to call to him but couldn't, then suddenly she was sinking and fading and no matter how he plunged his arms into the cold water, he couldn't reach her. From the churning depths there suddenly emerged hundreds of printed pages rising off the seabed as though torn loose from books. They filled the water below his spot on the rock, all sodden and spoiled and obscuring his view of the sinking woman until he was sure she had gone to the bottom.

Chapter Five

20ᵗʰ December

Magnús slept through the winds battering the little windows on the shore side of the shop. He was used to howling gales. What awakened him was the cold. *That* he was not used to, not indoors at any rate.

He was used to underfloor heating and endless, steaming hot water from the tap and never being more than a hammer's throw from a hot tub or a thermal spa at any time.

Borrow-A-Bookshop, however conveniently appointed for wonderful sea views and fun working holidays, was somewhat lacking in modern conveniences – like decent radiators, for example.

Climbing the stairs and stretching out his knotted back, Magnús was appalled to find the air growing colder and the building even more draughty the higher he went. He flipped the switch on the portable electric heater outside the bathroom door and turned it up as high as it went. Five didn't seem a promising number. Five couldn't tackle the wind sneaking in at the window edges and wafting the bedroom curtains.

Turning the lights on to combat the dark midwinter dawn – it was only just before seven – he saw his reflection looking back at him from the window pane. He thought he looked confused and a bit helpless, hunched beneath the low ceiling. A littler person might be able to lift themselves over the headboard and into the alcove window seat, but all Magnús could do was kneel on the creaky bed and lean his head and shoulders inside the cubby, his elbows on the cushioned seat. He peered down over his corner of Clove Lore towards the patch of dark sea.

From what he could make out there was nothing below him but a higgledy-piggledy mass of roofs and chimneys, treetops and hedgerows, a few flagpoles with green St Petroc's masts snapping violently in the wind, and as the village awoke, little bursts of colourful lights appearing as the Christmas trees were switched on in cottage living rooms.

He shivered. It wasn't too late to get out of here. What had he been thinking? He could have cancelled the budget flights bought so long ago, and returned Jón's money. He could be spending Christmas at home with his family and his old school friends – then again, that meant rubbing shoulders with old hook-ups he knew in town.

Running into old lovers was pretty much unavoidable back home. Hardly anybody did first dates in Reykjavík; in fact, he knew nobody who did. It was more a case of chatting online with a friend of a friend and then meeting at a club when everyone had drunk enough spirits to want to dance and to make kissing easy, and then, that was it. It was the way things had been since graduating high school.

He'd read an article about it in the Icelandair in-flight magazine on the plane over. It had said that Reykjavík was great for culture, history and shopping, but terrible for romance. He'd had to agree.

He thought of what he'd be doing tonight if he were back home. After his shift at the Vínbúðin liquor shop, he'd lock up, drink some beers at home with Jón and his friends, then after eleven, they'd head to a bar.

That had been the routine since Anna left him, and pretty much every time he went out he'd bump into her. Sometimes they'd end up back at her place for old times' sake. Some nights he'd end up in some other person's bed.

Yes, nightlife in Reykjavík was simple. He wasn't sure when exactly he'd stopped enjoying it, but the thought of doing it every weekend all winter long made him feel even colder.

He'd miss dinner and the Christmas Eve *Jólabókaflóð* with extended family, though. They'd all gather around the table with Uncle Tor asking when he'd get a real job, a job for life, like his grandfather and his *pabbi* had done – fishing, the aluminium smelting or working in tourism. Good steady work that the older generation exalted but just didn't exist any more, or if jobs *did* come up, they were casual and precarious. The older members of his family always wanted to know when he'd stick at something and settle down.

No one understood how on earth he could be happy going from being a businessman to a booze seller. He wasn't happy but, of course, he wouldn't tell them that, not in words anyway.

Even Jón had a proper job, had done since school, writing for the local paper. He'd recently been promoted to features editor and was responsible for weekend cover stories now. He was five years Magnús's junior.

If he stayed here in England he'd miss out on all their nit-picking, comparing and cajoling – even if it was all said with a smile, nothing too unkind. He'd also miss the exchange of beautifully wrapped gift books, all bought at someone else's bookstore.

Here, he wouldn't have to nod and smile as he watched fifty thousand króna worth of books being passed around, knowing in every house in town people would be doing the same thing while his dream shop stood empty.

Thinking about it, it might do him good to sit Christmas out here, alone and unbothered. Maybe he'd even play at being a bookseller like they wanted him to. He wondered what that would feel like, with no overheads and no worries. A meaningless game of putting money he didn't even get to keep in someone else's till?

He'd seen the prices on those books downstairs; pounds and pennies. There was no way this place could make a profit without the holiday let. A sham, not a real bookshop at all. Pretending. Playing at life. Faking bookselling. He'd done that once before.

His mood sank lower and a new preoccupation hit him. He was seriously hungry and there wasn't a thing to eat in the tiny room downstairs at the back of the shop that was supposedly the kitchen.

After changing his clothes (he wasn't willing to strip off and step inside that little bath with its clingy plastic curtain to stand under the dribbling shower; he'd face that torture this evening), he grabbed the shop keys.

There was a pub on the harbour wall, he knew that much, and they claimed to be a bed and breakfast. It was almost eight. He'd try there. He always felt better with a full stomach.

Only once he was outside and he saw the people hurrying down the cobbled slope towards the harbour and heard the shouting, did he realise something was wrong.

The wind blew stiffly and almost carried all other noise away but there was the distant sound of yelling and hauling from way below him. Before he knew it, he too was shuffling down the slope as fast as he could, his eyes fixed on the choppy water.

Could it be a whale in trouble? Did that happen here too? He'd never seen it himself, but the news reports of mass beachings from back home came flooding back to him now and his blood turned to cold mercury at the thought. He knew how these things usually went. What a way to begin what was supposed to be a holiday.

Turning the last corner of the row of cottages facing each other that made up Down-along, he saw it. The boat was tipped on its side in the splashing shallows on the pebbly grey beach, its brown keel aslant above the water and facing off against the turbulent sky.

There was a crowd on the harbour wall, sheltered from the high winds by the pub, passively watching. Almost all of them had suitcases. He put that fact to the back of his mind as irrelevant at that moment.

Two tall lads in waterproofs – fishermen, he reckoned – had just finished hauling the boat in, letting the rope drop. One had fallen backwards and was scrambling to his feet again; the other was making for the boat.

Magnús had read that there were two types of people in the world: those who run towards trouble thinking they should help and those who stand back out of fear they'll make matters worse, or maybe it's a primal terror they could endanger themselves. Magnús found out that morning he was a helper.

He bounded across the shore, stumbling awkwardly on the slippery pebbles – they were much bigger up close – the wind beating in his face, pushing against him with a force that took his breath away.

'Anybody aboard?' one of the lads called out. No sound came from the hull.

43

Making long strides, Magnús almost overtook the one that had stumbled and together they reached the prow of the cruiser just as the big black figure emerged from the cabin with a loud '*Ugh!*'

They were uninjured enough to be cross. Magnús thought that was a good sign.

'Let us help you,' one of the men told the figure, reaching his hands up to help lift them down.

Magnús couldn't speak at all.

He was too busy gaping at the woman. She pushed back the black hood on her great oiled waterproof and a mass of wet, white-blonde hair billowed up in the wind. She was scowling fiercely and terribly, deathly pale.

'Are you hurt?' one of the men shouted.

The woman was trying to manoeuvre herself out of the tipped cabin, but she seemed to have lost her strength.

'I'm Monty, this is my brother Tom. What's your name?' the same man shouted, and Magnús took a second to register that the two men looked near identical.

Still the woman didn't answer, only grunting and heaving, trying to right herself.

'She doesn't understand,' Tom told his brother, his day's fishing now completely forgotten, impossible in this squall anyway.

Magnús found his voice, if not his sense, and stepped right up to the cabin, his hand stretched out to the woman. '*Talar þú íslensku?*' he heard himself shout over the winds.

The woman blinked into his face.

'What?' She continued with her struggle, only now her hand was in his. He steadied her.

'I thought you might be Icelandic,' he shouted back, feeling stupid and not sure why. She was so fair and so tall and somehow familiar. He'd simply assumed.

'Pull me up,' she said, her voice salty and dry and followed by a coughing fit that made the Bickleigh brothers exchange worried looks.

'She's sick,' they both said.

Someone was now behind Magnús holding out blankets.

'Call for Morrison,' Monty shouted with all his lungs to Finan who stood on the wall outside his pub with hands cupped over his ears. The landlord caught the words and dashed inside.

With one heaving movement Magnús helped the woman out of the boat.

The fall was not at all dignified, but very much in keeping with the morning's messy scramble.

'*Uft!*' As the woman fell down on him, all the air was forced from Magnús's lungs. The back of his skull knocked against the pebbles but he'd tensed his body to catch her safely and he was surprised to find it only hurt a little.

She'd screamed as she fell, and the sound had penetrated his core, making his empty stomach somehow throb. The weight of her upon him set his heart beating again after his bloodless race over the shore thinking someone was drowned. They both breathed heavily as the woman pulled herself off his body, blinking wildly.

Mermaid, he thought, somewhere dimly at the back of his head. *She's a mermaid.* Then the notion disappeared as Mrs Crocombe came into focus, throwing a blanket around the woman's shoulders.

'Stop!' Magnús called, as the woman shakily clutched at the blankets. 'Take that off first,' he pointed to her great coat. 'Get out of the wet things, right away.'

The sodden woman nodded, her whole body now trembling, and her face even paler than before, all the pink from the fall now washed from her cheeks.

'Let me?' he said in a quieter voice, now up on his feet and leaning closer to her, instinctively knowing she didn't want any more shouting and yelling.

Passively, she nodded, looking like she might shrink away entirely. Her eyes darted around the beach at all the faces and then up at the crowd on the sea wall. She seemed afraid.

When she looked right at him as he pushed the great coat off her shoulders, Magnús felt himself weaken as though absorbing all of her exhaustion into his own body.

Her eyes were heavy-lidded and irises icy blue, truly like an Icelander. She was having difficulty keeping them open.

Why had she been at sea in these high winds? It was miraculous she'd managed to put in at the harbour at all. Perhaps she'd been washed ashore while she slept? Magnús watched as the woman pulled her dripping jumper up over her head and let it fall on the shore.

Mrs Crocombe – who was tiny in comparison to this woman – immediately wrapped her tightly in blankets and grabbed the wet clothes. She was shivering like a person in hypothermic shock and urgently needed to get warm.

'A hot bath will help her,' Magnús instructed nobody in particular, and the woman's eyes snapped to his once more, her expression dazed and unreadable. Was it a look of curiosity? He didn't have time to learn more; she was suddenly whisked off up the shore by the Bickleigh brothers who, without warning, had picked her up off her feet and were carrying her away like a great haul caught in their nets, making it look effortless and as though they netted mermaids every day of the week.

Magnús followed in their wake, unsure what to do now and feeling like he was no longer required. He was, after all, a failed bookseller, not a doctor.

Jowan and his little beige dog were waiting for the brothers on the old lifeboat ramp, long since decommissioned, and they placed the woman onto Jowan's wooden sled where she sat stiff and motionless before they hauled her up the cobbled street and out of view.

Mrs Crocombe placed a hand on Magnús's arm. 'She'll be all right now,' she told him with all the certainty of a soothsayer.

'Where are they taking her?'

'Jowan's cottage, the old B&B. Doctor Morrison will arrive soon, sort her out.'

The old woman was struggling in her wellies over the rocks, and Magnús slowed his stride to match her pace until they were at the top of the concrete lifeboat launch. 'You're shaking as much as she was,' she told him, looking up into his face. 'Come along, Finan can help you.'

Even though every muscle and nerve told him to follow after the mermaid, he let Mrs Crocombe tug his arm, leading him along the wide sea wall and into the pub.

Only once inside the deserted bar room with the door shoved shut did he realise how roaringly loud the wind had been and how cold his body was. He slumped into a chair by the crackling fire. All the while Mrs Crocombe shuffled about, finding Finan and ordering him to make a full English and a pot of sweet tea, and making Magnús take off his jacket and move even closer to the fire.

Magnús couldn't see anything other than that pair of blue eyes, wide and entreating, and the way the woman from the sea had looked down at him as he lay on his back on the shore like *he* was the one who had been shipwrecked and then dramatically, miraculously saved.

'I'll be off then,' Mrs Crocombe announced.

'Shouldn't you stay and have a hot drink, too? You were blown about just as much as everybody else,' Magnús asked with a croaky voice. Had he really been shouting that loudly over the winds?

Mrs Crocombe was already on her way out the door.

Bella appeared, placing Magnús's mug on his table, watching the woman leave.

'She'll have fourteen houses to call in at Up-along, spreading the gossip about the girl in the boat. She's better than the local paper, and usually more accurate.' She smiled, but not with her eyes, and walked back behind the bar, telling him his breakfast wouldn't be a minute.

A couple of holidaymakers with a grumbling, teething baby arrived and sat at the furthest table by the window, asking Bella for coffee as they passed. There was no one else around this morning, it seemed.

Magnús had the presence of mind to eavesdrop as Finan returned and informed Bella that the doctor had arrived and Monty was back in the kitchen to finish the breakfast service.

'Is she OK?' Magnús enquired weakly, but Finan and Bella had fallen deep in conversation, standing by the espresso machine.

'That's the last of our Christmas guests gone, except the Austens.' Finan raised a hand to the young couple by the window but they were too busy trying to get baby Serena in her highchair to notice. 'They've come too far to leave now, not with a little one and a ten-hour drive to get home,' Finan told his wife.

'All of them refunded?' Bella said.

Finan nodded. 'All but one room empty and our Christmas visitor takings wiped out by an amber weather warning.'

To Magnús, Bella looked a cheerful, robust sort; her voice now told a different story. 'Only the three breakfasts then,' Bella called through to Monty, close to tears as she turned back to her husband. 'There's eleven six-kilogram turkeys in the freezer. What am I supposed to do with them now?'

As Finan shrugged, Monty swept through from the kitchen carrying a plate. 'Did anyone recognise the boat?' he asked.

For a moment Bella and Finan only paused, looking at him.

'The woman's boat? Wasn't local. I never saw it before,' Monty added.

'What was it called?' Finan managed to ask, though he couldn't summon much interest. His eyes were now fixed on the till.

'Its name plate was off,' Monty replied, approaching Magnús by the fire. 'Along with half the starboard gunwale where she hit the harbour wall. Lucky for her she didn't go under a few feet farther out.'

He presented Magnús with his breakfast.

'You and your brother hauled her boat in?' Magnús asked him.

'Yep. We were on the shore. We'd just that minute decided it was too rough for Tom to take the boat out when we heard the crack. She was trying to put in by the harbour steps and was blown right onto the wall. Luckily, she threw out her rope and Tom waded in to get it. By then, her cruiser was filling badly. It'll be a long repair job, that. Hope for her sake it's properly insured.'

Magnús took in the information in silence and within minutes Monty, Bella and Finan had left him to his thoughts. After smiling politely across the room at the exhausted parents and their grizzling baby, he lifted his knife and fork and listened to the weather warnings on the radio, interspersed with incongruously merry Christmas hits.

For a man used to porridge, strong coffee and *skyr* for breakfast, the Siren's Tail's herby sausages, streaky smoked bacon, hash browns, huge field mushrooms cooked in butter, fluffy scrambled eggs and endless doorstop toast was a revelation. Monty's speciality spicy baked beans were the biggest surprise. Odd, he thought, but so good. He ate every bite and enjoyed it with the appetite of a ship-wrecked man realising he was still alive and put ashore on a bounteous island.

Every time he found himself asking why on earth he'd come to this curious place, Clove Lore seemed to provide answers in abundance. Sure, the weather was terrible, but he could add mermaids and amazing breakfasts to the best ice cream he'd ever tasted and access to his own book browser's paradise as reasons to want to stay in England this Christmas.

Chapter Six

Cake is Required

In spite of the buffeting winds, there was a crowd outside Jowan's cottage at the foot of the slope when Magnús left the Siren's Tail. They were talking in low voices amongst themselves and the sight was enough to make him change his mind about knocking on the door to ask how the woman was doing. He'd thought Reykjavík was a whispering place, but Clove Lore evidently surpassed it for news-spreading.

'There he is!' one elderly man in the crowd said, as Magnús tried to squeeze by on his way back to the bookshop. 'The one that lifted her out.'

Many faces peeping out from under hoods followed him. Magnús was sure he heard a slightly leery whisper about not realising there was a Viking in town, but when he looked around crossly, all eyes were innocently averted.

'Save her life, did you?' a woman piped up.

'*Nei*.' Magnús waved his hands in protest. 'No, it was... Monty? I think, and his brother.'

'Tom's in there now, with her,' another woman told him, and the words set off an instinct within him that Magnús didn't like.

Tom was laying claim to the shipwrecked woman like she was some kind of beach treasure, when it had been

51

him she'd gazed at with astonished eyes. Or, perhaps she had. He couldn't be sure. She'd been afraid and wishing herself miles away, that much he understood. She must be desperate to get away from prying eyes and grasping hands. And yet, deep down, he still wanted to be the one in there talking with her, not Tom Bickleigh.

He'd stepped up and knocked on Jowan's door before he knew what he was doing. The realisation made his blood heat in an uncomfortable way, as did the fact that his impulsiveness had an audience of overexcited locals.

'S'no good. They won't answer,' the oldest of the men, Jowan's neighbour, told him, just as the lace curtain at the upstairs window was pulled aside then immediately replaced.

Jowan seemed a sensible man, Magnús thought. Of course he'd know the woman's sudden appearance would rouse salacious interest in the village. He was protecting her by keeping the busybodies away, and Magnús had no desire to be included in their number.

With shoulders set against the wind at his back, he strode up the slope, annoyed and amazed he'd been rash enough to knock. He prized his own privacy above anything else. Why on earth had he tried to intrude upon the mermaid's? The realisation stilled his hand as he put the key in the bookshop lock.

'*Nei, hættu þessu.*' He'd stop himself thinking about her right now. Nip it in the bud. Whatever it was; this yearning wish to look at her one more time, to see if he could feel again the same electric jolt her eyes had sent through him. There was only one thing for it. He must occupy his mind. He had to open up this phoney bookshop and do some work.

Only it felt exactly how he remembered. Very real indeed, and not at all like make-believe.

No matter how much he set his mind to not falling for it, there was a familiar rhythm to pricing up the books which had been left for him in a crate by the till. He had taken his time and found it wasn't entirely awful.

Almost all of the books were second-hand, some positively antiquated and nicely bound in leather, some with beautifully faded gilt edges.

He lifted each title at a time, consulted the pricing websites on his phone and, based on its condition, took an educated guess at how much a holidaymaker might be willing to pay for it. Tourists spent more on holiday than they would when shopping at home, he knew, but even so, the bookshop seemed to have a policy of keeping its prices low.

He'd then found a cloth and made his way round the shelves but soon realised he was simply moving dust from place to place as opposed to eradicating it. So he vacuumed, using the droning old device he'd found in the tiny kitchen by the stairs when he'd made himself a cup of instant coffee. Someone had kindly left some milk in the fridge. Jowan, most likely.

The vacuuming and coffee had at least warmed him up, but he still swept out the ashes in the grate and set a new fire.

The glow from the hearth brought back the same comforting heat of last night. There was something about staring into flames and listening to crackles and sparks that soothed him, even if the furthest corners of the shop remained frigidly cold.

As he slipped the books onto the shelves, mixing up new and second-hand stock – which seemed to be the shop's way – he took time to familiarise himself with the shop's offering.

There were thousands upon thousands of books – some tatty, some treasures; Clove Lore picture postcards in a rotating rack, miscellaneous stationery that looked a bit dated, and in pride of place on the front desk were multiple copies of a bakery cookbook authored by 'Crawley and Son, Bakers'.

He turned down the corners of his mouth as he read the back of the book, which was more of a pamphlet, really. He wasn't at all sure why it was there, and he didn't give it any more thought, carrying on with his walk around the shop.

He shook his head at a first edition of *The Velveteen Rabbit* on the children's shelves priced at ten pounds, slightly foxed and missing half its spine. They could easily ask for ten times that amount, he complained aloud to the empty shop. Would anyone passing by be willing to pay that? He guessed not.

Although there was a newish-looking laptop on the desk by the till, he was surprised to find there was no shop website; no distance-selling of any kind. Even his dismally failed bookshop back home had had its own online storefront – not that it had attracted much business, but still. He'd met the market head on. This place was stuck in the nineties.

By eleven, he paused by the front door, at a loss for what to do next. It was dark outside but he knew it wasn't supposed to be. It was the grey clouds. The wind still beat strongly on the windows and not a single customer had yet set foot inside his shop. They were probably all waiting for gossip down at Jowan's cottage, if they hadn't all blown into the harbour by now.

Perhaps the locals would be more in need of coffee than books today? His eyes fell upon the low door at the far side of the shop, so low he had to stoop to pass through it.

The café was small and cosy. He was glad to find it had modern appliances and plumbing, including a scalding hot radiator. The oven was small and housed inside a little cubby behind a beaded curtain with shelves above stocked with homemade strawberry jam, its red colour jewel-like and vibrant in the white café. There were fresh eggs in the fridge and something called 'clotted cream' which, when he lifted off the lid, smelled sweet and inviting. There was a pack of salted butter, flour, sugar, and jars of fat sultanas. He didn't know they were for baking the cream tea scones the tourists came to Devon in their droves for year round.

He scratched at his beard, thinking.

'*Skúffukaka?*' No, there was no chocolate in the little kitchen, the key ingredient in Icelandic brownies.

'*Vínarterta?*' His *amma* had made it at this time of year when he was small, a kind of layered cheesecake and very comforting, but he wouldn't know where to start with those, and didn't that require spices and prunes?

The shelves weren't well stocked at all. It made him wonder if the other booksellers generally bought in their own ingredients. There was only one thing for it, he knew.

–

'*Mamma?*'

'She's not here,' Jón told him. He must be working from home again.

'Ó, já, that's right.' Their mother worked at the public library in the mornings now she was semi-retired, then she'd be drinking coffee with her macramé circle because it was a Tuesday.

'How's Devon?' Jón enquired.

'A little windy,' replied Magnús, enjoying the under-statement immensely. 'And there are no customers in the bookshop.' He waited for Jón's droll reply about how that was nothing new for him, but it didn't come. Instead there was an awkward silence before Jón steered them to safer ground. 'Have you met the local people yet?'

Magnús's mind flitted right past Jowan and Mrs Crocombe, Bella, Finan and the Bickleigh brothers, straight to the woman who had washed up on the shore.

'So? What are they like?' Jón pressed.

'They're uh…' A twinge hit him hard in the stomach, something like hunger, when he recalled the woman. It struck him that she'd have been driven home by now. She couldn't have come very far along the coast in that little cruiser. She'd be safely with her family again. Why did that realisation make him wince? He should have hammered on Jowan's door like Thor until he was forced to let him in. He'd saved her, hadn't he? Maybe just a little? That was what the local gossip-mongers in the crowd had said. He should have said goodbye to her at least, checked she was OK.

'They're… uh… interesting.' He tried not to follow his thoughts; they led to nowhere. She was gone. 'Listen, I have to bake something to sell in this coffee shop.'

'You're going to bake?' Jón was definitely laughing now.

'I can bake.'

'Uh, sure you can. What are you gonna make?'

'No idea. I thought Mamma might know.'

'It's Christmas, right?'

Magnús silently shrugged.

'You've gotta make *Jólakaka*.'

Yes! That was it. He scanned the café shelves once more. He could almost taste his mother's Icelandic Christmas cake, light and sweet and, he imagined, fairly easy to make.

'Want me to send you a photo of Mamma's recipe?'

'*Já*, I need it now.'

'There, sent,' Jón told him a few moments later after he'd rummaged in the kitchen for the notebook of family recipes. Jón asked if it was snowing.

Magnús didn't know if it snowed this close to the sea in England, but he delighted in letting Jón know everyone here was talking about storms coming in and this morning it had felt windier even than Stórhöfði and he was pretty sure that was the most windblown place on earth – even the tough little puffins were blown away by the end of summer there.

'Stay indoors and bake your *Jólakaka. Þetta reddast*,' Jón told him. There it was again, the family motto. *It'll be fine*.

'Of course. How bad can it be?' Magnús replied, and after Jón's usual farewell of 'Bless bless,' they hung up.

Peering through to the shop floor to make sure there were no customers in there – there weren't – Magnús rolled up his sleeves. He had work to do and no windy day or thoughts of the shipwrecked maiden, now long gone, could distract him.

Chapter Seven

Jowan's Cottage

'Is there anyone I can ring for you? Or the phone's right there if you want to use it?' Jowan prompted when the woman emerged from the bathroom after her long soak.

Mrs Crocombe was laundering her clothes for her right now up at her cottage. She'd shuffled off up the slope with her sopping bundle, having exchanged them for an oversized T-shirt that said 'Crocombe's Ices', fresh from its cellophane, and a pair of Scottie dog pyjama pants Mrs C. had intended as a Christmas present for her daughter. The ankles flapped around Alex's calves now as she made her way down the stairs.

She had to stoop under the low ceilings and even lower light fittings. Everything in Jowan's house – once upon a time it had been a fish salting loft – was diminutive, Alex was discovering, even down to the vintage kimono Jowan had given her to wear over Mrs Crocombe's offering.

For a moment Jowan gulped and couldn't seem to take his eyes off Alex, then he fixed his eyes on his cocoa mug and couldn't bring himself to look again.

'No, thanks, I don't need to ring anyone,' she told him, struggling to balance the fluffy towel over her hair as it bumped off the ceiling. What she really meant was, there was nobody she wanted to talk to.

The phone that had been in her back pocket as she tried to navigate her way to safety in the harbour wasn't there any more; she figured it must have fallen into the sea. It didn't matter. It had run out of battery power days ago anyway.

She wondered at how easy it had been to give up contact with her little community. Was this how people broke away from their old lives? She'd never have imagined a few years ago that she could cut herself off so entirely.

She perched on the sofa by the crackling fireside and across a low coffee table from Jowan where a cup steamed invitingly, waiting for her. Aldous, who'd been sleeping there, shifted closer to her, laying his bony little body along her thigh, immediately falling asleep again with a little snort of happiness.

'Thank you for this,' she told her host, touching the kimono sleeve which ended at her forearm.

'Isolde was a good two foot smaller than yourself – tiny she was, really, but only in stature, she was *some* woman,' Jowan said, his misty eyes betraying how difficult it had been to lift the gown from the closet and put it in the hands of someone else.

The robe smelled of cedar wood oil, lavender and something else, something salty like the sea breeze. He'd obviously taken care of it and aired it out often.

His Isolde, Alex realised, had been gone for a long time. She could see it in the careworn little 'V' between Jowan's brows that never dissolved entirely, even when his eyes crinkled into a smile.

'Mrs C. will be back shortly with your clothes,' he added quickly. 'You must want to be on your way home? Minty from the Big House has offered to drive you whenever you're ready.'

Alex sipped the hot chocolate – the old-fashioned, velvety kind made in a pan with full fat milk. Delicious. The warmth settled in her belly and, finding it empty, prompted a loud grumble. She clutched her stomach.

'After lunch though, eh?' Jowan sprung immediately to his feet and loomed over the fire. 'You're in for a treat,' he told her as he lifted two foil-wrapped bundles from the grate. 'My speciality...' He plopped them onto plates already set out on the coffee table and deftly opened the foil with fearless fingertips. 'Baked 'tato.'

How could something as simple as potatoes baked in a wood fire smell so appealing? Alex's stomach growled again in response.

'And... my secret recipe.' Jowan had slit the steaming potatoes in half and retreated to the little scullery for a second, coming back with a bowl. 'Creamy mackerel mousse. Ever had it?'

Alex shook her head and watched as Jowan cut two big pats of yellow butter in a dish before dressing their lunches with it, followed by a big blob of mousse. 'Mackerel flakes, fresh from the local smokery, crème fraîche, squeeze o' lemon, snip o' dill, black pepper, and there you have it. Tuck in, lass.'

The first mouthful made Alex smile for the first time in a long time. Jowan only nodded back, pleased she was pleased.

'This is a B&B?' Alex asked, remembering passing the sign attached to a vintage bike fixed to the garden railing outside.

'Was,' Jowan said, 'I retired in the autumn. Laundry, visitors arriving late and setting off early, all those fried breakfasts! It's a young person's game and my 'eart was never in it.'

Alex thought of her ferrying. She understood.

'It was Isolde's idea, when we realised her illness was serious. She wanted us moved out the bookshop and into a proper cottage. Then she made me promise not to waste away missing her, so I did what she told me to do. I opened the B&B. She said it would keep me out of trouble. Did it for years. Can't say I enjoyed it much.'

Alex smiled in sympathy. She definitely understood what it felt like to carry on doing something you really weren't keen on because it was immediately in front of you at a time of need. And now she'd gone and sunk her dad's beautiful *Dagalien*. It didn't bear thinking about.

'She wanted you to move out of a… bookshop, did you say?' Alex asked, trying to act as normal as she could under the circumstances, especially when Jowan was being so welcoming and unobtrusive. She at least owed him normal.

'Up-along. We ran it together for years, built it up from scratch. Another of Isolde's ideas. We were happy as two birds in a nest there, day in, day out, readin', chattin' and sellin'. I didn't want to stop, but she knew me better than I know myself, and insisted me and little Aldous didn't stay on alone with all the memories, making ourselves miserable.'

Keeping her fork in one hand, Alex let the other settle on the little dog's curly back. The poor mutt had lost his mum.

'So you sold it?'

Jowan brightened again. 'No, no, it's still there, only now it's a bookshop you can borrow for your 'ol-days. In fact, the lad who pulled you from your boat this morning is staying there at the moment.'

Aldous lazily lifted his head, annoyed that the woman with the cool hands had paused in stroking his back.

'The blue-eyed one?' she said, keeping her eyes on her plate, and trying to look for all the world like someone not all that interested to know more, but making polite conversation nonetheless.

A smile hitched a corner of Jowan's lips. 'Magnús. From Iceland.'

'Iceland?' She couldn't act cool about this. It was all coming back to her. He'd spoken in his own language as though she too would understand it, and… *oh no*, she'd fallen on him, sending them both flying.

No matter how much attention she paid her lunch or in fussing the little dog, she couldn't shake the embarrassment or the sense that Jowan knew what she was thinking (that the man had been so earnest and somehow solid and impressive) and that was what was making his eyes shine.

'He's only a hundred yards up the cobbles if you want to take a wander to find 'im,' he said. 'Mind you do it before the winds get any higher. Up-along's a tempestuous place to be when a gale's howlin'.'

'Good to know,' Alex replied quietly.

'Tuck in, there's another helping waiting for uz,' he told her.

Neither of them said a word as they finished their meal, Jowan because he was staring into the fire and taking big bites, and Alex because the simple comfort of this place made her feel like she was in danger of bursting into tears and making an even bigger fool of herself than she already had.

She shuddered. Imagine crashing her boat and needing to be rescued, then making that poor bedraggled doctor come out in this wind to see her when she was completely fine! Only exhausted and dehydrated, the doc had said. He'd prescribed fluids and rest and no more sailing. Some chance, with her ferry beached and broken.

But the fire and the food, along with Jowan's soft, quiet way made up for some of that shame. And he hadn't asked any questions, not even pressing her for her name. She liked that about him most of all. So she ate in silence, knowing the questions would come soon enough.

Questions, she thought with a sigh, such as, why had she been at sea all alone for so long, and so underprepared for a voyage, too? What was to be done about the boat? Who even was she and where on earth did she belong? And, the one that upset her the most, was there really nobody out there worrying about her right now and wishing they could reach her?

There was time enough to think about these things later. Right now, she was dry and warm, and there was a friendly mutt, a gentle-mannered host who put her in mind of a pirate that hadn't put to sea in many a year and, insinuated into everything in the little cottage, there was the feeling of being watched over somehow. It was the presence, Alex thought, of the woman who had once lived here and was loved so much she never really left. Jowan's Isolde.

The whole thing felt curiously like coming home, so she let herself indulge in the faulty feeling, like a cuckoo chick in a warbler's nest, singing to be fed.

So what if it wasn't real and she couldn't stay? She'd lie to herself for a short while and she could cry later. She was going to hold on to all of her secrets. Nobody was going to pity her or pry into her sorry situation here. They needn't even know her name. She'd be untraceable, and as soon as she was recovered, she'd be on her way again, to anywhere but Port Kernou.

Chapter Eight

Magnús Receives an Invitation

Magnús had burnt the first cake – not too badly but it was definitely singed. He'd been peering out the bedroom window, trying to crane his neck and catch a glimpse of the harbour – not possible at this angle, he'd found – and for a few moments forgotten he now had a café to cater.

He'd shaken his head coming down the winding stairs, telling himself to concentrate; there was a second batch of cake mix to deal with.

He'd been looking for her boat on the shore, he admitted, as though checking it was definitely real and not something he'd dreamt.

This morning's events had certainly taken on the haziness of a dream. He worried he was losing his grip on reality, and he'd only been here one night. What would he be like at the end of a fortnight? He couldn't explain his reactions at all. He was pragmatic and realistic, not at all the type to lose himself in daydreaming.

He weighed out the flour all over again, cracked the eggs and mixed and folded. That felt real, at least.

Just as the second *Jólakaka* went into the oven, Magnús's spine stiffened at the brassy sound of the bell ringing from the shop. An actual customer.

Two in fact, he discovered, as he stooped under the low door from the café. Men, his age, or a little older, he reckoned, and holding hands.

'Hallo,' he said, approaching the till. 'Welcome to my bookshop.' The words were already out but he still clamped his lips shut in surprise. What on earth? *My* bookshop? Not good. None of this was permanent – not that he wanted it to be more than a holiday. Not at all.

'You're Magnús?' asked the slighter of the two, and seeing the bookseller's surprise, quickly added. 'I'm Izaak, one of the volunteers, and this is Leonid.'

Leonid wore glasses and had thick, curly blond hair, with eyes as blue as Magnús's and an endearingly big gap between his front teeth.

Once hands had been shaken, Magnús asked, 'Can I help you, or are you here to help me?' He pressed his palms together awkwardly. 'There doesn't seem to be anything I need.'

'We're after a book, any books in fact, on camellias?' said Izaak.

'Camellias?' Magnús repeated, his eyes shooting around the shop. 'The flower?'

'Shrub, actually,' Leonid put in.

'Leonid is Minty's new gardener up at the Big House,' Izaak announced proudly, in what Magnús had decided was definitely a Polish accent. 'She brought him in to rescue the camellia grove that the gardens were once famous for.'

'A long time ago,' Leonid added, not telling Magnús that Minty had really brought him from Moscow so that Izaak, her loyal estate gatekeeper and groundsman, would have a chance of living with the love of his life who'd been languishing in a Russian university and unable to leave the country for years.

They'd married a few months ago in Exeter with none of their Polish or Russian families in attendance. Minty and Jowan had been the only witnesses and they'd stopped off for fish and chips on the drive back to Clove Lore in Minty's rusty old Discovery. And that had been it; a far too small celebration to mark the culmination of years of long-distance yearning, during which time the pair had read to each other in three languages every evening via Skype, wishing there was a way for them to be in the same time zone as one another.

Minty, for all her battiness, held the answer, and had arranged the paperwork, and provided the permits and the permanent address.

Now the husbands resided in Minty's converted attic rooms, which they'd turned into a jungle of hanging plants and climbing greenery, never quite daring to believe they'd actually been left in peace in England and always waiting for letters demanding yet more documentation to prove they weren't somehow aliens or – Leonid's deepest fear – simply telling him he must leave.

Perhaps that was why they clung to each other the way they did, like it was their last day in the other's company, and why anybody who so much as glanced at them could see their devotion.

The sight of their hands clasped so tightly made Magnús simultaneous happy for them and desolate for himself. He rubbed at the little twinge in his chest. All he knew was that these two were hard to encounter when he'd been so bleak for so long.

'Let's look,' Magnús told them and they scoured the shelves of gardening books, eventually turning up a general guide to acid-loving shrubs.

'You're coming to the donkey blessing tomorrow?' Izaak said, having held out his card to pay the four pounds fifty that made Magnús want to roll his eyes at the pricing system. That wouldn't even cover the cost of his favourite double-shot *íslatte* in a Reykjavík coffee shop. A timely reminder that this place was a sham, and he shouldn't be falling for its charm.

'The what?' He couldn't have heard that correctly. 'My English…' he began, even though he'd spoken English fluently for as long as he could remember.

'You heard right,' Izaak told him. 'A service for the village donkeys up at the Big House chapel. We'll be there.'

'Minty wants you to come,' Leonid said, gravely, making Izaak smile.

'I can't,' Magnús told them bluntly, hitting the buttons on the card machine and working the till. For all that this was a play shop, this part still felt good.

'You can't *not* come,' Izaak laughed. 'Trust us. Minty will only send Bovis to escort you. It's easier if you come of your own free will.'

Magnús appreciated his dry tone, and only nodded his acceptance.

'Six thirty tomorrow, drinks afterwards in the ballroom,' Leonid threw in, placing his new book under his arm.

'Do I bring anything to an English donkey blessing?' Magnús wanted to know.

'Just your incense and white robes,' Leonid smirked.

As they stepped outside again into the little cobbled square, Izaak called over the sound of the whistling winds, 'Is something burning?' making Magnús curse and run for his forgotten *Jólakaka*.

Chapter Nine

The Customer is Always Right

Alex peered around the door, making the little brass bell above her head chime. The bookshop smelled good, like a proper Christmas long ago: fireside, books and something freshly baked.

She would definitely have smiled more if it wasn't for the embarrassment and the nerves making her fidget. Plus, she wasn't exactly dressed for visiting.

Mrs Crocombe had brought her clothes back to her still warm from the dryer, but when she'd washed ashore that morning she'd been wearing the same thing she'd run off in; her boots (still rather damp now), inky jeans (from a high street store's 'tall' range), a white rollneck and the holey, oversized indigo jumper she'd been wearing every winter for years. The entire look was topped off with mismatched black woollen mittens, a brown scarf and an incongruously pink baggy beany she shoved her hair under on damp sailing days. If not exactly smart, it was at least fresh and dry. Mrs Crocombe had valiantly laundered and pressed the lot, and told her she must keep the T-shirt and pyjama pants too. How did you thank someone for that kind of goodness? Alex had wanted to cry. Instead, she'd kissed Mrs C. on the cheek.

Now she stood on the bookshop doormat under her voluminous coat, feeling totally ridiculous. What must the Icelander be thinking? He was immobile and stiff-necked, standing in the middle of his shop, and so far he hadn't said a word.

She'd come to thank him, but his look of incredulity made her wonder if he actually wanted an apology.

'Hi,' she said, raising an awkward hand.

'It's you,' Magnús informed her.

'Jowan told me you worked here.'

'I don't. I'm on vacation,' he corrected, before tutting at himself, which Alex thought a little odd.

'Well… this morning… you were great and…' Alex struggled, wishing he'd help her out by waving a dismissive hand, and saying *Oh that? It's nothing*, but he was just staring at her. 'I wanted to thank you.' Still nothing. 'And… I'm sorry I was… there.'

'I'm glad you were there,' he blurted unthinkingly, before turning his back on her in an instant and rearranging the self-help section, which to Alex's eye didn't look all that untidy or urgent. He seemed to be having some kind of argument with himself and was shaking his head crossly.

When he turned back, his expression was just as vexed but at least he'd found some words. 'Were you injured?'

'No, I'm fine. The doctor ordered me to rest for a few days, and to drink. I was dehydrated.'

'That's good,' he told her, his voice rising hopefully. 'That you're resting here, I mean, not that you were dehydrated.' He seemed to wince once more.

Alex told herself she'd made a mistake dropping by, and yet turning on her heel and leaving wasn't really an

71

option. English politeness stopped her, not to mention the fact this guy had run to her aid that morning.

Concluding that he'd reached the limits of his conversation skills for now, Alex took a few cautious steps towards the classic literature section. This seemed to startle the bookseller even more. He was looking at her the way a person watches up-close street magic.

Suddenly, with a blink of awakening, he retreated behind the till where he picked up a copy of the little baking book from the counter and read it so closely that it obscured his face.

She saw his shoulders slump as if in defeat. The whole thing was amusing – endearing, even – which made Alex ask herself if she'd been at sea for so long that she was just glad to be in the company of anyone new, even this odd fellow. He was handsome though, she had to admit, somehow concrete in his chest and shoulders, muscular in his arms and legs, a little soft around his middle, and tall like her. She snapped her eyes to the bookshelves.

'You're enjoying your holiday?' she asked at last, while looking at a modern paperback of Robert Louis Stevenson's *Treasure Island*.

'Am I?' he said in a thoughtful way, as if he wasn't sure. 'I arrived last night, I haven't really seen the place… and I've sold only one book so far.' He stopped to take a breath.

'Ah, well, let me help with that.'

She could have sworn he took a step backwards as she swept towards the till, book in hand. 'I'll take this, please. I didn't bring anything with me to read on the…' She almost said 'on the *Dagalien*' but quickly swerved for 'on the boat.'

Taking the paperback from her hand seemed to calm him. '*Treasure Island*? That's one of my favourites.'

'I've never read it.'

'*Ha!* Then you are in for an adventure. Let me know what you think of it when you're done.'

His sudden enthusiasm threw her. 'Oh, well, I'm a slow reader, I…' Alex didn't know where she was going with this, only that she didn't want to admit she'd really quite like to stay put in Clove Lore for a while, sitting still on dry land and reading and not having to think about things or explain herself to anyone. The idea struck her as utterly lovely. 'I'll be gone before I finish it, probably,' she heard herself saying.

'*Já*, right, of course. So, let me see,' he peered at the book's inside cover. 'That will be… two pounds sterling? *Of course* it will.' He was shaking his head again.

What a strange person, Alex thought, but his grumbling, fumbling way still made her want to smile.

She pulled a pearl-coloured coin purse from the pocket of her great coat and handed over the money, just as the shop door rattled violently on its hinges and the wind roared. Their heads snapped round to look at it.

Magnús made an impressed, 'Woah!'

'This storm isn't calming at all,' she said.

'You should drink coffee,' he told her, as though that somehow followed, and seeing her surprised smile he added, 'before you walk back to Jowan's, I mean. For warmth. Also I made cake and nobody's tasted it.'

'Well…'

That was the clincher. That and the fact she had nowhere to be and nothing to do. The call to the insurance company could wait until morning. Jowan and Aldous weren't at the B&B to greet her, though he had given her a key and told her she could stay as long as she needed, which she'd taken to mean a couple of nights max. He couldn't want her there over Christmas.

Jowan and the little dog had accompanied her as far as the turning for the bookshop and then they'd walked on up to the Big House to visit the mysterious Minty, who Jowan, no matter how devoted he was to his late wife's memory, kept talking about. A bad case of mentionitis there, she'd thought.

Alex knew all about mentionitis now. Ben had caught it weeks ago. It had been *Eve said* this and *Eve likes* that. Funny how she hadn't suspected a thing at the time, but the constant name-dropping now told her that Eve had occupied his thoughts.

Maybe he'd tried to stop himself? Maybe he'd fought the attraction at first? Tried to be loyal? Who knew? None of that mattered since she'd walked in on him and her best friend practically eating each other before springing apart in their shock at being discovered.

She'd been too trusting or – and the thought made her mood sink like an anchor – she'd been only too willing to be fooled, just so long as she had some kind of family to fit into.

'Cake would be good,' she conceded, trying not to sound too weary.

For the first time, the Icelander smiled. 'I'm Magnús Sturluson,' he said, and the frank way that he held his hand out across the counter weakened her resolve to remain incognito. She confessed her name was Alex. No surname necessary.

The warm clasp of his hand took them both back to the beach that morning, and Alex felt the last remnants of her brave face slipping. He'd seen her at her absolute lowest point, suddenly washed ashore when she'd wanted to hide away from the entire world for at least another few weeks. And she'd squashed him flat on his back on the beach. *Ugh!*

Just before another crushing wave of humiliation washed over her, Magnús led the way through the shop and into his café.

His silence felt like a promise. He wasn't going to pry either. Just like Jowan, he understood she was holding on to her sorry story out of self-preservation. If she told it out loud – the awful truth about Ben and Eve, and all the rest of it – she'd be surrendering the last little fragment of pride she had left, and in front of strangers too.

If she explained herself she'd lose her mystery, the only thing she had to her advantage, the one thing that stopped the sympathetic looks or well-meaning but painful comments and the insensitive questions, and she'd had enough of those growing up without her mum. She wouldn't stand for any more.

'So, what's on the menu?' She knew her voice was shaky with emotion. Forcing her hands into her pockets helped. *Get it together*, she scolded herself.

'*Jólakaka* and… something like a cappuccino. There's no machine,' he told her, busily washing his hands in the little sink behind the café counter where, inside a glass dome, sat a golden loaf cake studded with fruit. 'Or you can have tea?'

She pointed to the cafetière now in his hands and found she was glad to see he was filling it up for the two of them.

'The Icelandic Christmas cake is a family recipe,' he added, as Alex pulled up a high seat at the counter.

'Whose recipe?'

'My mother's, and Amma's before her. I mean, my grandmother's.'

Alex accepted a big slice of cake and watched as Magnús heated some milk then frothed it with a noisy little electric device that looked a bit like a screwdriver. He stayed on the other side of the counter until she asked him to join her. 'You can't stay on your feet all day, sit.'

He poured out their drinks then did as he was told.

'So how do we do this?' he asked eventually.

'Do what?' Her eyes widened in panic.

'Have a conversation without you telling me anything about what happened to you this morning or who you are?'

So he did get it. Alex's heart swelled with the relief, but there was embarrassment too. Clove Lore people were picking up on how prickly and sensitive she was. That wasn't an altogether nice feeling.

'We could talk about the storm,' she put in quickly. 'Jowan said this morning's gales are only a storm front and we'll have a better day tomorrow, and then the second storm they're forecasting might miss us altogether, move back out to sea or something.'

'Or we might get absolutely battered by the second storm for Christmas? I heard that too, on the radio.'

Alex fell silent again as she tried to picture where she might find herself on Christmas Day. It was a blank. She knew where she didn't want to be, that was for sure: alone in her little house in Port Kernou.

She broke a corner off the cake and tasted it. The sweetness brought her round and she realised Magnús was drinking his coffee, not even trying to fill the silence in the café.

'*Mmm!* You're a good baker,' she said.

'Only good? In Reykjavík my *Jólakaka* is famous.'

'Oh wow, really?'

'No.' He shook his head. 'This was my third attempt. I burned the others.'

'You were joking?'

'I was.'

'You don't smile when you tell jokes?'

'I *am* smiling,' he told her, his mouth forced into a straight line, but his eyes shining wickedly.

'Yeah, hate to tell you this, but you're really not.'

'Well, I'm incandescent on the inside.'

They both smiled now and everything felt a little easier.

'You're lucky, growing up eating like this.' She took another bite and Magnús mirrored her with his own mouthful.

The café was warm in spite of the wind rattling the door and the thin lace curtains at the windows failing to seal out the dark, gusty afternoon.

'Christmas food doesn't taste the same since Amma died,' he said, matter-of-factly. 'This is not as good as hers.' Yet, Alex observed, he was still taking big bites and reaching for the knife to cut a second slice.

'I'm sorry to hear that,' she told him. 'Oh, go on, then.' She accepted another piece too.

Something about seeing him relax and the quietness in the café made her give way a little.

'My mum had her own café, actually. Well, it was more of a diner,' she said, keeping her eyes fixed on her plate as she licked a finger to dab up the crumbs. A few tiny details about herself couldn't hurt, surely? He'd been so kind and welcoming. 'By the harbour, in a village a bit like this really, except it's all on the flat.'

She shook her head dreamily at the memory and imagined herself walking in through the familiar white door and up to the counter where her mum would stoop and lift her into her arms for a hug. 'It had a sort of sixties vibe going on, all red-and-white checked tablecloths and those tomato-shaped squeezy bottles. Remember them?' Magnús didn't. 'She made the best milkshakes in the whole of… the village.'

She remembered to be guarded. She couldn't have word getting out about where she was from or they'd all encourage her to go back there, but her caution wasn't enough to stop her reminiscing. She loved talking about her mum whenever she could. 'Hands down, her strawberry shake would beat anybody's. I'd eat there every night after school. Same thing every day; milkshake, Mum's cheddar, ham and tomato toasties, a side of chips, and a big square of chocolate crispy cake for pudding. And mum would be grabbing sips of cold coffee and being worked off her feet.'

Alex didn't mention that her dad also worked late into the evenings all summer long from his spot on the quayside just across the square from the diner. He'd wave in the window at them both every time he got back from ferrying the tourists in search of evening meals and sunset strolls across the river.

'I loved it there,' she sighed. 'Songs on the radio and all the old ladies chatting. Mum would let me write the specials on the chalk board. It's funny, the little things you remember.' She took a gulp of coffee. 'I don't like to go back now, though. Somebody else bought it.' The words slipped out as the grief bloomed fresh in her chest. It was amazing how the sadness could hit her all these years later and still knock her breathless.

Magnús only nodded. 'You don't have her any more, your mother. I am sorry.' None of it was enquiring. He didn't want details, only to say he felt for her.

He topped up their coffees from the cafetière, then added more frothed milk.

After a moment, the horrible realisation hit her. 'Oh no!'

'What's the matter?'

'My photographs!' She turned to face Magnús. 'They're still on the boat. Only a few, stuck inside the cabin. I need to get them back.'

'*Jæja*, yeah, OK.' He seemed to inhale while the sounds came out, as though he didn't want to waste time exhaling before agreeing with her. He was nodding, too. 'I'll come with you. In the morning. But it's too dark now. Too dangerous,' he told her, and his straightforward rationality stilled her again.

Of course it was too dangerous. She'd almost risen and made for the harbour there and then. Stupid really, typical of her new impulsive streak. 'Thank you. I'd appreciate that.'

She thought of the *Dagalien* on the pebbles, the swell tide now submerging her, most likely, the wind and waves forcing the poor craft farther up the beach, her varnish scratched off and the stones tumbling inside her prow. What would be left of her by morning? Everything felt so hopeless.

She felt the tears stinging her tired eyes and without saying anything, Magnús stood and reached for the shop keys in his pocket. 'Sleepy?' he asked.

Yes, let's pretend I'm sleepy, she thought, before polishing off the last bite of cake and draining her cup. *Sleepy is easier than cheated on, stranded, lost and alone, and feeling utterly sorry for yourself.*

'I will walk you home.' His accent was as soothing as his actions.

She didn't remark on how much she liked his voice. She guessed he heard that a lot. Yet, his voice *was* wonderful to her ear, with its lilting upward inflections – which for all the world sounded kind of Canadian – and the 'w' sound that mixed with every 'v' as it left his full lips, along with the deep elfin softness that took her back to box-set evenings in Middle Earth. If she wasn't mortally afraid of spilling all her secrets or bawling her eyes out in front of this man, she'd like to listen to him talking all night long.

Once out on the cobbled slope, they found the wind had changed direction and was now hurling itself at their backs as they turned Down-along. Magnús still hadn't said a word since promising to walk her 'home'.

Alex tried hard to pretend she *was* being walked home. Nothing weird about that. Earlier, Jowan had shown her a low white bed, flouncy and floral, in a small upstairs room. She wished it really was hers.

How easy life would be if she could go on pretending she was a castaway with no baggage whatsoever. A fresh start, though impossible what with all the mess left behind – not to mention strewn all over Clove Lore's beach – seemed blissfully easy in comparison to facing up to all her losses. She tried not to sigh for herself and the shambolic life she was running from.

It was far too windy to speak, and they had to hold tightly to the metal railings and gate posts that lined the wide path between the sloping rows of cottages that made up Down-along.

There was bracken, branches and sand strewn on the dark path beneath Alex's boots and they made gravelly crunching sounds as she took careful sideways steps.

Just as they reached Jowan's cottage door and Alex slipped the key in the lock, she felt a panic rise in her chest. She'd be all alone in there with her thoughts, and she didn't like that idea at all.

Magnús, however, held out two packages, both of which he'd taken the time to place in white paper bags. 'Your book, remember? And also, some cake for your bedtime snack. Read yourself to sleep. The storm will be gone in the morning if what they say is true.'

He was reading her mind, surely?

It struck her as she took the bags from his hands that they were the same height and she had to fight the urge to lean forward and kiss his cheek, like she had Mrs C.'s. Or maybe not *exactly* the way she'd kissed the elderly woman. She had a feeling she'd like very much to press her lips to the smooth-looking skin of his fine cheekbones framed by sculpted dark blond stubble. Which was precisely why she wasn't going to do it. She turned the key in the lock.

'Until tomorrow,' he told her.

She watched from the cottage steps as he powered himself up the slope and out of sight, unable to tame the feeling that she had caught a little of the glow he claimed to have always inside him, even when he was straight-faced and serious. 'Incandescent on the inside,' she said with a smile, as she shut the door and made her way to bed.

Chapter Ten

Returning to the Dagalien

She'd done just as Magnús had instructed; read until she slept.

Treasure Island had swept her away into another world of buccaneers and buried gold, of talking parrots with long memories and secrets they spilled on repeat like a broken record, but the descriptions of churning seas and their uncharted depths had unsettled her too, and she felt herself out on the water again in her own little boat. It was only really hitting her how risky putting to sea all by herself had been.

She could have died out there, and because of Ben? 'Not worth it,' she told herself as she'd drifted off, shortly after she heard Jowan letting himself into the cottage and whispering to Aldous, 'It's all right, our castaway's safely home again. Her coat's there by the door.'

Just knowing Jowan was there, her own pirate Jim Hawkins, one of the good guys, had been enough to send her into a deep sleep.

For breakfast, they'd shared the last of Magnús's cake and a pot of tea in front of the fire before Jowan announced he had a book-buying trip that morning, now that the storm had abated. He asked if she would like to go with him, but the knock on the door halted their discussion.

—

'*Hæ hæ*,' Magnús greeted her, holding out the bundle in his arms.

'What's this?'

'You have no clothes. I brought you clothes.'

Alex held the soft jumper to herself. It was thick and long-bodied in creamy white with a deep–blue patterned yoke that swept down over the shoulders. It looked a lot like the one that Magnús was wearing, though his was soft grey and black.

'It's a *lopapeysa*,' he informed her. 'Traditional Icelandic jumper, very cosy. It's yours.'

'Thank you. I'll give it back—' She hadn't finished the sentence before slipping the jumper on over her white rollneck.

'It's yours to keep,' Magnús interrupted. 'Castaways need to stay warm.'

Thanking him, Alex's eye was drawn to the white cottages behind Magnús, their walls glaring in the December morning light. 'The sky has the audacity to be blue? After all that grey?'

Magnús seemed frozen, watching her lifting her long hair out from the neck of the jumper. She may even have swished her locks a little more than was natural, suspecting he was transfixed.

'Shall we, *ah*, go to your boat?' he said with a gulp.

Alex steeled herself with a deep breath. 'If there's any of it left.'

After saying goodbye to Jowan, the pair made their way the last few metres down the cobbled slope and onto the harbour wall where the concrete path split away down the beach.

Alex was dimly aware that, being the same height, Magnús naturally matched her stride. Just another way she felt comfortable in his presence and now here she was, wearing his jumper. What was going on here?

Nothing about the last week and a half made sense to her, and to that she could add the pleasant, sparkling sense of liking Magnús's company to this surprising degree; it was not something she'd experienced with a guy before. She had felt something similar with Eve, however.

They'd hit it off so easily last year, and Alex had always looked forward to their Friday nights at the pub or their stolen chats by the quayside between sailings. They'd laughed like drains and everything had been easy between them, right from day one. *Just goes to show how wrong a feeling can be*, she reminded herself. It hurt, losing her best friend.

Thinking about Eve made her lose her courage as she approached the boat, not wanting to look but knowing she had to.

'Oh my!' Alex stopped dead, gaping at the sight on the shore.

Great piles of kelp and seaweed were strewn across the pebbles, covering almost the whole beach in a gleaming mass of green and gold. Gulls and waders picked through it like treasure hunters hoping for coins washed up in the storm.

Instead of the *Dagalien* lying forlorn on her side like she'd expected, she was astonished to see the boat raised on a roller trailer attached to a beaten-up old Land Rover, and beside it was Tom Bickleigh, lighting a cigarette.

'Morning!' he called with a cheery wave as the pair made their way over to him.

'You did this?' Alex's eyes were all amazement. 'Thank you, Tom!'

'Me and Monty, at first light. Borrowed Minty's Discovery.' He pulled a phone from his pocket, its screen dead. 'This dropped out onto the beach when we righted her. It's yours?'

Alex's face fell as she took it from him and turned it over in her hands. In her haste to leave Port Kernou she hadn't grabbed a charger so the batteries had run down within twenty hours' sailing, and in that time no one had called her.

'Where would we be without our phones, eh?' Tom was asking. 'You'll have a million messages waiting for you.'

Alex slipped the phone into her back pocket, aware that Magnús was watching her with an inscrutable expression. After years of reading about them in novels, she finally understood what 'penetrating blue eyes' looked – and felt – like.

Tom talked on. 'Took the liberty of ringing my mate Charlie from Bideford. He's a shipwright. Reckons he can sort that gunwale and get you watertight again.'

'He can? How long will that take?' Alex may well have managed the maintenance on her ferry but it had never before been damaged like this so she had no idea about timeframes. A small internal voice was chiming, *let it be ages, let it be ages*.

'Depends what your insurance company has to say about it.'

'Oh, of course.' Her burning awareness of the phone in her pocket returned and she lowered her eyes, not wanting

Tom to see her reluctance to rejoin the real world quite yet. Or indeed, ever.

It wasn't the idea of being left on hold for hours with the insurers, or the inevitable paperwork and evidence-gathering that she minded. It was what would come along with it. These things couldn't be sorted out remotely. She'd have to go home, back to her empty house where she had a horrible feeling all the policy documents were.

Magnús had wandered away around the boat to look at the damage and, seeing his chance, Tom took it. 'Going to the donkey blessing tonight?'

'*Uh*,' Alex blinked. 'The what?'

'Up at the estate. Everyone's going. Should be a laugh, at any rate.' He paused, expectant, taking a draw on his cigarette.

'I'd better sort this mess out, I—'

'See how you feel later, eh?' Tom seemed undeterred, but changed the subject anyway. 'Isn't your harbourmaster looking for you? Expecting you back?'

'What? *Oh*…' The panic she'd been swallowing down for days spiked viciously at the thought of Bryony Black-well.

It was her job to monitor the comings and goings in the estuary, make sure nobody was moored up at the quayside who had no right to be, and generally keep an eye open for everyone's safety, especially in bad weather. She must have watched Alex from her post, binoculars to her eyes, as she set out onto open water. She'd have been wondering what on earth she was up to. Bryony never missed a thing.

Of course, it was Alex's boat to do what she liked with, and there was nothing stopping her leaving her ferrying for a while, other than the dogged sense of filial duty that had kept her at her dad's post all these years. The other ferry operator, Lizzo, used to take her cruiser off around the headland and into open water whenever she wanted something from the big supermarket or when she visited her sister down at Greeb Point for a few days so it wasn't unheard of for boats like the *Dagalien* to leave the village, but at first she had worried Bryony would panic and alert the coastguard that she was acting out of character.

Yet, no calls had come in to her cell phone that first day and she'd heard nothing over the radio, so she'd assumed Bryony hadn't thought much of her sudden sailing away, or, more likely, that she had heard about Ben and Eve and it had all made sense. That didn't mean she wouldn't be getting concerned about Alex and the *Dagalien*'s whereabouts now, however.

Tom laughed, and the sound jolted Alex's frayed nerves. 'There isn't a manhunt going on for you, is there? Where are you from, anyway?'

Struggling to retain control of her breathing, she pressed her hands to her stomach. It didn't help. That was the problem with pretending your problems didn't exist; the looking away made you afraid to look back, in case they'd got even bigger. 'I don't feel well,' she said, her voice small and shaky.

'*Woah*, OK!' Magnús was suddenly by her side and reaching for her. 'May I?'

She nodded, feeling the dizziness overtake her.

'In you get,' he told her, one hand clasping hers and the other on the small of her back, supporting her so she could climb up onto the trailer and over the gunwale. Once inside the boat, she sat down on one of the wooden benches the tourists sat on while being ferried.

Tom carried on with his task of unhooking the trailer from Minty's Discovery, glancing back at Alex with a look of concern but obviously deciding against approaching the pair.

Magnús stood on the beach, only his head and chest visible to Alex over the side of the boat.

'He asks a lot of questions,' Alex whispered. Entirely valid questions, she knew.

'Permission to come aboard?' asked Magnús. 'Is that what you say? I'm not a boat person.'

Magnús easily clambered inside the *Dagalien* and sat beside her, keeping his eyes on the deep blue winter horizon. 'Just breathe,' Magnús said, so quietly Alex wondered if he was saying it to himself.

His closeness settled her anxiety, as did Tom shouting his farewells and climbing into the Land Rover. Alex called back to thank him for his help, but he didn't turn around, only waving out the window as he drove away. Magnús let Alex settle into silence again.

She clasped her hands between her knees and looked at nothing at all, too many feelings circulating within her for comfort.

'Let's get your photographs, *já*?' Magnús said in his soft, gruff way.

Without replying, she stood and made her way inside the cockpit alone. Magnús chose to keep a respectful distance, just like she somehow knew he would. Still, it was comforting knowing he was nearby.

And there they all were, Blu-tacked to the dashboard as if they weren't the most prized of her possessions. Pictures of her mum and dad in the cockpit of the *Dagalien* where she sat alone now; a shot of Alex as a five-year-old in a captain's costume at the river gala, the ferry decorated with black-and-white bunting, everyone smiling; and a shot from a rare holiday at Praa Sands with a lanky, gap-toothed Alex holding a drippy 99, her mum beside her in a stripy sundress.

The photos may well have faded but they were enough to prompt the memory of what it had felt like, having her parents right there with her. Now the pictures were damp. They'd need to be dried quickly in case she lost the images forever. She slipped them carefully into her coat pocket.

Rifling through the cockpit, her hands fell upon some of the documents she'd need: the bill of sale, ancient now and signed in her dad's hand; untidily kept maintenance records and safety certificates held together with elastic bands; but no insurance papers – they were definitely at home. There was some comfort in knowing that Tom hadn't searched through them, thank goodness. They were all clearly marked with the name *Dagalien* and with her Port Kernou address stated on the registration documents. She could hold onto her secrets a little longer.

She glanced around the cockpit, her back slumping. Decades of her family history were now dripping with salt water; the electrics shorted and the wood splintered. She couldn't imagine ever sailing the *Dagalien* again. A growing belligerent streak piped up inside her brain, telling her she didn't ever want to.

Every day, back and forth, handling all the pound coins and fivers, fishing for change in her pocket, pulling pink tickets from a reel in all weathers. Smiling and making small talk with the tourists, pointing out the sea birds and occasional dolphin out in the open water.

That had been her dad's life, not hers. Had he meant for her to carry on with his work? He'd never actually told her so. She'd taken it upon herself, and she wasn't sure why any more.

Of course she'd felt a connection with him here, and it had kept her busy and stopped her from being alone but it had, she was realising, stopped her from doing anything else.

If Magnús hadn't been aboard, she'd have shut herself inside the cockpit and cried. Turning to look at him through the door, she found he wasn't watching her; in fact, he was standing to greet someone approaching the boat. She had seconds to pull herself together before making her way out into the glare to join him.

'All right, you pair?' a cheery, Scottish voice called out. It belonged to a small woman with a big smile coming down the lifeboat slope carrying a basket.

Alex slipped into a spot on a passenger bench and watched her approach.

'You don't know me, but I know you, Magnús,' the woman said. 'I handled all the emails on your booking. Jude Crawley?'

'*Ó, já,*' Magnús offered her a handshake over the side of the boat.

Alex thought it so formal and polite she stopped worrying about her predicament and stared up at him as he straightened his back again.

She had the curious experience of seeing Magnús through Jude's eyes. She must see how his eyes were as blue and pale as the wind-blown winter sky. She must see how rugged and outdoorsy he looked in his super high-tech waterproof jacket. He had the look of a man who'd enjoy yomping up the side of a volcano before stopping at the top to read a moody European thriller and have a slice of cake. How could someone be so fit and fierce and yet so soft too? Did Jude see how his hair was shaven at the sides and the short velvety buzzed areas looked so soft and blond and touchable?

Wait! Alex had to stop herself.

Nothing in the way he'd treated her had been anything other than respectful and, well, really kind of noble, and here she was thinking how nice it would be to run her fingertips through his hair?

She had never thought of Ben like this; properly lustful thoughts that bloomed effortlessly in her brainstem and sank down her spine where they settled in the treacherous muscles of her core and set to work maddening her with longing sensations for this Icelandic stranger who, weirdly, didn't feel at all like a stranger when she was beside him.

Jude had reached a hand out to Alex by now and, in a bit of a daze that made her blush and apologise, Alex shook it. 'Sorry, I was just… it's the shock of seeing the boat again.'

'Looks like you're staying a while?' Jude said, surveying the damage, but not waiting for an answer. 'You'll be needing a wee bit of brunch, I reckon.' She was already in her basket pulling out a paper bag. 'You're Cornish, aren't you? Jowan said so. Hope these live up to expectations. Pasties. I'm experimenting with something new.'

Alex took the bag, now fully awake and functioning with as much adult rationality as she could muster. 'Thanks, I love a pasty. My mum's were legendary.'

This drew Magnús's eyes down to her but she kept hers fixed on Jude, just in case there was pity in his expression. She didn't want to see it from anyone but especially not from Magnús. All she wanted from him was more of that light and warmth that had radiated from him last night.

'While the weather's dry you should make the most of Clove Lore,' Jude was saying, with something provocative and insinuating in her voice, even though she was trying to suppress it. 'Have a walk together.'

'That might be a good idea, now we have a picnic,' Magnús said, acknowledging Jude's gift.

'The waterfall's well worth wandering to, along the beach.' Jude pointed a finger, making them both turn to look over their shoulders at the cliffs along the bay.

'We'll do that,' Magnús told her, making Jude smile to herself.

'I'll away drop these in at the pub, then. Not that they have many guests now. Bella told me their Christmas bookings are almost all cancelled; the storm warnings are putting everyone off travelling. Still, they might get the local lunch crowd.' Jude held up her basket and gave it a little shake. 'Anyway, you enjoy your walk, and your pasties.'

When they'd thanked her and she'd gone on her way to the Siren's Tail, which looked a little sorrowful today without any lights on inside, apart from in the bar room, Magnús turned to Alex, and some of his reserve returned.

'Would you like to see this famous waterfall, with me? And some… pasties?'

Alex's laughter told him she accepted his offer and she shoved the documents into her pocket beside the photographs and clambered out of the *Dagalien*, closely followed by Magnús.

They began the slow trudge over the pebbles and slippery kelp heading away from the lifeboat station and along the bay, all the while staying close to the foot of the cliffs rising above them in a sheer, black craggy wall.

Alex took the opportunity to fill Magnús in on what exactly a pasty was, opening the bag to show him the fat half-moon pastry cases, telling him how they were designed for the dirty hands of Cornish miners to hold the crimped crust and keep the beef, potato and swede pie clean and safe to eat. Magnús had raised his fine brows when she told him there was even a version of the pasty that had a divide down the middle and one side was filled with meat and the other filled with sweet dessert.

'What did they do with the crust?' Magnús wanted to know.

'*Hmm?*'

'The miners?'

'Oh, I've no idea? Feed it to the canary?'

'*Huh?*' Now Magnús was lost.

'Never mind,' she said, waving a dismissive hand and laughing before glancing back at the *Dagalien* now a good distance away and looking far less forlorn and battered from here. Alex liked being unseen out here on the empty beach and, from the set of Magnús's shoulders, he too seemed to be relaxing more the farther they wandered from Clove Lore's prying eyes.

After a moment's silence when they both took in the wide view of the clouds far out on the water, the pale blue overhead, and the dark, dripping cliffs to their right, Alex found herself wanting to get back to the way they'd been when it was just the two of them talking on the boat, or in the bookshop's café. Could she re-establish that easy connection now there was nobody around spying on them or interrupting?

'You said you're not much of a boat person?' she tried. 'Your ancestors are Vikings, aren't they? Sailing's in your blood.'

Magnús frowned at the word. '*Nei*, coffee and books are in my blood. I like dry land.'

'Me too, actually. The dry land thing.'

Magnús nodded, apparently accepting that a person could arrive in a port in a storm wearing a great, waxed ferryman's coat and still not think of themselves as a sailor at all. 'OK,' he said.

'You like books about Vikings, at least?' she asked.

'*Já*, of course. I was raised on Icelandic saga and Norse mythology.' Now he was getting enthusiastic. 'Everyone I know was.'

'Makes you proud?' Alex asked, thinking of the Cornish myths her dad had told her: Tristan and Iseult, Merlin and Arthur, Cormoran the giant, and the mermaid of Zennor. She'd been so deeply steeped in those legends they'd become a part of her identity as much as any lessons learned at school.

'Sure,' Magnús said, 'but being brought up on tales of legendary men doing brave things and killing monsters doesn't do much for your ego. Those guys are remembered for a reason.'

Alex broke into a smile. 'I'm not going to feel sorry for you because you're not Thor.'

'Let me feel sorry for myself then. I don't even sail. My ancestors are ashamed of me.' Magnús was smiling, flashing straight white teeth and unwittingly drawing Alex's eyes briefly to his lips before she realised she was in danger of staring. 'Boats in books? I know those,' he said, apparently not noticing the fight within Alex to avert her gaze.

His voice was so light and laughing, Alex knew they had stumbled into his comfort zone. This man was soothed by storytelling and escaping in books in ways she recognised in herself.

'Do you know about Gudrid Thorbjarnardóttir?' he asked. 'Ah, look, over there,' he said, pointing to the white water falling down the vertical black rocks; the waterfall was just becoming visible now they were rounding a shallow promontory. Their boots carried them towards it over increasingly large, smooth rocks.

'Goodrid–tor–barn–otter?' Alex echoed.

He repeated the name and Alex attempted it again. Magnús's level look told her she'd garbled it.

'Close enough,' he let her off the hook. 'Gudrid was from Iceland.'

'I figured that much.'

'And she sailed all the way to America five hundred years before Christopher Columbus had even seen his first bath tub.'

'What? You're making it up.'

'*Nei*, it's all in the *Vinland Sagas*. She had the good sense to come straight back home and forget to tell anyone about the place.'

'Really?' Alex stopped, a few feet before the waterfall, wanting to look at Magnús even more than the natural wonder of the waterfall.

Magnús stopped too. 'Gudrid was brave and pioneering and, as you proved, almost totally forgotten.' The heavy pattering music of the waterfall seeped into their conversation and they broke their fixed gaze and turned to face it, but Magnús talked on. 'She died an old lady on her farm. Every time I read the old tales I wonder how she lived with the memories of doing something like that, so amazing and unexpected, sailing right off the edge of the map, and then just going back to her old way of life as if she hadn't seen a whole new world.'

Both of them thought hard, lifting their faces to where the water cascaded over the cliff. The water had worn the rock precipice into a deep bite high above them.

Alex spoke first, after a long while. 'Going back home must have been more appealing than starting a new life there, I guess? Or it was safer or easier to head home and just do what was expected of her. Gudrid, I mean.'

Magnús glanced at her briefly before saying they should find somewhere to eat their pasties. He led the way towards the waterfall and found the water disappeared into a deep, dark cavern in the beach surrounded by jagged wet rocks.

'There's a cave behind the waterfall,' he called back to Alex who seemed stuck on her spot on the pebbles. 'But we'll get wet trying to get in there. Here.' He took off his waterproof and spread it on a flat boulder a little distance from the cascading water. 'Sit down.'

They squeezed together onto the rock. 'Won't you be cold?' she asked, but Magnús reminded her with a fist to his chest that he was a fierce Viking and they smiled and opened the bag.

'Jude knew I was Cornish,' Alex said, before taking her first bite. 'So did Jowan.'

'Your accent?' Magnús offered.

'I guess. Do you know Cornwall? It's the next county down.'

'Cornwall? Nei. I've only been to London on a school trip.'

'You haven't travelled much?'

'I have. New Zealand, Canada, Rome, Sweden, a lot of places, with my parents on summer vacations.'

'Oh.' Alex hadn't expected this, somehow. She waited for Magnús to ask her about her travels, but he didn't. She'd never been anywhere anyway.

Not that she'd had any big travel plans of her own, but she had barely left Cornwall. It struck her she hadn't made it to London when even Magnús had seen the place. Still, she was glad he wasn't prying. In fact, he was taking big bites of the pasty and telling her how good it was while looking back at the waterfall. She got the feeling he was trying to make her feel unobserved; he was so exaggeratedly focusing his attentions on anything but her.

If he knew the truth, he'd want to know how on earth a twenty-six-year-old could be so independent and so work-worn and yet so inexperienced at the same time?

She couldn't bear strangers knowing how she'd never left the county, never done anything special after leaving school, always living in the same home, keeping to the same old routines. It made her feel sad and sorry for herself. She bit it down, along with another mouthful of the really very good pasty. Not as good as her mum's, of course, but good.

She was an oddity, she was realising. A young woman who'd known terrible grief as a child and who, at eighteen, had inherited a weight of responsibility that many middle-aged adults would find daunting.

She'd coped with it all by adopting a hardened, dogged spirit of determination to just keep going, getting through one day, then the next, and so on, never giving up and never breaking down, and yet for all her independence and competence, she hadn't really grown up. Comparing herself to the worldly Magnús, brave and pioneering, she was still a kid. A kid with bills and responsibilities and chores, but not a fully fledged adult.

There were so many things she'd never experienced that most of her school friends had: girls' holidays abroad, working under bosses, climbing career ladders, making a home of her very own, decorating, throwing house-warming parties and engagement parties, planning

97

hen-dos. Instead, Alex had clung to the few things she'd known as a child, and the things she'd lost, she'd tried to recreate with Ben and the Thomases.

And yet, she was like the pioneering Viking Gudrid. She'd seen further than her peers at a young age, sighting new, frightening dangerous places – death and grief – no child should have to trespass in, and she'd come back a changed person, only to live a small, simple, fearful life.

Losing your mum when you were a little girl would do that to a person, she thought – convince you that the future was so risky there was no point in making plans. Life would do what it wanted to you anyway, no matter how hard you tried to forge ahead on your chosen path.

Alex sank deeper inside herself, forgetting Magnús and the waterfall and the blue sky entirely.

Why were these thoughts, so clear and so disquieting, only coming to her now that she was in Clove Lore? How long had they been forming at the back of her mind and settling in the pit of her stomach, heavy and dull? Had her break from the relentlessness of the endless estuary crossings given her time to actually think for the first time in years?

She supposed it was only natural, now that she couldn't sail for a while, that she'd weigh up her options. On one hand, she could restore her father's historic ferry and relaunch it, continuing the work he'd begun and carrying on his legacy, or she could… she could…

No alternatives whatsoever presented themselves to her. She'd never allowed herself to dream any bigger than that.

Magnús shifted on the rock. His movement stirred her and she found herself talking.

'You called me a castaway earlier, but I'm not. I'm more of a runaway.'

'Me too,' Magnús told her, and they both turned to inspect the other.

She didn't know what to say next but the faintest smile twitched Magnús's lips, enough to reassure her he really wasn't going to ask her what she was running from, and he wasn't going to tell her about the life he was taking a break from either. Magnús scrunched the empty bag in his hands. 'I ate the crust,' he told her blankly.

He was so disarmingly odd and so considerate of her privacy she couldn't help shaking her head in surprise. She held up the crimped crust of her own pasty for his inspection before throwing it onto the pebbles.

Within seconds, the gulls descended and fought noisily over it. Pulling out his phone, he snapped a picture of the birds but he didn't turn the lens towards her, which was a relief of course, but there was a tiny part of her pride wishing he'd tried.

Didn't he want a memento of their brunch at the beautiful waterfall? Didn't he want a shot of her to keep? She told herself off for wanting privacy while harbouring this new sneaking desire to share herself with him. She couldn't have it both ways. She had to decide which desire was stronger. Keeping her sorry story to herself and getting out of here scot-free when the time came, or encouraging Magnús to open up to her more.

She wanted to know him better, and yet, she knew that wouldn't come without a cost. The thought of Magnús pitying her then trying to persuade her to reach out and contact her loved ones back home overwhelmed her thoughts, and she shook them away.

'You're not opening your bookshop this morning? Now that Tom's saved the boat and I have all my stuff here, you don't have to stay.' She sprang to her feet, putting her hand against the papers and pictures in her pocket. It was pitiful, really. So little to show for a life.

'My bookshop?' Magnús stood too and shook out his jacket. 'Almost all the guests from the pub left when the storm hit, and the reports of another weather front coming in won't have tourists rushing back. I have no customers. I heard on the radio this morning they've named the second storm now, Storm Nora. They don't name an approaching storm unless it's going to cause trouble. And anyway, the locals are busy getting ready for Christmas, and they don't seem to need books either. I have nothing to do.'

'Rubbish, you have a whole shop to play in.'

Magnús's voice was abrupt. 'I don't want to play at being a shopkeeper.'

Alex squinted at him.

'*Ugh*, OK.' Magnús's shoulders dropped an inch as he exhaled. 'It's a long story but I didn't choose to be here, not really. Now I'm here I don't know what to do with myself.'

'I get it. You feel like you're holding a treasure map but there's no X marking the spot,' Alex said, looking down at her boots.

'Exactly. I feel, I feel… *stefnulaus*?'

'Lost?' Alex guessed.

'Aimless.'

'Ah! That's it. Nail on the head. I'm the runaway, you're the castaway. We're both a bit stef-la-noose.' She pronounced it terribly to make him smile again and it worked.

'*Já*,' Magnús agreed. 'So what do you want to do now?'

She fixed her eyes on the tiny dot of the *Dagalien*. 'I need to get my phone working. If it *can* work again. I'll go see if Jowan has a charger.'

They started the walk back, slow and reluctant.

'Listen.' Magnús sounded cautious. 'I know you can't tell me about yourself and I'm sure you have good reasons, but I can help you if you want it. They,' he tipped his head towards the harbour, 'don't have to know. I can keep a secret.'

This set all of Alex's instincts and feelings warring against each other again.

'There is something you can help with,' she said, looking for a way out of the maelstrom.

'Name it.'

'You can take me to the donkey thing this afternoon.'

'Í guðanna bænum!' he laughed. 'You know about this too? What is it with everyone and donkeys around here?'

'We can go?'

'We can go. I don't think we have any choice, but yes, let's go.'

Slowly they walked back to the harbour, making the smallest of small talk, and Alex felt her resolve weakening with each step, the words threatening to spill out: *I've lost my family, and my second family; now I'm alone and I've nothing to offer anyone. I've wrecked my dad's boat, put myself out of a job, and I can't bear the idea of being alone for Christmas so I'm hiding out here, terrified you'll all send me back home when you realise who I am. There! I'm not what you think I am. Spent my twenties playing at being an adult. Never even left England. Slept with one man and he cheated on me. Had one best friend and she betrayed me. I'm a shipwreck of a person. Hollow and sad. How'd you like me now, Magnús Sturluson?*

Chapter Eleven

A Blessing in Disguise

'I know I'm supposed to love all animals, but Moira really is a pain in the arse.'

Elliot observed the elderly donkey from the far side of the stable. At the first sight of her halter she'd stuck her nose firmly in the corner and parked herself there, as immovable as a caravan up on bricks.

'You don't have to love her,' said Jude, only just realising what she'd got her boyfriend involved in and feeling guilty. 'You're not Saint Francis of Assisi, let's just get her in her hat and up to the Big House.'

'Her... *hat*?'

Jude pointed to the straw boater that Minty had left for them. It had holes for Moira's ears and winter ivy and berries all around the brim.

Elliot's eyes blazed. 'Pretty sure that counts as cruelty to animals. And getting that thing on her definitely amounts to cruelty to vets. I won't do it.'

'OK,' Jude conceded. 'Shall we at least try to get Bon Jovi in his cape?' She held up the green velvet fur-lined affair for Elliot's approval. 'I think he'll look lovely in it.'

Bon Jovi, the littlest of the stable's mules, skittered about on the cobbles knocking over their feed bucket and making the donkeys in the surrounding stalls hee-haw loudly.

One of them, Mushy Peas, generally known as the most biddable of the lot, was proudly dressed in a red festive jumper with a sprig of crocheted holly between her long spiked ears.

'God's sake. Give it here.' Elliot took the cape, and so began a half hour's muttering and cursing, accompanied by what he could have sworn were the sounds of donkey laughter.

By the time they made it to the little chapel the winds were getting up again and the sky was clear and star-spotted, Bon Jovi had lost his cape on a spiky hedge way back at the entrance to the estate, and Moira had tossed her hat onto the bridleway and trodden it into the mud. Elliot, in spite of his size and soft-heartedness, was utterly cheesed off and very tired. Jude followed up the rear with the angelic Mushy Peas plodding along beside her.

The chapel, Elliot had to admit, did look inviting, even with the light spilling out through missing tiles on the roof. There were candles at every little window.

The chapel had been a simple construction, built by Minty's grandfather in the early nineteen-twenties for his increasingly devout French wife. Though if you listened to village lore, the holy Mrs Clove-Congreve made use of her private chapel to escape the demands of the Big House nursery and her noisy brood of children – and then, later on, her husband. As if to support the notion, when she died, a well-thumbed stash of Barbara Cartlands and hidden Turkish Delight boxes had been discovered beneath the front pew.

There was room for roughly eighteen people sitting and the same number standing around the pews and squeezed into the narrow vestibule, and tonight the chapel was full indeed, probably for the first time since Minty's parents' wedding day.

Minty didn't go in much for religion, even though she enjoyed having the parish vicar at her beck and call for odd jobs such as donkey blessings or the opening of a fox and field day or a fete in the summer months.

Reverend Morgan dabbed his brow as the donkeys were led into the chapel. All the children had been given flameless candles to hold and only a few of them had been tempted to take out the double A batteries and roll them around noisily on the little shelves on the backs of the pews.

Everyone Minty invited had turned up, so naturally she was delighted.

Jowan, with Aldous under his arm and snoring loudly, took the front row alongside Bella and Finan, who didn't look all that pleased to be dragged away from the quiet of the pub. Their only remaining inn guests, the Austens, were with them on the pew, Serena fast asleep in a sling across her dad's chest.

The Bickleigh twins were together as usual and Tom winked at Alex when she arrived late and sneaked in at the back, though his face fell when Magnús arrived a second behind her, reverently pulling off his woollen beanie because he thought that was probably the sort of thing you should do at a Devonshire donkey blessing in a draughty chapel.

Mrs Crocombe was with her daughter and son-in-law and a gaggle of blonde children wrapped up warm and cooing over the animals as they clip-clopped up to the altar.

The rest of the village had turned out too, on pain of Minty's disapproval, including the teaching assistant from the local primary school, Monica Burntisland, her husband, who hadn't taken his eyes off his phone screen since they arrived – he was something big in finance – and their own three children. Anjali the vet was at the back with her parents and grandparents, smiling broadly at her colleague Elliot who had very much drawn the short straw tonight.

Leonid and Izaak had arrived early and helped Minty arrange the winter greenery in the brass vases that decorated the pew ends, half of which Bon Jovi had knocked onto the stone flags and then given a disinterested nibble before deciding it wasn't for him. He was now snuffling at the children's pockets and mittens looking for sweets.

Some of the busybodies who had gathered outside Jowan's cottage the day before hoping for a glimpse at Alex were there too and making no secret of discussing her appearance at the service.

Generally there was much chatter and excitement and the poor vicar had to do his best to talk over the whole rabble until it was time for the school children to come up to the front and murder 'Little Donkey' on their recorders, which they did with utter solemnity while their parents caught it all on camera.

The whole time, Alex and Magnús were wedged firmly together in the crush right at the back of the crowd and every time Magnús fought to stifle a laugh, Alex felt his shoulders shaking and it set her off again. Even with the holes in the roof, their little corner of the chapel seemed to be growing warmer.

When Minty took over proceedings, announcing that each creature would now receive Holy Communion and the vicar had spluttered and looked terrified at this renegade break from their plans – not to mention every church practice in the land – Magnús had almost burst with joy. Alex had to turn away entirely to hide her face in his shoulder as Minty presented each creature with a slurp of Ribena from a silver bowl and a Jacob's cream cracker slathered in Dairylea.

The whole affair was wonderfully bonkers, wholly unnecessary, and right up Minty's street.

When the vicar finally regained control, he wisely took the decision to cut the Lord's Prayer, ditch the final carol, and dismiss everyone as quickly as possible with an anxious, 'Merry Christmas everyone, and to all God's creatures,' before he bustled out of the chapel, past the donkeys still licking at their fuzzy chops. No doubt he was on his way to put in a pre-emptive call to the arch-deacon in case he got wind of it, to explain that the whole irreverent mess was Minty Clove-Congreve's doing and if they'd only met her they'd understand his predicament. She really was impossible to say no to.

Minty didn't mind one bit. High on the success of the evening, she clapped her hands, startling all the donkeys into a fit of loud braying, and declared the cocktail party would begin in a few moments in the ballroom.

'Shall we?' Alex asked Magnús, wiping her eyes, her cheeks burning pink. 'Ah, that was amazing!'

–

Alex looked around in wonder as Minty gave her and Magnús the grand tour of the oak-panelled lobby and ballroom – the only two of the party who hadn't visited the Big House before.

At first, the Christmas tree and the paperchains did a good job of hiding it, but as Alex's eyes grew accustomed to the candlelight she noticed the thick cobwebs at the highest points of the ceiling, the peeling paint around the cornicing and the big bits of stucco missing from what must once have been an impressive frieze depicting a fox hunt racing all the way around the room.

There was a sad single bulb where a chandelier must have dazzled long ago. The bulb was doing its best but the many white candles in rusting sconces all along the panelled walls had to make up the shortfall.

A black grand piano stood at the centre of the room. It looked very old and valuable. The oak floor was shining, freshly polished for Christmas, and judging by the stern look on Bovis's face at the sight of Mrs Crocombe's daughter's stiletto-heeled boots, it had been his handi-work. The young mum paid him no attention. This was her first night out in months and she was making the most of it out of sight of the school kids and parents who'd gone straight home after the service. She'd taken two cups of festive gin punch from the drinks table in the lobby and kept both for herself.

Minty was speaking proudly about how, decades ago, a young Winston Churchill had danced her own mother – a little girl at the time and in her nightgown – around the ballroom when she'd stumbled into one of Grandfather Clove-Congreve's legendary after-hunt parties.

Minty didn't hold with hunting, but she did hold with other traditions as far as she could. Alex listened as she told them how all the portraits had been sold years ago when the estate ran into debt – all but one. A rather foppish-looking man in hunting pinks stared down at them from his frame on the wall. 'Grandfather Clove-Congreve,'

Minty told them. 'I couldn't part with him, even if he is going a bit fusty up there, poor chap.'

'Great moustache,' Magnús said, so seriously that Minty thanked him.

'He was always rather dapper,' she added, gazing up admiringly. 'Mad as a brush, unfortunately, and rotten with cash. But still, traditions must hold. He's staying on the wall, and that's that.'

'No paintings of your own parents?' Alex asked, just as the murmur of chatter in the room dipped and everyone heard her overloud enquiry.

After a beat, during which Minty's face grew suddenly haggard, she said, 'No,' and the coolness in the word was enough to stop Alex asking any more questions.

'Don't worry about her,' Jude whispered, once Minty had strode off to discuss something with Jowan. 'She's hard to work out at first, but once you know her story, you can't help feeling sorry for her. She doesn't mean to be brusque.'

'She doesn't mean to, only its tradition,' Elliot said dryly, before shaking hands with Magnús and introducing himself.

Elliot had thrown out all his resolutions about having a carb-loading, lean Christmas and downed a beer in seconds, his reward for getting those donkeys back in their stables while miraculously remaining unkicked and unbitten.

Jude was more sympathetic. 'It can't be easy for her. This whole place was her family's, and now she's confined to just these rooms, a wee kitchen and a bedroom while the rest of the house is turned over to developers, apart from Izaak and Leonid's attics. Her dad squandered their entire fortune apparently, until her mum had had enough and disappeared to somewhere sunny. Where was it again?'

'Madeira,' Elliot put in.

'That's it, and Minty couldn't keep the house going any longer. She's got no brothers or sisters to help out, either. They're turning the place into private lets now. The builders moved in last month; they're gutting the place.'

'That's a shame,' said Alex, watching Minty across the room. 'So she was saddled with an inheritance she didn't want.'

'She was, hence all her "must stick with tradition" stuff and her desperation to attract visitors to the estate gardens.'

Elliot, still brooding about the donkeys, had lost interest in Minty's misfortunes and was talking with Magnús. 'We were at the bookshop before you, back in the summer, you know?'

'That's where we first met,' said Jude, suddenly drawn in. 'We arrived separately, not knowing each other. It was a double-booking mistake kind of thing.'

'Best mistake of my life,' Elliot smiled.

Mrs Crocombe seemed to have sniffed out that the conversation was turning to singledom and slunk up behind Magnús, making him flinch when she began explaining how she'd been responsible for bringing Jude and Elliot together and that they were likely to get married soon.

'*Eh!*' Jude flustered, 'Cool your boots, Mrs C. There's no wedding bells ringing in Clove Lore any time soon. Elliot, shouldn't we check on the…' She pointed to the door where they'd come in, and Elliot caught on quickly and agreed that yes, it was indeed time to go and check on that thing, and the pair said their goodnights and bustled off.

Alex heard them whispering as they left, about Mrs Crocombe being relentless and how she wouldn't be happy until they'd gifted the local school with triplets.

Jude was still laughing brightly as she and Elliot swept out into the dark night and away from the village match-maker. They had zero plans to emerge from their cosy home until after Christmas now that Elliot was on holiday and Jude's uni assignments were in for the year.

Left alone, Alex glanced over Mrs Crocombe's head towards Magnús as though sending a wordless SOS through sheer willpower. The older woman was drawing a notebook from her pocket and asking Magnús to kindly spell his surname and if he had any plans to stay in the country after his holiday was over. Alex's heart turned hummingbird at the thought of the inquisition being directed towards her next.

'Mrs C?' Magnús stooped a little to talk to her. 'Is Minty married?'

'Married? Goodness, no. She's been alone all her life, running this place. Married to the estate.'

'And yet?' Magnús said, tipping his head to indicate Minty and Jowan standing by the blazing fireplace, 'I think she has a partner?'

Jowan and Minty were absorbed in telling Aldous what a good boy he'd been at the blessing. The little dog wiggled in Jowan's arms, his neck stretched ceiling-ward for scratches, supremely happy with his lot in life. Minty fished something from her bodywarmer pocket and slipped it to the little dog – a piece of cooked liver from the kitchens – and all the time Jowan was smiling placidly into Minty's face, agreeing with everything she said.

'No-o,' said Mrs Crocombe, slapping a hand to Magnús's chest. 'They're old friends, those two, going way back. They're not a match.' And yet, Mrs Crocombe kept her eyes fixed on the pair. 'They couldn't be. Not with Isolde occupying so much of Jowan's heart.'

'And yet, hearts change. They make room,' Magnús said sagely, setting wicked, gleaming eyes upon Alex who tried hard not to giggle as Mrs Crocombe took the bait.

'He does talk about her a lot,' Alex added. 'With admiration.'

Mrs Crocombe's eyes narrowed upon the cosy three-some by the fire, lit from behind by its rays which shone out around them in a glowing halo, a little holy trinity with Aldous, their special boy, at the centre, the site of interchange of Minty and Jowan's affections.

'She does seem to like that dog very much,' Magnús added, knowing only another little nudge was all it would take.

Mrs Crocombe's brain worked. 'I'd better not stand here talking all night,' she said distractedly, still peering at Minty and Jowan, as though running through all the recent interactions she'd witnessed between them. 'Better… mingle,' she said, and with that, she glided away, seeking out Izaak to pump him for information about his boss and whether she'd been having an increased number of visits from her old friend of late.

'I thought she'd never go,' Alex's shoulders drooped with relief.

'Poor Jowan, he's in trouble now!' Magnús added.

'But we should leave, shouldn't we?' Alex suggested. 'Before she circles back round to us. Jowan told me that notebook in her hand is her betting book. There's a whole village sweepstakes thing going on, taking bets on who'll get it on with who.'

'And we don't want to end up in her book.' The upwards inflection in Magnús's accent made this sound very much like a question.

Alex downed her champagne. 'I don't, no.'

'Of course not. Me neither. *Mmm-mm*, no way, José,' Magnús rambled, looking like he wished someone would stop him talking. His brows formed their tight little 'v' once more and Alex couldn't help smiling at the sight.

She led him back through the once grand ballroom to the draughty foyer where the punch bowl and champagne were set out. Lifting another two glasses of bubbly, she pressed one into Magnús's hands.

'Cheers to that,' she said, and took a long drink. It was delicious and definitely the expensive stuff, no doubt from Minty's wine cellar. Alex wondered aloud how rich people could plead poverty but somehow managed to find the ready money for things like this. She had no idea Jowan had paid for it all, as his Christmas gift to Minty. 'God, that's nice. You can see why Churchill liked it here.'

Magnús mirrored Alex, throwing back the whole glassful, then wiping at his mouth.

'When did you last drink champagne?' she said with wonder, more to herself than to him, but the words halted Magnús's hand as he set the empty glass down.

'When I opened my bookshop in Reykjavík.' His face closed like shutters slamming.

A little alarmed, Alex lifted two more glasses and led him to the cloakroom. 'Naughty not to have another, when it's almost Christmas, and it's free.' Glancing back to check he really was following, she shoved her way through the coats and scarves hanging on rails and sat down on an ancient wooden chest emblazoned with the words 'Master

Clove-Congreve. Clove Lore,' and underneath it a crest she didn't recognise as belonging to Eton College.

The bubbly in her bloodstream told her to pat the box beside her, and obediently, Magnús sat down. 'Your bookshop opening sounds like a good story to tell on a winter's night in a creepy old house.'

'OK, if you really want to know? I warn you, it's kind of scary!' His voice was wry but he still took a deep breath and let the words flow. 'It all began when I left school and did a degree in bookselling.'

It was news to Alex you could study such a thing, but she didn't interrupt. To her surprise he told her all about it, the hours of studying, the weekends gaining work experience in bookshops all across the city. He laid it all out, every laborious step on his way to winning, and losing, his bookshop.

'After I graduated I spent years working in a tacky juice shop for tourists. Man, I hated that place, but I finally had enough money saved up to look for a business start-up loan and… that was it. I opened Ash and the Crash. Best day of my life.'

The light in his eyes dimmed as he went on to tell her about Anna leaving when things were at their worst. By then, Alex found herself lulled by the music of his voice into somehow shifting her body so she was facing him. Their knees were so close to touching it was almost all she could think about. Then he explained how he'd ended up here on this crazy getaway. All the while, his voice was low and his eyes cast down at the glass in his hand.

When he was finished he remarked that he'd definitely had too much champagne but still took a long drink and let the silence settle. The sounds of Minty demanding everyone sing around the piano while Jowan played a carol reached them and they both smiled when the chords of a slightly out of tune 'The Holly and the Ivy' rang out.

'So you see,' Magnús lifted his eyes. 'I can't really go home early. My family are expecting me to have fun on vacation, and yes, spending time out of Reykjavík is good for me… but I don't know what to do here. The Borrow-A-Bookshop, it's so…'

Alex tipped her head, inviting Magnús to maintain eye contact, which he did. 'So…?' she encouraged.

'So fake.'

'I was in there yesterday, it seemed pretty real to me.'

'It's not the shop, it's… it's me. If there were actually some customers in the village maybe I could sell some books, get that feeling back of being a bookseller. Ah, I *loved* that feeling. And I could do inventory, and order new stock. That's what I want to do. To prove that maybe I can actually do it. To remember I wasn't so bad at it, after all. But the place is dead. The storms chased everyone away and I'm just sitting there alone, like I was before. And I don't like so much time to think; it feels bad, and all those unread, unsold books on the shelves!' He seemed to shudder at this. 'It reminds me too much of my…' Magnús's words tailed off.

'Say it. It'll help,' Alex urged, entirely forgetting she'd have run a mile if he'd been pressing her to vocalise her feelings like this.

'My failure. It reminds me too much of my failure.'

Alex was right. Saying the words aloud loosened the hard knot he'd been carrying in his chest, and other words followed, tumbling out of his mouth.

'I had everything I wanted and it went wrong, and I don't know why, honestly. I have *no idea* what went wrong for me. My teachers, my parents, they told me if you work for something and you really fight for it, it will happen. So that's what I did. I studied, I worked, I saved. I spent every hour I could at my shop and I still lost it all. And now I don't know how I'll ever get back that enthusiasm, that drive, you know? I failed, and it's gone. Does that make sense?'

Alex thought hard. 'I think so. I mean, I haven't been in the same position.' It struck her that she'd never striven the way Magnús described. She'd never had the same ambition, or courage. 'I've always done my best, I suppose. But I've never had anything I really, really wanted, like your Ash…'

'And the Crash.'

'Right.' She gulped, feeling dizzier by the second at the feelings rushing in. 'You really went for it. I admire that. I've always just gone along with life.' Saying it out loud for the first time pained her almost as much as seeing the sorrow in Magnús's eyes when he beat himself up about his business going under.

In her mind, she replayed how she'd tumbled headlong into humdrum. The day after the funeral, lifting her dad's keys and going to the riverside, walking like an automaton, not knowing what else to do for the best. She'd started the motor and written the crossing times on the chalk board and within half an hour she'd ferried her first customers. It had been as easy as that to fall into. There'd been no intention or planning behind it, only a feeling of being lost, and maybe a sense of duty and of wanting to stay in the same familiar pattern set by her father. A horrible thought struck her.

'I didn't put in any of the work you did, and I still lost everything anyway.' Her voice shook. She took a gulp of champagne to disguise it.

'So you're damned if you try and damned if you don't?' Magnús said. 'I hate that.'

This made Alex shake her head. 'No. No, that can't be right. Some people get their dreams, right?'

'*Já*, plenty.' Magnús was surprised to find himself thinking of Izaak and Leonid and the story they'd told him. They'd achieved their dream jobs, a happy home, and real love all at once.

Magnús's hand made its own way to the throb in his chest and he rubbed at it. He said once more that he'd had too much champagne. All the while, Alex's eyes were darting and flickering in the half light as she sifted through the thoughts coming to her.

'I won't accept that you can't have your dream,' she said at last.

'What's this? You're having some kind of inspiration?'

'We'll open your shop,' she told him, a smile spreading. 'We will?'

'Yes!' She was emphatic. 'Tomorrow, first thing. Why not? You want to prove you're not some faker or a failure? Let's open the shop and sell books all day and... do whatever booksellers do. And I,' she rose to her feet, 'I could run the café!'

These last words had flown from her subconscious straight out of her mouth. She froze at the sound of them resounding in the cloakroom.

'You want to do that?' Magnús narrowed his eyes.

'*Um*.' She thought, suddenly becoming still. 'Yes. I really think I do.' More emphatic nodding followed, her mind catching up with her mood. 'I think I'd really, *really* like that, actually.'

'Like your mum.' Now Magnús was the one wondering at his words. He'd risen to his feet too. 'Sorry.

I shouldn't have said that. You got me all worked up about the shop, I was just excited.'

'No, you're right. I think I'd like to be in that café and see what it feels like.' The last of her words got lost in a hurried gulp of emotion.

Where was all this coming from? She knew she wanted to hide away in Clove Lore until she worked out what to do next, but now she was volunteering to run a café?

'What will you sell in your café?' Magnús was grinning at her now, even though her adrenaline was spiking and eyes widening like saucers.

'I guess, milkshakes and toasties and chocolate crispy squares?'

'OK,' Magnús laughed, and he took her hands in his. 'OK,' he nodded, wanting to reassure her. 'Let's do that. And we won't play, we'll really do our best. Bookselling and feeding people.'

Magnús's touch sparked another level of light-headedness in Alex and she found her gaze lifting from where he clasped her fingers to meet his shining eyes. He really was glowing on the inside, she could feel it.

One of them was breathing loudly but she wasn't sure which, and their feet seemed to have shifted closer, closing the distance between them until their joined hands were pressed between their chests.

She felt her eyelids growing heavier as her gaze settled on Magnús's lips, soft-looking and full. All she had to do was lean in.

She knew instinctively that he wasn't going to make the move. He would hold still, making sure the kiss was definitely what she wanted. The faintest, most intimate, gentle smile at the corners of his mouth was all it took to make her tip her head and…

'*Carriages!*' Minty called from somewhere nearby, her footsteps getting closer. A brash light came on over their heads, entirely breaking the magic.

Alex gasped. 'Everyone's leaving.'

She and Magnús sprang apart and made a show of searching at opposite ends of the rails.

'Ah, there you are!' Minty announced on discovering the pair rummaging unconvincingly.

Alex's voice was pitchy. 'Magnús is helping me find my hat.'

The whole party was gathering by the cloakroom now. Mrs Crocombe's right eyebrow was arched in a knowing way which Magnús hadn't seemed to notice but which worried Alex terribly.

'Walk you home, Alex?' Jowan was saying, as he pulled on his jacket and tucked Aldous inside.

Wordlessly, after throwing an apologetic smile at Magnús, Alex squeezed through the crowd and made for the door in Jowan's wake.

With that, the evening was over and Alex had somehow, in her zeal to help Magnús repair some of his hurt pride, decided to step into her mum's shoes as a diner owner. The impulse had come from somewhere so deep within her she hadn't even known it was there, but now that the agreement had been reached she couldn't wait for morning, and if playing in Borrow-A-Bookshop all day was going to delay her rejoining the real world for a little longer, all the better.

Chapter Twelve

Bottled Messages

Alex had drifted back Down-along that evening, talking with Jowan about all the ingredients she'd need if she was to help out in the café tomorrow, and she had seemed cheerful on the surface, yet on the inside she'd felt a numb, but not unpleasant, kind of shock.

All the way home in the drizzling rain, all the way upstairs and into bed, she'd held it together, smiling and saying goodnight to Jowan, but her brain was crackling with activity.

She'd almost kissed Magnús, and even though it had felt like he was going to kiss her back, she had been the one instigating the whole thing.

She replayed it over and over, looking for anything she might have missed. He'd held her hands. That was all him. But she had been the one stepping closer and leaning in, closing her eyes, wanting it.

What had she been thinking? Runaways didn't go getting involved in cloakroom clinches with near strangers, no matter how much those strangers radiated warmth from their very insides; not even if being near them felt like reaching a life raft after days floundering in the ocean.

Shipwrecked women were supposed to lie low and concentrate on survival. If she were on a desert island right now, she'd be focused on sorting out her basic needs: food, warmth and shelter. Yet these were all things Magnús seemed to represent.

He'd given her a jumper, baked for her, made her sit and drink coffee when she'd been unsure what else to do, and it had all been so easy, and she definitely felt safe with him. *Dammit!* This was not at all what she'd planned.

Getting in the *Dagalien*, sailing off into the horizon – she was supposed to be running *away* from everything, not running towards the first hot landlubber she laid eyes on. And he *was* hot. She'd felt it when he'd pulled her from the boat, and she'd seen it when they'd talked in the café, but with all the champagne and Christmas carols and the feeling of being the only two sane people in the entire county she'd been hit by the full effect of it tonight.

He was magnetic somehow, pulling her in, and frankly everything he did, from his straight-faced joking to the way his blue eyes lit up like dawn over the Atlantic whenever he was listening to her speak, was completely delightful to her.

What on earth was going on? Was this how it worked for other people? How was it possible to take one look at a person from a faraway land and instantly connect with them?

That was not how it had been with Ben. She'd known of Ben's existence since she was at primary school, even though he was in the year below her, and she'd been to discos and youth clubs where he'd hung around with his mates and hadn't given him a second glance. When they were older, he was always at the local pub at the weekends and they'd chatted now and again but it had taken an unexpected New Year's Eve kiss at midnight after lots of Sambuca and then weeks of shy, tentative dating to decide she might quite like him enough to kiss him again.

Even then, after falling into a cosy cycle of work, dinner, telly, bed, she'd never experienced the same electric current of attraction passing between her core and someone else's like when she'd stepped close to Magnús tonight. That jolting, buzzing magic just hadn't been there with Ben and until tonight, she hadn't even known it had been missing.

She stroked at her hair in bed with the brush (Isolde's) that Jowan had let her use, wearing the oversized T-shirt that read 'Crocombe's Ices' with a big strawberry sundae printed on the front.

As she brushed, she gave herself a stern talking to – which was the kind of thing a sensible person might do if they wanted to protect their heart and stop themselves making an even bigger spectacle of themselves in a strange place where they'd already been a bother.

She told herself she'd have to leave Clove Lore soon, no matter how cosy she was getting. She told herself Magnús wasn't even from around here. He'd be going home after Christmas, maybe even before then if she failed in her mission of reminding him of the highs of running his own bookshop. There was also the small problem of having run away and left a million messy loose ends she had no idea how to untangle.

So she vowed to stick to her plan. Yes, she'd help Magnús, as any grateful friend would. She'd have fun in the café tomorrow. She'd keep her distance, and her secrets. Then she'd move on. Unfortunately, that was the part of the plan where she still drew a blank. 'What am I going to do after this?' she asked the night.

At that moment, as she pulled the brush through her hair with one last static crackle and laid it down, her old life burst into the shore-side sanctuary she'd made for herself.

Her phone, which had dried out all day long and was now attached to a charger, suddenly awoke, its screen garishly bright, and one after another, loud notification alerts buzzed and pinged, making the screen flash with missed calls and messages.

The blood rushed to her cheeks and made them burn. She found herself hunched over it on the bed, reluctant to touch the thing and wishing the storm had taken her and her phone to the bottom when it had the chance.

She read the messages first. The first one she'd seen ten days ago but hadn't had a chance to reply. It was from Ben's mum and seemed so sweet now, it winded her.

> Just nipping to Waitrose to recce the smoked salmon for Christmas Day. Did you prefer the smoked slices with dill or the moussey parcel things we had last year? You decide, love, Mum

Mrs Thomas had sent it while Alex had been ferrying and, unbeknown to them both, her son had been doing his best to delve into Eve's knickers.

Alex ran her thumb over the word 'Mum'. She wanted to ring her there and then and tell her she'd be back soon and not to forget about her, and not to stop calling herself Mum no matter what she'd heard from Ben, but that was impossible now. She wasn't her mum. They weren't going to be a cosy family any more. Tears blurred her vision as she scrolled and clicked the next message.

Where are you? I'm at my place on my own. Will wait until you get here. I can explain everything when I see you. It definitely wasn't how it looked. I promise. I love you. Come back. Ben x

He must have sent it when she was newly put to sea and with a weak signal. It hadn't got through to her at the time. Alex blinked hard. *It wasn't how it looked?* How could the evidence of her eyes be wrong? Ben had been holding Eve's face in his hands and the whole thing had looked horribly heated and intense.

Was he really going to gaslight her? Did he expect her to believe she'd read it all wrong and he was *innocently* pawing at another woman in her living room? And at lunch time on a Monday, too, which made it all the more insulting.

Alex couldn't remember the last time she and Ben had done anything remotely romantic on a Monday lunchtime, or in the daytime for that matter. Kissing was a Friday night after the pub, lights off and under the duvet kind of thing with them now – had been since the start, if she was honest with herself.

The whole awful shambles was beginning to feel painfully real, unavoidably so. Here were the consequences of her actions coming to get her and they stung. She kept scrolling.

The next message alarmed her so much that her heart thumped and her face flushed. It was from Bryony Blackwell, sent two days ago.

> Please confirm co-ords. Radio contact lost
> with Dagalien. Other shipping sightings:
> Penzance harbour; Lamorna Cove;
> Longships; Cape Cornwall; Godrevy; last
> seen off Boscastle, Dec 17th. All stations
> alerted 19th December 8pm.

A second message from Bryony showed as being sent from a different phone.

> Please just ring me, Alex. We heard about
> Ben and Eve. In fact, he ran down the
> quay after you with no shoes on. If you're
> licking your wounds just let me know.
> They're planning a search, launching
> Christmas Eve, if no further sightings.

So she *had* been spotted on her mad dash north, lots of times. How could she have been so conceited to think a missing boat wouldn't cause a commotion? It had been a few days between the last sighting of the *Dagalien* and the storm that sent her into Clove Lore, so chances were that nobody knew she was there, and there was no harbour-master in the village to record her arrival and tip Bryony off.

Alex tapped out a reply, the sickly sense of panic and shame still stealing her breath away.

> I'm fine. No search needed. Tell Ben's
> parents as well. I'm so sorry. Please don't
> worry, Alex.

She sent the message into the ether and scrolled on, feeling wicked and selfish for worrying everyone. Everyone except Ben, maybe.

> I understand you wanting to get away but if you'd just ring me I can explain. I miss you so much! Please say you're all right. I miss you. I love you. Ben, x

There were a further three from him, all sounding increasingly desperate. One said he knew he'd hurt her but they could sort it out, he was sure of it. A second told her it wasn't fair leaving Lizzo Johnstone to run the only other Port Kernou ferry all by herself (that had only made Alex swear), and there was a third and final plea that she come home for Christmas, telling her his mum and dad were frantic. Alex held back guilty tears at this.

The message to Bryony would quickly put a stop to all the worry. She'd have received it by now and would be relaying it to everyone in Port Kernou. There'd be no need for the Christmas Eve search. The thought of wasting resources pained her. Thank God they hadn't started a search yet. Alex understood the cost of each lifeboat launch, and the risks too.

Ugh! She'd been thinking only of herself while a whole village — well, maybe not a whole village, but a handful of people — were wondering where she was. There'd be plenty gossip too.

She pictured the barflies at the pub saying how she'd caught Ben at it with the new girl from the post office and run off, furious and mad. She knew how these things went and somehow she'd be the crazy woman in all of this.

There was another message from Ben's mum, begging her not to let her boy's 'silly mistake' keep her away from 'her family'. That was the last message, sent yesterday.

It struck her now, how few people had her mobile number, and how small her life had shrunk. Something deep within her cruelly told her that if she kept scrolling there'd be a message from her father telling her that he loved her and advising her what to do. This was of course impossible and ridiculous. Alex sobbed over her phone, worrying how detached from reality she had become, how selfish and stupid she'd been.

The last of the notifications cluttered the screen. She had voice messages. Eight of them were from Ben, all saying the same thing as his texts. Her heart only hardened, hearing his voice. What right did he have to cry like that? Finally, there was a message she was not expecting.

'Lex, it's me.'

She gasped at the sound of her friend's voice. It was Eve, obviously nervous.

'I know you don't want to hear from me but please, just listen. The whole thing was my fault. I'd had another fight with Maxwell and come round to see if you were home for lunch. I was upset and you know how lonely I get and it just sort of happened. We barely had time to think and then you were there and… I swear we didn't do anything. He was in pieces, ran straight out the house after you, but you were gone. I haven't seen him since, I swear, but everyone knows he's distraught. He's been sitting by your mooring waiting for you. Me, Maxwell and Stevie are leaving. So if it's me stopping you coming home then you don't have to worry. I've put in my notice at the post office and we're going back to Maxwell's mum's at Truro.

We're going to try starting over again, *again*. So, Lex, come home. Ben's waiting for you and it's Christmas and… I'm just so sorry.' She sighed shakily and the message ended.

Alex hit delete.

'It *just sort of happened*?' Alex said through gritted teeth. 'They *barely had time to think*?' Alex threw her phone on the bed and spat a long string of expletives into her pillow, making sure Jowan wouldn't hear.

Her tears turned to the hot angry kind, mixed in with searing shame and guilt at all the trouble her disappearance had caused. At least now she'd fixed that. Bryony would have put out a call to all shipping and she'd be forgotten about, like all those castaways and runaways who disappear over the horizon in all the old books are eventually forgotten, and life goes on without them.

After a long time crying into the pillow, she lay on her side and let the tiredness come for her. The last clear thoughts she had were accompanied by an image of Ben sitting on the mooring post on the quayside watching for her. Could that be true? Or was Eve making it all up like she'd bemoaned her poor husband and his neglectful ways? How much of that had been true? It sounded very much like she'd cheated on him before, and that *she* was the problem with that marriage. Then finally, she thought of Eve and Maxwell's little boy, Stevie, only four and a half and so tiny for his age, and so very pale and quiet. What on earth had that poor lad lived through, shunted from pillar to post, moving house every time his mum messed up again?

Eve would never be happy wherever she went and the thought of her little family trailing after her galled Alex even more.

How on earth could Ben have thrown himself at her when he too had met their little boy umpteen times? There was even a box of Lego under her Christmas tree for him back in Port Kernou. He could cheat on Alex in the heat of the moment, sure, but he'd been able to forget about that kid and Eve's husband too, willing to cast them gleefully aside along with his shirt.

Alex sank into a heavy sleep, more determined than ever to stay away from the whole embarrassing, awful affair. At least now she didn't have to worry about the village looking for her.

If she'd been calmer and less tired, she might have checked her phone once more before switching it off that night.

She might have seen her message to the Port Kernou harbour mistress bouncing back undelivered.

Unaware, Alex slept and dreamed of spending a whole day in a peaceful little bookshop café, the very idea of which felt very much like the excitement of a near kiss with a handsome man, the anaesthetising magic of champagne bubbles, and the thrill of Christmas coming, all rolled into one.

Chapter Thirteen

Booktelling

Magnús was turning the sign on the door so it read 'open' when Alex arrived along with Jowan and two big bags of ingredients they'd picked up at the visitor centre shop at the top of the village.

Magnús had chosen his outfit a little more carefully than usual; boots, black winter cargos and a thick black jumper over a fitted grey Henley had seemed appropriate, and he'd spent time scrubbing his cheeks and tidying his beard. He'd pressed cologne to his neck while looking in the steamy bathroom mirror, telling himself it would all be fine. 'Þetta reddast. It's just a normal working day.' Yet he hadn't been able to face his morning coffee. He blamed the champagne while knowing full well this wasn't the same as any kind of hangover he'd had before.

A nervous hunger lay in his stomach when he welcomed Alex into the shop and he was immediately hit by a wave of something sweet.

'You smell good.' The words were out even before he'd said good morning.

Jowan hadn't been able to hide how amusing he found this as he made his way past the pair and into the café with the shopping bags.

'Thanks.' Alex seemed more shy this morning, and somehow more ethereal. She was pale, like she hadn't slept until the early hours, much like Magnús. 'I tried on some perfume up at the visitor centre while we got the stuff for today. This one's called Highland Coral Beach.' She lifted her crooked wrist to his nose, and the action softened his insides. Why was he being like this?

He was going to ask her if she'd bought herself a bottle but decided not to. He had no idea how she was financing her Clove Lore escapade or what she did for a living back home, wherever that was exactly. Did she have any money for luxuries like perfume? Instead, he told her he liked the scent very much.

Alex didn't move from the doormat and Magnús's feet seemed somehow stuck as well, so they stood in her soft aura of lavender and heather mixed with the chilly sea salt air she'd brought inside with her.

Timidly, they assessed one another. Was she going to mention it, Magnús wondered? The way they'd almost kissed? He'd thought of little else since yesterday, half tortured by the idea that she must regret their champagne-fuelled closeness, and half maddened by how much he wished he'd ignored his natural reserve and instead pulled her closer and pressed his lips to hers like he'd wanted to.

Now it was daylight, and there was only coffee, no alcohol, and they had work to do. It wouldn't happen again and it was dawning on him that not kissing her would be his biggest regret about this whole trip.

'Right, anythin' else you two need?' Jowan was back and rubbing his hands for warmth. 'There's fresh logs outside by the steps. Better keep the fire going all day.'

Although it was hard to turn away from Alex's face, so soft today, and so sleepy, Magnús thanked Jowan.

'Oh, and I'll be back down in a mo'. I've a Christmas gift for you both, well, for the shop. Just nippin' up to get it from Minty.' He tapped the side of his fine nose with a finger and winked before starting for the door.

'Tell her we said thank you again, for last night,' Alex said hastily. 'It was lovely.'

'That it was,' Jowan replied, as if thinking back to standing by the ballroom fireplace, head bowed over Aldous in his arms, talking in hushed voices with the lady of the manor.

'Give uz an hour, I'll be back,' he told them with the cunning look of a man who might be cooking up a secret plan to bring a little Christmas cheer to the Icelandic bookseller who always looked so serious and weary except, he and Minty had observed, when in the company of a certain Cornish girl.

'We'll be here,' Alex chimed, as Jowan drew the door closed and the shop fell silent.

Magnús kept his eyes fixed on his guest as she glanced around the shop like she were seeing it for the first time.

'It's beautiful, isn't it?' she remarked, her eyes dancing between the hand-painted signs in curly gold script above each set of shelves, all the late Isolda de Marisco's work: *Philosophy and Psychology, Sciences and Mathematics, History, Biography, Geography, Popular Fiction, Poetry, Literature and Rhetoric, Queer Lives and Loves, Natural Sciences, Arts and Crafts.* The Borrow-A-Bookshop had it all.

On the low shelves and in willow baskets under the spiral of cast iron stairs crouched the *Children's Literature* area with its own pretty sign in gilded lettering and bright rugs on the floor for kids to sit upon and read, and beside that, the low armchair in front of the dark hearth.

'Your fire's gone out,' Alex told him, avoiding his gaze, and for a second Magnús wanted to tell her it really hadn't; he was still burning ardently inside.

'Ó, Já! I'll bring the logs in.' He was sure he heard Alex chuckle as she made for the café.

Turning for the door, his insides butterflied at the exasperating, astounding way she affected him. How was he supposed to do this?

They'd committed to a day's bookselling, but all he really wanted to do was stare at her. Ridiculous, not to mention impossible. These feelings, whatever they were, were all startlingly new to him, and they were accompanied by a sense of needing to practise caution.

Alex seemed even more of a rare treasure now than she had when he'd pulled her from the sea. Seeing her looking fatigued and pale this morning had awakened a desire within him to look after her; another new sensation for him. Even so, something told him Alex would not appreciate this impulse. She'd already shown him she wasn't delicate or some kind of sea-maid in distress. When she'd spoken last night, she'd practically fired sparks of enthusiasm and self-will from her body.

That excitement, he reminded himself, had come from her bursting desire to run the café today – an opportunity she clearly hadn't known she wanted until last night.

With a swallow, he told himself that if anything was going to spoil her day, it wouldn't be him. This might be her only chance to do this thing, to connect with her mother. Whatever she gained from washing ashore here, and whatever it was – in addition to her grief at losing her mother – that she was running from, Magnús was determined that she'd be allowed to enjoy this respite. He wouldn't make it awkward or unhappy for her.

No, he told himself with stern conviction, he'd keep his distance and let her play until her heart was content and he'd keep all thoughts of kissing her buried away.

He dragged the sack of logs inside, their bark sparkling with frost and smelling deeply of English forests. He let himself inhale it as he set to work on his knees before the fire. The bark was soft and speckled with green moss, damp and sweet, an olfactory reminder that Christmas was within touching distance.

As if to test his resolve about leaving Alex in peace and to stop fantasising about himself as some kind of romantic hero and she some mythical being come to upend his world, the sound of soft singing came to him from the café.

Alex, rustling shopping bags and placing down jars and packages on the countertop, was making herself at home.

'Soft, hear the merfolk, sing I.
I call to thee, boy of the shore,
My pretty one, my pretty one,
Hear me sing my water song.'

Her voice, Magnús thought, was beautiful. 'She's happy,' he told himself, drawing a line under any inconveniently soft feelings she might be provoking in him. Instead, he worked at the hearth and listened to her sing.

It was a song Alex had been sung many times as a child, most often by her dad. A song about a family of merfolk, one of whom falls in love with a human and lures him to her in the waves where the siren keeps her lover with her forever, far away from land where the boy had been so lonely.

Alex hadn't thought of the song for years but now it played in her head and she was glad it accompanied her while she worked.

—

Alex started on the sweet stuff first. It was only nine o'clock and if anyone came into the café in the next hour or two they'd want coffee and cake, most likely. She could think about lunch orders later.

The kettle boiled and hissed water from the spout while she tipped the crisp cereal into a big bowl. As she reached for the chocolate bars, she remembered her mum always wore a pinny when working and grabbed the long white chef's apron from the hook on the door that led into the bookshop. She kept the door open so she could hear Magnús's boots clomp back and forth as he set the fire and tidied the (already very tidy) shelves.

Pulling the apron over her head felt somehow like anointing herself, a serious part of the baking ritual she'd watched her mum undertake many times, even if it was just crispy chocolate squares she was making. The thought made her smile as she drew the strings around her middle and tied a bow.

The bain-marie was soon set up, just a glass bowl over hot water in a pan. She took her time snapping the milk chocolate squares and dropping them in to melt. The aroma was too sweet to resist and she let herself taste a piece, just like her mum would.

After stirring the melting chocolate until it was slick and glossy she added her mum's secret ingredient, a great big dollop of her favourite hazelnut spread which melted in to the liquid chocolate. When it was ready, she poured it into the cereal, mixed it thoroughly, then pressed the whole mixture into a high-sided tray and ferried it to the fridge, still singing to herself.

As the base layer cooled, she prepared the thick, sweet caramel middle layer by heating condensed milk, brown sugar, and yellow Devonshire butter in a pan until the whole café smelled of hot molasses.

Even with her back to the door she was aware that Magnús had popped his head into the café, his nostrils flared and sniffing, and his eyes fixed hard upon her, but when she turned with the spoon in her hand for him to lick he'd ducked back under the low door and was gone again.

What a shame. She'd wanted to show him what she was up to and to say out loud to somebody how her mum always told her, 'Life's too short not to lick the spoon!'

Instead, she poured the thick caramel mixture over the chocolate cereal base, now nicely chilled and put the whole thing back in the fridge.

In a minute or two she'd add another layer of smooth milk chocolate on top before drizzling over thin zigzags of white chocolate for decoration and her Port Kernou Quayside Diner luxury crispy squares would be done. Perfect.

She smoothed her hands over her apron and surveyed the little café. Actually, it wasn't quite perfect. It was the twenty-second of December; the place should be festive and sparkling, but from the look of the café it could be any old winter's day. If they were going to have a good day's bookselling and baking, it ought to at least look like Christmas.

Alex didn't know it, but Jowan and Minty had already taken this into consideration in their plans for Magnús and his surprise guest.

Chapter Fourteen

Minty and Jowan, Alone

'*Pfft*.' Minty swept a hand at the cobwebs in the Big House basement. She hadn't set foot down here in months. 'Is that flashlight working?'

Jowan, stepping carefully down the stone stairs, greasy with damp, turned on the heavy flashlight used once upon a time by Minty's father for night-time rabbiting with his retinue of estate men.

Those fields, teaming with rabbits, had been sold off long ago, along with the entire village itself. All its cottages and the Siren's Tail, the estate's Victorian model dairy (long since gone), and historic herd of Red Ruby cattle, which had been in the family for generations, had all passed into private owners' hands in the estate's desperate bid to keep the Big House going.

Minty's entire domain now consisted of her few rooms in the Big House, an overgrown rhododendron valley leading down to the crumbling chapel and what was once a pretty camellia grove behind it. She'd also retained the softly undulating lawns that the house sat in, along with the formal parterre and patio at the back of the property overlooking the Atlantic breakers. In total, only a few acres amid what had, in the middle of last century, been Clove-Congreve land for as far as Minty's antique field glasses could see.

'Would you look at this!' Minty lifted a floppy leather folio from the top of an overflowing crate and opened it. 'If we hadn't sold off our library this would be displayed in pride of place.'

Jowan lifted the lamp to help illuminate the black-and-white photographs of the fine camellia grove.

Minty wasn't really seeing them. Instead, she was picturing the old library in her mind's eye; floor-to-ceiling leather-bound wonders from the eighteenth and early nineteenth centuries when the family had been thriving on tin mining, cattle farming, and clever investments overseas.

Young Araminta had spent hours in the library, which was always warm and dry, unlike the bedroom she'd shared with the string of au pairs who never seemed to stay very long, some packing up and disappearing while she slept. She hadn't understood at the time how her father's wandering eye – not to mention his hands – had chased them away, in much the same way as his tiresome behaviour had kept her mother away from home for months at a time.

Throughout it all, the library had been a constant source of comfort. Most of all, she'd prized her late grandfather's globe that stood always in the window recess. How she loved to spin it on its smooth axis and trace with a finger all the places her wandering mother had told her about: Constantinople, Paris, Strasbourg, Cannes, Monaco, Venice and all the others! Places that sounded to young Araminta impossibly glamorous, wild and appealing, much like her mother appeared to her.

Mrs Clove-Congreve was rarely at home, and on the occasions she at last came sweeping in, unannounced, she'd bring crates of gifts and antiquities that Minty's father would blanch at.

'Think of the cost, Margaret, my dear. Please,' he'd tell her, begging her not to venture out of Devon again until he'd accumulated some capital. He'd plant his feet and raise his chin, indignant with his wife, as if anyone truly believed he was about to turn over a new leaf. As if he wasn't already well on the way to frittering away the very last of their money on horses and house parties.

Minty sighed, scanning around the cellar while Jowan pored over the pictures. 'I remember those camellias,' he told her. 'T'was where I proposed to my Isolde. Whole grove smelled of lemon and anise.'

This drew Minty's attention again. She didn't have to say much to her old friend to let him feel her sympathy.

'It did,' she nodded. 'It really did.' A deep sigh escaped her.

Jowan knew where her thoughts were taking her. 'Don't be getting maudlin on me, Mint. You're doing a fine job with the estate. If you're not proud of the way you've kept it together, then let *me* be proud for you.'

Minty wasn't a sulker or a brooder. She was made of sterner stuff. Only here, amongst the damp relics of her old life, she allowed herself a little leeway. 'Will it ever be a grand estate again, Jowan? Like we remember? Surely it's too late for all that?'

'Nonsense!' Jowan turned the page again, revealing a picture from between the wars of a band of young toffs in Pierrot costumes and Venetian masquerade gowns, all exquisitely posing for the camera, louche, happy and care-free. 'Well, perhaps you won't be wantin' to return to this sort of thing.'

Minty looked too and let out a sharp laugh. 'Hah! Perhaps not.' She folded her arms across her body with a shiver. 'I'd like to keep the roof over our heads though, and keep my staff on, paying them properly, keeping their families away from the food banks that are springing up left and right. Don't think I don't see it, the decline. I'm not so much in my ivory tower I don't know the whole world's struggling.'

'Never thought you were,' he assured her in the dry, humorous tone he kept for her when she was feeling down. 'You're not like these ones. Livin' for pleasure. You're a new breed, Minty Clove-Congreve.'

This provoked another laugh. 'Am I? Well good. Something needs to happen to shake this place up. Now the developers have helped clear all the estate's debts, you could say we've a clean slate for the first time in three hundred years, but what to do with it? And the coffers almost empty.'

This made Jowan snap his head to hers. 'Oh?'

Minty sighed once more and put her hand on the flashlight, lowering its glare to the earth floor. She didn't want Jowan to see her when she told the truth. 'You can't tell anyone, but there's only enough money to pay the workers until July. After that, I don't know what we'll do.'

Jowan frowned. 'But Leonid's residency depends on his having a job here, doesn't it?'

'Partly, yes. And there's Izaak and his caretaker's job, the undergardener and his trainee, Bovis and his two men in security, Mr Moke at the donkey sanctuary. They all depend on the estate making enough money from visitors to pay their wages, and with the last couple of years we've had, well…' She shrugged, despairing.

'We'll think of somethin'.'

'That's exactly what my father used to say; went to his grave still racking his brains for what to do.' Minty gave a wry laugh and closed the album. 'Come along, let's get what we came down for.'

Yet, Jowan stilled her hand upon the book with his own, hoping she wouldn't mind his rough-skinned touch. 'We will think of somethin'. You and I, and you can stop livin' with all this worry. I make my promise to you, Mint, I won't let you, my oldest friend, go through this alone.'

Minty stood frozen before him, her lips moving and eyes blinking like a malfunctioning machine. She only stopped when Jowan lifted his hand away and swept the flashlight around the room.

'Right,' he declared. 'Let's get these decorations down to the bookshop. You're sure you have enough?'

Minty fought to regain her poise, straightening her bodywarmer with a firm tug and clearing her throat. 'Goodness yes, there's all manner of old baubles and bells down here. And Leonid furnished you with a decent tree, yes?'

Her clipped efficiency never left her for long. This was the old Minty that Jowan knew, fierce and capable. She only ever let her guard slip in front of him, and not all that often either. Only recently it seemed to be happening more and more. Perhaps the invasion of the builders last month had done it.

'Yep,' he told her. 'Fine tree, ready for delivery. Do you want to help me take them down the slope? I'll treat uz to a bite of whatever young Alex is making at the café.'

Even though Minty was rummaging through a box of threadbare tinsel and who only knew how many spiders, there was a note of girlishness in her voice when she agreed that yes, she'd like that very much.

Chapter Fifteen

A Christmas Gift for the Borrow-A-Bookshop

It didn't matter if Alex's first customers of the day were only Minty and Jowan, or that they'd dragged a five-foot fir tree complete with bits of straw, moss and insects into her freshly cleaned café.

The two big bags of decorations – also a gift for the shop, apparently – didn't look all that promising either, but she'd forgotten all that when she served up their toasties and milkshakes.

Minty wasn't sure she liked milkshake but Jowan had persuaded her to try one and everyone was relieved when she announced it was 'excellent'.

'It's Mrs C.'s strawberry ice cream that makes it,' Alex told her.

She'd nipped Down-along earlier that morning to buy a big tub. Mrs Crocombe had been pleased to see Alex still in the village but her ears had really pricked up when she heard Alex was helping Magnús run the café for the day.

'So you *are* staying for Christmas, dear?' Mrs C. had probed, but Alex hadn't been able to commit either way, which had caused the old matchmaker no end of frustration.

'The storm coming in might help make up your mind,' Mrs C. told her with a knowing chuckle as Alex paid for her ice cream and left.

She'd stopped in the middle of the slope to look seaward at the endless grey rainclouds blanketing the sky and dropping icy drizzle over Clove Lore. Alex had seen skies like that before and they always spelled trouble for people living along the coast, but her only thoughts right then were focused on her café and the day ahead.

After a couple of slices of crispy cake – a step too far for Jowan who didn't have a very sweet tooth so Minty had to finish both of them – Alex's first patrons paid in cash and left.

Alex overheard Jowan asking if Minty wanted to pop down to the cottage and walk Aldous with him, and she'd protested weakly about the drizzle before pulling a clear plastic RainMate with white dots from her pocket, covering her hair and saying, 'Oh, go on then!' as though it were a terrible bother to her. Jowan had only smiled and offered her his arm which she took with a look that was both comfortable and coy.

Alex let the café's lace curtain fall when she saw for sure they were turning Down-along together. 'Good,' she said to herself, feeling every bit like meddling Mrs Crocombe – a not entirely pleasant realisation.

'Everything good?' Magnús enquired from the shop floor.

'We've, *uh*, been given a gift, from the Big House,' she called back, and waited for Magnús's curiosity to bring him through to her a few seconds later.

'It's a tree, and we've to decorate it with this stuff, apparently.' Alex pulled one of the bags open.

'What are we waiting for?' Magnús asked.

'Some customers, maybe?'

'If we get really busy doing something, that might bring customers in.'

'How would that work?' Alex asked, but she was already lifting the bags and carrying them past Magnús into the bookshop. 'Let's put the tree in here,' she told him. 'A bookshop needs a tree at Christmas.'

'We should have some Christmas music,' he told her, and when she replied that she hadn't brought her phone – with a queasy stomach-churning feeling that memories of last night's messages dredged up – he'd pulled out his own and searched Spotify for Icelandic Christmas music, which soon filled their corner of the shop near the, now glowing, fireplace.

They placed the spruce in its antique stand, Magnús tightening the rusty vice that held the trunk upright. Alex fearlessly picked the living creatures from the branches and let them loose on the big potted palm tree in the square outside.

'Did you sell any books this morning?' she asked as they both went through the contents of the bags.

Magnús was glad to tell her he had. 'Two children's picture books, to one of the women from the party last night.' He meant Monica Burntisland, the school's teaching assistant. 'Stocking fillers, she said.'

'Two books isn't bad. Do you do stockings in Iceland?'

'Of course! Where else would the yule lads put their presents?'

'Yule lads?' Alex echoed incredulously. 'You're pulling my leg.'

'Not at all. There are thirteen Yuletide lads. Each one comes down from the mountains in the days leading up to Christmas and they leave a present in a stocking.'

'Really?'

'Or a shoe, or they open a window and drop the present inside.'

Alex narrowed her eyes. 'I can never tell if you're joking or not.'

'Serious,' Magnús insisted. 'I can't believe you don't have *Jólasveinar* where you're from. Next thing you'll be telling me you don't have a Yule Cat either!' This was said with a wicked sparkle that told Alex he already knew for sure yule cats were news to her.

'And what does he do? Chase the yule mouse and unravel the yule yarn? Leave a fur ball on the *Jólakaka*?'

'You're making fun of Iceland's sacred festive traditions?' He placed a hand to his chest, exaggeratedly offended, making Alex laugh. 'No, the Yule Cat is a big black hairy cat with spiked teeth and a hungry belly and he lurks around ready to pounce upon and eat any children who don't receive new clothes at Christmas.'

'Oh *that* Yule Cat. Sure, everybody in England knows about that guy.'

Now Magnús was laughing.

'Is that why you gave me your jumper?' she said. 'So I wouldn't get eaten by a demon cat?'

'*Jæja*. That's right. I'm actually kind of offended you haven't given me anything, not even a pair of socks. It's like you want me to die.'

'I'll be sure to give you something to ward him off, don't worry. Can you wait or is it likely to strike this afternoon?'

'I'll wait.'

The smile seemed fixed to Magnús's face as he took on the challenge of untangling a string of coloured fairy lights, trying to contain his delight that this had for all the world sounded like a promise that Alex didn't intend to leave Clove Lore any time soon.

Their task was further interrupted by no fewer than three sets of customers. The first were a couple – hardy tourists in hiking boots who'd persevered through the rain to buy a Matt Haig, two crispy cakes, a milkshake and a black coffee. The second was a local looking for wrapping paper which Magnús had to admit he didn't stock but he'd managed to sell them one of the baking books from the counter.

The third customer was Bovis.

He'd stumbled inside the shop and looked around wide-eyed as if buying books was an entirely new experience for him.

'Can I help you?' Magnús asked, rising from his spot by the tree where he was winding lights around the lower branches. Alex took over from him, wrapping the tree in sparkling colour.

'I, *er*, need sommit for the mistress,' Bovis announced.

Alex interrupted from across the shop to prevent Magnús jumping to the wrong conclusion. 'He means Minty.'

''S'right, the mistress,' Bovis confirmed. 'She likes books an' that.'

'Any particular kind of book?'

Despite Magnús's efforts to draw out Bovis's knowledge of his boss, they drew a blank, until a suddenly brainwave stuck.

'She likes… organisin', I s'pose.'

Magnús clapped his hands in triumph and led Bovis to the stationery selection by the till. 'A woman like Minty will enjoy a notebook.'

'Reckon?' Bovis was unconvinced.

'Definitely,' Alex put in. 'And a nice pen… or two.'

'S'not much, though, is it? For the mistress,' Bovis added, looking down at the fine watch on his wrist that she'd bestowed upon him last Christmas, engraved on its back, '*To loyal Bovis, with gratitude, A. C-C.*'

'Add some reading material from our bestseller shelves?' Magnús suggested, gesturing to the colourful jackets at eye level on the shelves behind the till.

'What do ladies like to read?' said Bovis, surprising them all.

'Can't go wrong with *Pride and Prejudice*,' Alex said with a shrug. 'It's a classic. *Very* Minty! Lots of horsey types and long walks. It was my mum's favourite – well, when it was on the telly. She loved Mr Darcy!'

'Can't say I've 'eard of it, not much of a reader, but I'll take it.'

'Good choice,' Magnús congratulated him.

'An' wrap it up, brown paper, if you don't mind,' Bovis added furtively, having spied the cover, a photographic still of a handsome man with chestnut curls, a riding crop and a damp-looking frilly shirt.

'She'll love it. Guaranteed,' Alex pitched in.

Bovis pulled the money from his wallet with a pained expression before turning his thick neck in the direction of the café. 'What you cookin' in there?'

'Ah, let me show you.' Alex swept him and his purchases across the room and under the low door.

Within fifteen minutes Bovis was sitting, contented as a schoolboy, tucking into a toastie and a pot of tea. Alex placed his crispy slice on his table and left him scrolling through the news sites on his phone. He, like everyone else in Clove Lore, was tracking the storm warnings.

Back in the shop Alex glanced through the glass. It was indeed growing dark, and it was only one o'clock. The palm tree in the square was bending and bobbing in the wind and the fire in the hearth struggled to fend off the cold whistling around the doorframe.

Magnús however, only topped up the logs in the hearth, turned up his music, and continued to pass Alex the strands of tinsel and the really rather wonderful vintage baubles, all a little faded and tired, but every one prompting them to fill in its imagined history.

There was a tiny silver samovar, a china bowl of cherries, blown glass clowns and clothes peg fairies. Some of the oldest ones were so shabby it was hard to tell if they had once been painted Father Christmas heads or pinecones. They'd both grimaced as they pulled out a monkey face bauble which Magnús hung round the back of the tree where it couldn't scare any children.

'Where do you think this one's from?' Alex asked, holding up a fat, iridescent teardrop. It had a round window pressed into one side and inside that concave was a picture not of Mary or the baby Jesus – not even a snowy Santa – but of Lenin himself.

'Wow! Somebody in Minty's family was a secret Bolshevik,' blurted Magnús.

'*Shh!*' Alex shushed, pointing to the café where Bovis sat. 'That's his boss, remember?'

To keep Bovis from overhearing, they turned to whispering instead, keeping their heads together and thoroughly enjoying the cosiness of having something distracting to do whilst keeping each other company as the rain fell harder outside.

'What's this?' Magnús said when he reached the bottom of the bag and pulled out a bottle. 'Red wine?'

There was a parcel label tied around its neck. Alex reached for it and read, 'Merry Christmas, stay out of the storm, from all at the Clove Lore Estate.'

'Save it for later?' Magnús asked, his brows raised, wondering whether Minty and Jowan had wagered money on Alex and him in Mrs C.'s little book.

Alex waited a long moment before answering, during which Magnús regretted asking. 'Yeah, let's keep it for closing time,' she said, watching for his reaction.

When he looked away and scratched self-consciously at his beard, she grinned and stood up, pulling a long tangle of metallic paperchains from the second bag. 'Time to do the café?'

Bovis was still sitting where Alex had left him. His notes lay on the table for her to put in the cash box, and his plates were so clean she wondered if he'd licked them.

'More tea?' she asked, but he didn't reply. He was watching a news report, the screen held protectively away from them, earphones relaying the sound.

Magnús held up his end of the crumpled paperchains for Alex to fix above the counter. They bustled around Bovis, tying a gold star against the glass in the café door and running a set of fairy lights in a zigzag across the kitchen shelves.

Soon the shop bell called Magnús away to serve what turned out to be his last customers of the day, the young family from the Siren's Tale in dripping cagoules. They told him they were increasingly worried they were going to be stuck indoors the whole time and baby Serena had a tendency to wake up and cried every time they put the telly on. He sold them a big pile of emergency paperbacks to keep them going until they checked out on Boxing Day (a Stephenie Meyer, two P.G. Wodehouses, one Arundhati Roy, and one each of the Smiths: Zadie and Dodie).

Another seventeen pounds in the till. It felt good, and the shop looked so warm and welcoming he couldn't help surveying it from his spot by the door, arms folded, chest puffed.

He was proud of what they'd achieved, in spite of the weather and all of his reservations about the place. Still, he had to admit today wouldn't have been anywhere near as fun without Alex here insisting that this was all worthwhile and making the place feel like a real business with real meaning.

He set about mopping the raindrops from the floor while Alex sang the same lyric she'd been stuck with all day, '*I call to thee, boy of the shore. My pretty one, my pretty one, hear me sing my water song.*'

She positioned the last of the decorations around her café. Everything was good and warm and comfortable, just how she had wanted it to be, and Bovis, seeming to have made himself a permanent fixture in the café, scrolled on.

Alex was too busy to notice him stopping abruptly on the BBC Devon and Cornwall news pages and hitting 'play' on a video story with the headline: *Concern Grows Over Missing Port Kernou Boat Woman.*

The reporter was standing on a Cornish quayside that Bovis had visited as a child. It looked inviting with its festive lights. Bovis was ready to swipe on to the next story, only something stopped him.

The reporter handed over to a young man in a zipped-up jacket. An older man, who looked like the youngster's father, stood behind him with a protective hand on his shoulder and a furrowed brow. The man, introduced as Ben Thomas, was pleading into the lens, 'Alex, please let us know you're all right. We're all missing you so much. Please, just come home for Christmas.'

'What state of mind was Alexandra in when you last saw her?' the reporter asked, jabbing the microphone closer to the young man's face.

'Well, *uh*, she was… fine. Happy? Looking forward to Christmas.'

Bovis knew a liar when he saw one and this lad was terrible at hiding it, gulping and tugging at his jacket collar like it was choking him. He really did appear to be worried, though more for himself maybe than his missing girlfriend.

'Had you quarrelled at all?' the reporter wanted to know. They too seemed to know there was more to the story than he was letting on.

'I wouldn't say we'd been *quarrelling*, more that… she got upset, and she ran off. Spur of the moment sort of thing.'

'You only reported her as missing yesterday. Why?'

Panicked, he spoke quickly. 'She'd been spotted all along the coast so we knew where she was, and she's a good sailor. We all thought she'd have turned back by now.'

'Yet, there have been no sightings of the ferry known as the *Dagalien* since the seventeenth of December, and no radio messages at all. We understand that the search was initially planned for Christmas Eve but has been brought forward to start later today due to the storms. Will it find her, do you think?'

'I hope so,' the man gulped, and his eyes swam with tears.

Bovis wondered if it wasn't just the wind whipping at the lad's face doing it. He didn't like the look of him one bit, but he felt sorry for the older man standing behind him, visibly anguished.

'Ben Thomas, thank you very much.' The reporter turned back to the camera, telling of the mounting Storm Nora that was expected to make landfall in the next twenty-four hours and how if the search didn't turn up any clues as to the missing ferrywoman's whereabouts soon, there'd be little chance of finding her until after the storm passed, which could, the reporter warned, be many days.

Bovis peered at the still image of the missing blonde woman on the screen, angling his body so he could compare it with the woman wiping down the counter and singing a song to herself. His eyes narrowed.

Wordlessly he stood, flicking the news site shut. As he left through the café door, making the five-pound notes on the table flutter to the floor, he talked into his phone. His words were caught up in the wind and carried away, out of Alex's hearing.

'Coastguard? The runaway girl? She's 'ere at Clove Lore.'

Chapter Sixteen

The Calm before the Storm

'So maybe we didn't make a fortune,' Alex said, counting out her profits and adding them to the bookshop till's takings. 'But it was fun, right?'

Magnús didn't want to say he had loved every second. 'We did well. Sixty-three pounds and seventy-five pence. It's still a profit.'

There were many days back at Ash and the Crash where he'd have given anything to have banked that much. Meanwhile, Alex could make three times that amount on a busy day's sailing, but she kept that to herself.

'Have you turned the sign?' she asked.

Magnús strode round the counter and displayed the word 'closed' to any passers-by crazy enough to step out in this rain, now falling at a slant and drumming upon the cobbles.

Bovis had been the café's last customer of the day and he'd left over an hour ago. The rain and winter darkness had chased everyone else back indoors.

Under its thick blanket of cloud, Clove Lore smelled of chimney soot, wet sand and hearty meals being cooked in cosy homes. Somewhere nearby, a winter garden bonfire had been snuffed out and the resinous smoke still lingered around the rooftops. The scents insinuated their way into the bookshop, mingling with the heady aroma of fir tree warmed by the log fire.

Magnús surveyed the shelves, wonderfully illuminated by the tree's twinkling lights – red, blue and green. The star on the top branch, attached by a perilously thin vintage cord to the mains, gleamed gaily, casting a gentle glow over the wonky-beamed ceilings.

He had kept the firewood topped up all afternoon, just as Jowan instructed, so the edges of the room were finally warming to a comfortable temperature. The sounds of raindrops pattering on the roof and the windows only made the place cosier.

'Did you enjoy your day?' Magnús asked, as Alex dropped the coins into the till and locked the drawer with the key.

She thought for a moment. 'I'll be honest with you. It was the best day I've had in a long time.' She shook her head and repeated the words. 'A *long* time.'

'Me too.' He really meant it. 'Thank you for helping me. I think we're good at this.'

The Christmas music from Magnús's phone filled the silence as Alex pressed the toe of her boot into the floor. This morning's awkwardness was threatening to creep back in now they were alone again, and she refused to let it.

'We should eat something. I'm starving,' she told him.

Cooking together in their newly decorated café was as pleasant as Magnús knew it would be when she suggested they both try her toasties and milkshakes.

Alex was smiling and moving deftly around the room, while Magnús tried his best not to get in the way, but two tall and broad-shouldered people working in close proximity behind a café counter brought its own difficulties.

'Oh, sorry,' Alex said, having nudged Magnús hard in the stomach with her elbow while working the bread knife.

'*Ups!*' he murmured, having dropped a ball of ice cream onto the floor instead of into the milkshake glass in his efforts to prevent their bodies touching when Alex squeezed past him to get to the fridge.

In the end they'd been forced to laugh about it, and on her last sweep past to rescue the toasted sandwiches from the grill before they burned, she placed her hands fast against Magnús's arms from behind him, making sure he didn't suddenly step backwards into her as he plated up the chocolate squares for dessert.

He'd instinctively flexed, hardening the muscles beneath her fingers, before apologising goofily. 'No idea why I did that,' and they'd had to laugh to get through the weird excitement neither of them could contain.

Just being near her set off all of Magnús's enthusiasm and brightness, and Alex responded by letting herself relax.

She loaded their food onto a tray as Magnús found cutlery and wine glasses.

'You seem happier today. Have you heard from… anyone?' Magnús had no idea how to end the sentence.

'I've contacted them,' Alex said, turning off the grill. 'Everything's sorted, for now.'

'Hah!' Magnús was pleased for her. 'So you can enjoy yourself now? Call this a kind of holiday, even?'

'I think so.'

What Magnús wanted was for her to unburden herself, to tell him all her secrets, but he wasn't going to push her. She was happy, as though the invisible thing that had been chasing her had lost her scent and she was free to just be herself. It was heartening to see her smiling like this.

Following her through to the bookshop as she carried the tray, Magnús collected the wine bottle from beneath the branches of the Christmas tree and uncorked it to let it breathe a little. He took the opportunity to remind himself to breathe too. Why were his nerves jumping and his blood racing so much? All they were doing was sharing a meal.

'Wine after the strawberry milkshakes, right?' he said, watching from across the room as she settled onto the floor in front of the fire.

'You take the armchair,' she told him.

'No way.' He carried himself to her and sat cross-legged on the hearth rug, pushing the armchair a little farther away. 'Now *this* is Christmas,' he told her.

'It's a shame there's no TV, we could've watched a Christmas movie,' she said, handing him his plate.

'There's the shop's laptop?'

'No, it's OK, let's just sit. I can't remember the last time I sat in front of a log fire and just did nothing.'

'*Jæja, já, já,*' he said on an inhale, nodding in agreement, wishing she'd say more.

'What is that?' she said, biting her sandwich and tipping her head.

'What is what?' Magnús froze.

'You sort of breathe in while you're listening to me; you say *ya ya ya.*'

'You think it's funny?'

'No, not funny, just interesting.'

'It's the *innsog*. Icelanders take a big breath while saying yes to encourage you to keep talking, or maybe to show you we really, really agree. Or maybe to show we just *can't wait* to agree with you so much we don't even take time to breathe.' He was laughing and bringing a knee up to sit more comfortably, shifting a little closer to her and not even realising he was doing it.

'It's nice,' Alex said with a lift of her shoulders. 'If I could, I would do it back. I like you talking.'

This was a step too far for both of them, and yet not nearly far enough at the same time. They both pretended to be absorbed in eating the triple-decker toasted sandwiches, so crisp and gooey, and watching the flames, feeling thankful for the Christmas music pouring from Magnús's phone speaker.

Magnús handed Alex her milkshake and lifted his own. 'So this is your mamma's famous milkshake?'

'It is. Go on, try it,' she urged, before taking a long drink from her straw, her eyes falling to his lips as they pursed softly and he sucked up the pale pink drink. His eyes widened as he drank, not stopping for a comically long time. Half the glass was gone when his lips released the straw and he exclaimed, '*Ljúffengur!*'

'Loo fenger?' Alex echoed.

'Delicious.'

'Ah!' Alex took another drink and they let the fire crackle between them and the music fill the room.

Yes, everything about this evening was delicious, and neither of them was going to let it end too soon.

When the crispy squares had been eaten and Magnús had winced at the sweetness before concluding it was something you got more accustomed to with every bite and he'd licked his sticky fingers clean and hoped there was more left for later, he poured the ruby wine into glasses and shoved the tray stacked with dishes away from them with his boot. The last thing he wanted was Alex springing up and offering to wash plates.

Alex stretched out her legs in front of her, leaning her back on the armchair, signalling to Magnús there was enough room for him to lean too.

There wasn't. Both of them could see it, but he still plucked a book from one of the baskets below the staircase and settled himself beside Alex, his boots close to the fire.

Shifting awkwardly so their shoulders didn't clash, Magnús soon gave up trying to fit and lifted his arm instead. 'Can I?' He reached out across her back.

'You can,' Alex told him, already leaning into the nook under his arm and slipping her hand around his back so her fingertips came to rest on his belt loop while her other hand clasped the stem of her glass in front of her.

'You're not worried about this storm coming in, are you?' Alex asked after a while spent watching the flames dance and pretending being close like this wasn't sending fireworks crackling throughout her nervous system.

'*Nei, Þetta reddast,*' Magnús said, feeling very much like his level-headed, pragmatic old man back in Iceland. 'It'll all be OK. You'll see.'

Curling their bodies closer to one another like foxes deep in their winter den, Magnús opened the book and read. '*T'was the night before Christmas and all through the house...*'

Alex closed her eyes and enjoyed his voice rumbling in his chest against her ear. His body was soft on the surface and hard underneath and he easily supported her as she let her weight sink against him.

When he finished the story and closed the book against his stomach, Alex heard herself talking.

'My name's Alex Robinson. I'm from Port Kernou. I had a ferry there; that's the boat I rammed into the Clove Lore harbour wall.' She rolled her eyes but he couldn't see her face to know. 'And now I'm here. I've got no job to go back to. I do have a house, though. My parents are both dead, years ago, and I miss them so much and *umm*, that's me.'

She waited, her head still leaning on his chest, listening to him breathing.

'It's nice to meet you, Alex Robinson. I've been wondering when you'd show up.'

It was enough to make her laugh and lift her head.

'Anything else to tell?' Magnús asked, holding her gaze. 'These were the secrets you couldn't mention?' He tipped his head. He knew there must be more to her running away than that.

Alex's mind raced. Was there anything else left to tell? Perhaps, but nothing she felt like saying right this second. She thought of Ben and Eve, Mr and Mrs Thomas and the family she'd come to think of as her own. Yes, losing them hurt; it ached in fact, but with this new distance between them and the fresh clarity she'd found about Ben and her so-called best friend, it was a little more bearable. And yes, she had been embarrassed about running away and worrying everyone, but there was no need to let it eat her up now; she'd dealt with that by messaging Bryony.

'There are still some practical matters to deal with,' she told him. 'But it's OK.'

She knew she was making light of her dad's wrecked boat, and the fact she still had to make a living somehow – the little money in her bank account wasn't going to last forever – but in Magnús's embrace it didn't seem so pressing. And wasn't she allowed to take some time off, after all these years? Couldn't she just enjoy Christmas, and this man's company? He'd be leaving for Iceland soon enough. She'd face the real world then.

With her eyes locked on Magnús's soft gaze, she found there was nothing else she wanted to say.

'Can I ask something?' he said.

'OK,' she replied, a little too cautiously.

'How old are you?'

'Oh,' she let out a laugh. 'I'm twenty-six.'

'Twenty-nine,' he said, pointing a thumb at himself. 'Thirty in August.'

'Me too! I mean, I'm an August baby too. But I don't like birthdays.' She tucked herself into his chest again.

'Cake? Parties? What's not to like?' Magnús asked before thinking better of it. 'Oh, I get it, I'm sorry.'

'Yeah,' she said. 'You try having a birthday with no parents. You just kind of want to forget it.'

'Not even a cake?'

'I banned birthday cake, and cards, and all the rest of it. No birthdays for me.'

'Alex, that is so sad.'

She pulled away so she could look at him, his eyes so sorrowful thinking of the things she'd been through. Right at that moment, she didn't feel sad or sorry for herself at all, and she told him so. In fact, she felt nothing but comfort and warmth.

It took only a few electric seconds for them to abandon their wine glasses and for the book on Magnús's stomach to slip to the floor.

Magnús brought his fingertips to her cheek.

'You know, I wanted to kiss you very much yesterday,' he stated, his voice so low Alex felt its effect upon her core.

She only let out a held breath and allowed her eyes to dip to his lips.

This time it was Magnús who leaned in, determined not to let anything come between them.

He pressed his lips to hers with a fiery yearning and they sank even closer, the softness of their mouths touching and the heat from the hearth melting away the last twinges of tension in their muscles, their nervous energy dissipating and turning into something else, something spellbinding.

The awareness of having not only all night but all of the Christmas holiday stretching out before them helped Magnús pace the kiss, even when Alex drew him down onto the rug so they lay in each other's arms.

The exquisitely slow pressure of his mouth and the tantalising way his tongue parted her lips and coaxed her to deepen her kiss told her that he was going to take his time, and the way she let her hands roam down across his back to press at the base of his spine told him that was what she wanted too.

He rolled her with him so he lay on his back, loving her weight laid out upon his, and she pressed herself against him all the more while his head rolled back, her mouth finding his throat.

He gasped like a drowning man, holding their cores together with the firm pressure of his hands spread across her back.

The growl in his throat as she mouthed his earlobe and bared her teeth against his skin was enough to send Alex reeling and all thoughts of her old life left her consciousness.

All their awareness reduced to only the heat from the fire, the hardness and softness of each other's bodies as they pulled away winter layers and took in every tiny detail of the other's skin and how it felt to collide and sink together under green, blue and red Christmas lights.

For Magnús, there was nothing but Alex, the woman astride him, her white-blonde hair falling over his chest. There was no mermaid, no mysterious runaway, no faraway bookshop, failed or otherwise, and none of his old bruised ego either. There was only their fingers clasped tightly, palms pressed together, their kisses and gasps mingling over now distant music.

For Alex there was only their bodies rolling together like the ocean tides and deep, unthinking, breathless pleasure and the promise of a long stormy night ahead to do it all over again and again.

–

As the fire grew low and Alex shifted in the spot on the hearthrug where they'd both collapsed into a sleepy heap, Magnús lifted his eyelids drowsily.

'Are you cold? We can move upstairs,' he said.

'Not cold,' she murmured. 'Happy.'

'*Mmm*.' Magnús held her close, his hand across her stomach. 'Alex Robinson?'

'Hmm?' Her eyes were closed again.

'I like you.'

'*Mmm*,' she smiled, absorbing the words.

'I like everything about you,' he said again, softly kissing her shoulder.

Alex's sleepy, dopamine-soaked brain mulled this over and her smile spread. He liked her. Not love, thank goodness. Liking everything about her somehow sounded much, *much* better than love. A sore spot at the back of her brain wanted to know whether she had been much liked before now, but she was too relaxed to follow the thought.

'I like you liking me,' she said in a whisper, squeezing her shoulders closer to Magnús's chest. He brought his legs up to cradle hers all the more.

'OK then,' he murmured, low and dozy.

'And you are also nice,' she said in a robotic voice, making him laugh.

'I don't talk like that,' he protested.

'I like how you talk. I like everything about you too.'

She kissed his wrist and tucked his hand into the spot below her chin, holding him tight before they feel asleep once more.

Magnús, thinking himself a changed man, smiled in his sleep, knowing that tomorrow they would lazily eat breakfast and light the fire once more, turn the sign on the door, and open their shop and café again, ready to welcome last-minute gift shoppers braving the weather.

It would be another perfectly happy day, he told himself, and not one brooding, dark synapse in his sleepy brain fired a warning, like it would have done on any other night of his life, to remind him that nothing good ever came this easily to tormented, striving Magnús Sturluson.

Chapter Seventeen

23rd December – Rescue

The knock at the shop door was so soft it hadn't awakened Magnús, but it sent Alex scrambling for her clothes and grimacing at Jowan who was politely averting his eyes behind the glass.

It was still dark by the time she'd dressed and tiptoed sheepishly outside to greet him. The wind swirled wildly in the little square as though it wanted to knock her clean off her feet.

'There are some people here to see you,' he shouted over the gale.

She'd followed him Down-along through the blast of icy rain, her heart sinking further with every step.

It had rained steadily all night, not that she'd been aware of it, and the cobbles now ran with clear water between the stones.

The first thing she saw, apart from the thick white clouds lying oddly low in a wide band above the shoreline and fringed with long fingers reaching towards land, was the little crowd around the *Dagalien* on the beach.

Tom Bickleigh was there with a man in overalls and a yellow sou'wester who she didn't recognise. They were drilling something into the port side gunwale so the whole thing could be wrapped in a new tarpaulin. Tom had told her he'd help and here he was, as good as his word.

The other figures shifted on the shore and it took a moment to register who they were. She wasn't prepared to see Ben standing with his hand raised to the back of his head, and his dad beside him.

For a moment she watched their backs from the harbour wall. She'd have obeyed her instincts and run in the opposite direction if it wasn't for the sympathy in Jowan's eyes now fixed upon her.

'Just see what they have to say. I'll be right here,' he told her.

That was when she noticed Bovis, sheltering from the rain under the gable of the old lifeboat house. She knew from his sharp eyes and redder-than-usual face this was something to do with him.

There it was again, the guilt and shame, and the feeling of being a nuisance and an embarrassment even though she hadn't asked anyone to go to any trouble on her account. She wasn't sure how they'd found her or what they wanted; still, her whole body reeled from the feeling of being ambushed.

With heart thumping and legs weakening, she left Jowan's side and made her way down onto the pebbles, just as Ben's father spotted her.

'Alex! Darling.' With his arms outstretched and his expression breaking into undisguised relief, the sight of him made Alex suddenly want to fold over with sadness.

'Dad!' Her feet carried her towards him. She loved him, even if she wasn't going to be his daughter-in-law. He'd been nothing but kind to her over the years and she desperately wanted the hug.

He held her without an ounce of animosity about the worry she'd caused. 'Thank God,' he said, over and over, rocking her in his embrace even if he was fully a foot shorter than her. 'Thank God.' When he broke away, he kept hold of her wrists, examining her at arm's length as though looking for injuries. 'You're all right, not hurt at all?' And he turned her with his hands, trying to somehow examine her back through the layers of her rollneck and her father's long coat.

'I'm completely fine. Why are you all here? How could Bryony know I was here from a text?'

Mr Thompson turned her right into Ben's path. He was crying.

Already feeling trapped, now Alex wanted to simply dissolve like sea foam. Anger seemed to creep up from her toes and build as it hit her gut. The fact that he'd pulled off his hood and the rain was soaking into his hair and running in rivulets down his face like he thought he was the dashing hero in a rom-com somehow made her even more livid. He was crying like he was the victim here.

'Oh, Alex!' he gasped, his mouth making a great O. Alex thought ungenerously how like a fish he looked, all wet and gaping, his eyes bulging in amazement. Then it was his turn for the *thank God*s as he made his way towards her. She was ready to tell him to go back where he came from and leave her alone when he stole her words away.

Lunging, he reached for her and pulled the lapels of her coat, kissing her hard on the mouth, a desperate lover's kiss, making her lose her footing on the pebbles.

That was when Magnús arrived.

He'd awakened at the sound of the bell over the shop door tinkling. Finding Alex gone, he'd pulled on his trousers and thin Henley and dashed down the slope after her in unlaced boots only to freeze at the sound of Alex calling that strange man 'dad' then immediately handing herself over to the younger guy who was now practically bending her backwards with his kiss while the father clasped his hands together and smiled soppily. Alex's hair was lifting in the wet gusts and wrapping itself like sea kelp around the man kissing her.

That was when Magnús realised what he'd been doing; running after her, half asleep and not at all properly dressed for this and not at all wanting to be seen.

He retreated, but not before Bovis sidled over and informed him that he'd been the one to reunite her with her fella. 'And that's her father-in-law,' he added. 'Maybe it's one of 'em cases of amnesia you read about in the papers? Forgot where she was from?' Bovis looked very much as though he expected to have his head patted for being such a good boy.

Magnús didn't oblige; instead, he pounded back up the slope alone and unnoticed by anyone in the beach party.

Alex was so stunned she didn't even think to slap Ben, but she *did* shout, in fact she roared at him as the wind rose and the waves crashed against the sea wall and the few boats tied in the churning harbour strained at their moorings.

Mr Thomas turned away, letting the two have their tiff, his head bent, focusing discreetly on his shoes as they scuffed over the pebbles.

Tom Bickleigh watched the entire thing too, hood up, his cigarette hanging loosely from his lips, looking extremely put out to realise he'd gone to all the trouble of getting his mate Charlie over from Bideford this morning to help start work on the boat when Alex, the mysterious woman from the sea – who he'd been telling everyone he was sure he had a chance with – in fact had a boyfriend.

They'd all converged on the shore at the same time this morning; the result of Bovis's quick-thinking phone call to the coastguard last night.

Bryony had been immediately alerted, and she'd left her post at the quayside cabin and run to tell the Thomases the good news.

Ben and his dad had wasted no time in jumping in the car and driving the eighty miles to where Alex had been spotted but could find no one out and about in Clove Lore to direct them, except for Jowan who'd been attempting to drag Aldous (who hated the rain) outside for his night-time pee.

Jowan had invited them into his cottage and out of the weather, telling them she'd likely not be long coming back and feigning innocence about where Alex might be.

The awkward evening hours had passed – during which time Ben had filled Jowan in on the story of Alex's impetuous overreaction – until the fact that she wasn't coming back to the cottage that night couldn't be ignored and Mr Thomas and Ben had been forced to bed down at Jowan's until morning.

At dawn, Tom Bickleigh and Charlie – who'd driven over specially to help his old mate – had started work on making the *Dagalien* watertight, which was all they'd manage today in this weather. They'd been surprised to discover the strangers on the shore shaking their heads and wringing their hands at the state of the Port Kernou ferry they knew so well.

Jowan had taken the opportunity to slip away and recover his missing houseguest and now tempers were flaring as strongly as the winds were blowing.

'Get your hands off me, Ben,' Alex yelled, forcing as much fury and volume into her voice as she could, but Ben seemed to be hearing something entirely different over the boom of the wind. He was smiling indulgently.

'Let's get you inside, you poor thing. You're soaked. Come on,' he told her.

Mr Thomas held his hands out behind his son and his girlfriend, as though shepherding sheep, and even Jowan joined in trying to get Alex to move, though perhaps more out of pity and a sense of decorum than wanting her to do what these strangers were telling her.

'I'll make us some tea,' Jowan shouted over the wind. 'At the cottage. It's perilous to be out in this weather.' At this, a loose slate from the roof of the Siren smashed down on the harbour wall.

'Please come inside, won't you?' Jowan added, more softly, and Alex let herself be led through the rain towards the B&B that only a day ago had felt like a sanctuary to her. Now it looked like what it was: Jowan's cosy home where she'd intruded, breaking in on his peace, overstaying her welcome and spoiling Isolde's memory by touching all her things and getting in the way.

She began to wonder as they fussed around her with towels and brought extra coal for the fire and hot sweet tea if, in fact, she did still belong with them.

All their talk about getting back to Port Kernou for Christmas left her wordless. Everyone had missed her so much, Mr Thomas told her, and there were presents under the tree waiting for her from all the family, and wouldn't it be nice to sleep in her own bed under her own roof and get changed into her own clothes once more?

Ben kept his distance, furtively packing her few belongings in a plastic bag.

The car was waiting in the beach car park behind the pub, Mr Thomas told her, and they'd be home in a couple of hours if they got on the road now.

The *Dagalien* was going to be taken by trailer to Bideford where it could undergo repairs to its hull in the New Year. By then the insurance would be through, and life could go back to normal.

They had it all figured out for her, and then Ben's mum was suddenly on the phone. Someone held it to her ear, and she was sobbing so much that Alex started to cry too, and she'd tried to say, 'I'm sorry, Mum,' but all she'd managed was to sob and shiver as though she'd only just been pulled from the sea a few moments ago.

What had she done, hurting all these people who loved her and wanted her home so badly? They were all crying and so relieved to have her back and she felt something like relief too, and if not relief, at least the mindless numbness of not having to make any decisions and being swept along in other people's plans for her. It was certainly easier than putting her foot down. Hadn't she lived this way for years? Wasn't this the way of things?

It didn't occur to her that their love felt so tight she could hardly breathe. Instead, she let herself be patted dry, made to stand and moved about. She only stared at their faces, not really understanding anything other than her growing awareness of how wild and reckless she'd been lately, how unthinking and selfish.

Her vision swam and the warmth from the blankets and Jowan's fire made her drowsy. It felt like being loved very much, even if there was something nagging at the back of her head, stopping her from being happy. Mr Thomas took her cup and helped her into a pair of her old slipper boots he'd brought from his house where she left them for visiting after work. The sight of them, pink and fluffy, made her somehow deeply, deeply sad and sorry.

'Don't cry, my love. We've got you now,' Mr Thomas said, helping her to the door. 'Let's get you home before this storm really hits.'

Chapter Eighteen

Storm Nora Makes Land

'Get yourself inside! Haven't you heard the weather warnings?' Mrs Crocombe called from the door of her ice-cream shop as Magnús stomped up the slope, his heart pounding and eyes wide in disbelief at what he'd just witnessed on the shore.

'What?' he stopped to shout back, even though they were only feet apart.

Mrs C.'s white hair was set in curlers, her frilled apron fluttering in the wind at the doorway. 'Storm Nora! Upgraded from amber to red. Met office is telling folks to stay indoors out of the way of flying debris. It's to last all day and night, they say.'

Magnús absorbed the information, but he only felt numb. What was this storm to him? What did it matter if this whole cursed island was blown inside out when Alex was down on the beach kissing someone else? She'd been reclaimed by her family and he'd been forgotten.

The urgency in Mrs. C.'s eyes stirred his conscience.

'Will you be OK?' he asked, just as the hanging baskets of winter pansies and trailing ivy on either side of the ice-cream parlour door blew horizontal. One basket unhooked itself and landed in a twiggy fuchsia bush two gardens Up-along.

'It's not myself I'm worried about,' Mrs Crocombe returned. 'There's two hundred litres of ice cream in these freezers. If we have a power cut, that's my winter stock spoiled.'

'What can I do to help?' he asked, but Mrs C. had pre-empted his offer.

'Just get indoors, get your fire lighted and make it through this as best you can. That's what I'm going to do,' she told him, hiking her thumb at her living quarters above the shop.

Accepting this, he walked on, only for Mrs Crocombe to call out behind him in an afterthought, 'Where's the girl?'

'Gone, I think,' Magnús shouted over his shoulder as he marched into the little lane that led to the bookshop square.

Mrs Crocombe squinted in confusion before thinking better of running after him, instead forcing her door shut against the wind.

The big terracotta pot that had stood for years at the centre of the square with its raggedy palm tree had blown over. It now lay up against the bookshop steps and was badly cracked. Pink earthen shards, sweet-smelling wet compost and stringy roots were strewn everywhere. Magnús picked his way through them and into the shop which, he was amazed to find, he'd left unlocked, its door flapping open in the wind, the keys still in the lock inside.

'Hallo?' he called out after forcing the door closed behind him, finding himself breathless.

Nobody replied. He was alone again.

Like a robot, he cleared the plates and glasses from the hearth, trying not to look at the pile of rugs, jumpers and books they'd made into their nest last night.

The fire had burned out long ago and was now cold and ashy.

He washed up the mess in the café sink. Cutlery she'd held, cups her lips had touched – the detritus of what had been the most romantic, connected night of his life.

Images of the last few hours played through his mind. Had he and Alex not been on the same page? Had he imagined their connection was something bigger than it actually was? If so, how could he have got it so wrong? He'd been swept up in a dream once before and discovered he'd been fooling himself. Had he really done it again?

If Alex really had come to play – playing at running a café, playing at being a bookseller, playing at falling for him – she had been utterly convincing.

He had to look at the facts. She was gone. In spite of everything he'd believed last night, she hadn't stuck around. Although, he had to remind himself, she hadn't actually promised she would stay. They hadn't made any promises whatsoever.

He tried to unpick every little thing she'd said, coming unstuck when he remembered her making fun of the way he didn't laugh easily like British lads must. She'd mocked the calm way he spoke. That had been a clue, right there. He'd thought she was flirting, finding him adorable even, liking everything about him. Had she too found him cold and robotic, like Anna had?

He stooped to lift the jumper he'd given her to keep the cold, and the Yule Cat, at bay. When he'd put it into her hands he had meant for her to keep it and here it was, abandoned.

And yet, she'd seemed so genuine, so heartbroken and lost, like she too was desperately in need of a home and a harbour. She'd sung in the café like she was truly contented there and she'd told him that yesterday was the happiest she'd been in years. How could he have misunderstood all of that? He must be in worse shape than he'd realised. Perhaps he'd been so desperate to fix his bashed pride that he'd handed it over to anyone feigning interest in it.

Those men this morning – they'd looked so intent on reclaiming her, the same way Tom Bickleigh had looked when he'd hauled her in off the beach like he'd caught a real-life mermaid.

When he tried to replay the scene at the beach this morning it was hard not to wonder if Alex did this kind of thing all the time. Maybe it wasn't the first time she'd bolted from home and had to be picked up and taken back. What kind of messed-up family drama had he got himself involved in?

The way she'd called out 'Dad' like that – it had set the doubt spiralling into distrust bordering on horror. He could still hear the tremor in her voice. You can't fake emotion like that. Maybe he was her real dad. The way he'd hugged her had said as much. Was it all lies, about her parents being dead? Was she a fantasist and a liar?

'*Nei!*' he cried out in the empty shop while the wind whistled down the chimney and scattered white ash over the hearth stone. 'I won't believe that. She wasn't lying about that. She couldn't have been.'

He searched his memories of the night before. She'd told him she'd sent a message and everything was going to be fine now, hadn't she? And she'd seemed so peaceful at last, after so long being locked inside herself and fretful.

He knew she was struggling with real loss, just like he was, in a way. He'd felt it in everything she did and said

– or rather, it was there in the things she couldn't bring herself to say out loud.

'Was one of the things she couldn't say that she was in love with someone else, and that he was coming to get her?' he muttered, shaking his head, trying not to allow himself to be convinced he'd been conned.

'*Nei*,' he said again, quieter this time, holding the jumper to his face and taking a deep inhalation. The perfume she'd tried on at the visitor centre still lingered there, mixed with her own good, clean smell. 'There *was* something between us, something bigger than whatever escapist fantasy brought her here. She really was happy yesterday, I know it. *We* were happy. We were…'

His thoughts were abruptly halted by the loud sound of the bedroom window cracking.

Bounding up the spiral stairs and pushing the door aside, he found one of the little panes had a crack running the length of it and, outside, a long piece of snapped iron guttering hung down, bumping off the glass in the wind.

Unlocking the undamaged pane and reaching out into the cold air, he grabbed the rusty piece of piping, wrenching it free. He let the whole section drop down into the overgrown shrubbery below.

Wild wind rushed into the Borrow-A-Bookshop and whistled downstairs and through the shelves. The front door bumped and rattled in the stiff gale that was now tormenting the entire coastline.

With some effort he closed the window. He'd have to tape over that crack and quickly or the whole pane would end up in pieces across the bedspread. It was getting worse out there and the cracked glass had sharpened his mind.

'Red weather warning?' he said, thinking of Mrs Crocombe's words. Was Alex really leaving in these perilous conditions? 'Think, Magnús!'

Had she embraced that other guy when they kissed? Hadn't her arms in fact been flailing around like a person knocked off balance? Had she really wanted to leave or was she being whisked away against her will? She hadn't said anything like as much but he could piece the puzzle of Alex Robinson together and conclude she'd more than likely set to sea in her ferry boat to escape them.

He pressed the heels of his palms against his temples.

Where was Alex now? Was she on the road already? Was she safe? He had to know. He threw open his suitcase and pulled out waterproofs and warm layers. He was going to find her. He was going to get answers.

–

The birds all along the coast already knew what the people had been too distracted to grasp. The robins, always so smart and the first to recognise a threat on the horizon, had flitted to their hidden winter pockets in hedgerows and potting sheds, watching with black eyes as wrens darted for cover and the blackbirds turned silent.

The dairy tankers struggled to get along muddy B-roads while the farmers brought every living thing under cover and shut up their barns.

All the hard-working sheepdogs would spend the day ahead dozing by the fire, sleepily unfurling their ears at each creak and clatter outside. It was a day for Christmas movies accompanied by the kettle boiling and home comforts.

School children across the county had already forgotten term time and last week's nativity plays and were so deeply entranced by the wonder of Christmas Eve coming tomorrow they didn't mind the storm one bit, while their parents fretted about relatives driving for Christmas visits.

The news reports ran on a loop. Windblown reporters planted their feet for pieces to camera on wild promenades where waves leapt over sea walls or on motorway gantries overlooking high-sided lorries lying prone on the tarmac. With hoods blown back and microphones buffeting, their voices distorted by the gales, they all repeated the same grave words of warning: *Do not attempt to travel. Wherever you find yourselves now, the Met Office urges you to take shelter there.*

This was to be the great one-hundred-year storm our scattered little islands had been waiting decades for, hoping it never came, praying it was a myth.

Red ticker-tape banners ran along the foot of every news channel. 'Danger to life from falling trees and debris; Flash floods likely,' they read.

The whole of Devon and Cornwall held its breath while some blithely shared comic Facebook posts about flying trampolines and wrecked fence panels and Father Christmas giving up on his journey and heading home to the North Pole where they were enjoying better weather. It was all rather fun, in a way, if you were safe at home with loved ones.

Alone in Port Kernou, Mrs Thomas wrung her hands and wished her husband, son and the girl she wanted as a daughter-in-law were back already, safe and sound. She had everything prepared, the perfect Christmas; enough food and wine and chocolates to last until January even, if only they'd walk through the door right this minute, but as much as she stared out at the rain-soaked driveway and wrung her hands, they still didn't come.

Chapter Nineteen

Summoning Jowan

The silver weathervane on the turret top of Clove Lore Big House span like a merry-go-round. The visitor centre car park at the summit of the precipitously high and winding village was long since closed off, the girls from the shop had been sent safely home, and the donkey sanctuary stables locked.

Up here, there was no shelter from onshore winds determined to lift tiles and rip away Victorian guttering. So far, the Big House held firm, an indifferent old matriarch in her dotage, refusing to budge for anything.

Minty, wishing she was as impervious, had watched the storm coming in off the Atlantic from her childhood nursery window.

The whole west gable end of the attics belonged to Izaak and Leonid and while they'd been misting their Calathea collection – Leonid's absolute favourites – Minty had rapped at their door and begged a spot at the porthole window which she knew had the highest and best views in the house.

She'd come armed with a newish pair of field binoculars – 'new' to Minty meant anything from the eighties onwards – and climbed the ladder attached by runners to the attic walls up to the vantage point.

'What can you see, Captain?' Izaak asked, standing at the foot of the ladder with a cup of Leonid's excellent black cherry tea for her.

Minty didn't reply for some time.

A massive blue-and-white container ship was perched precariously on the thin navy line of the horizon, a car transporter, she reckoned, probably a couple of hundred metres long, a great high-sided tub of a thing. It was listing badly. The undercurrents must be giving it hell.

Overhead, a helicopter droned past the house on its way out to sea and Minty prayed to a god she'd never believed in to save all the souls on board and noted grimly that if *that* ship was in trouble, what luck would smaller boats out there have?

'These gales are enough to blow the horns of the devil himself,' she said eventually, looking down with a stoical smile, before refusing Izaak's tea.

Izaak sat by the ladder and drank it himself while Leonid stared broodingly from the low window at the far side of the attics. Below him were parked the developers' vehicles, all in a row upon his beautifully manicured front lawns, lush and free from weeds even in December.

The builders had checked and re-checked the scaffolds on the entirely empty shell of the east wing before downing tools and calling the Christmas holidays early this morning. The house was quieter than it had been in weeks – or would have been, were it not for the wind whipping down the chimneys.

Rain had fallen heavily all morning and puddles were forming in great patches the size of golf-course bunkers. 'The rain is lying on the lawns. It is not draining,' Leonid called back to his landlady-boss.

'Let's hope the drainage channels are up to the job of taking any run-off safely down to the sea,' she said.

From where she stood, Minty could see all the way down over the jumbled rooftops of the village to the harbour and the Siren's Tail. She also had eyeball on a certain old B&B cottage and the comforting sight of smoke rising from its chimney, which today was being whipped away and diffused by the wind no sooner than it escaped the mossy old pot.

She fixed the crosshairs upon it today with a deeper interest than usual. Jowan had promised to bring Aldous up to the house for lunch and maybe then stay until the storm had passed, but it was past noon and there was no sign of him yet. It was never his habit to be late.

Her eye was drawn by the sudden appearance of the Icelander, out on the slope. She turned the focus ring of the glasses, setting her sights on him, sharp and clear. Even from this distance she could make out the fact that he was struggling against the winds. He was turning left and right as though unsure which way to go, when another figure, sandy-haired, bearded, and with a second, fluffy head peeping out from his coat, appeared. It was Jowan, at last.

The men talked together for a moment and Jowan gestured with a pointed finger coastward. The holiday-maker leaned intently towards him, perhaps straining to hear over the sea-blast. Minty observed him seem to shrink, shoulders dropping, and Jowan patting his arm. The Icelander was shaking his head disconsolately and turning back the way he'd come, back to the alleyway that led to the bookshop – the safest place for him.

What was he thinking, striding about in the storm – and a stranger, too, who couldn't know all the little cut-throughs and safe spots in the village like those born here did?

A plume of litter rose high into the air, a twister of trash – chip wrappers and ice-cream tubs. One of the bins Down-along must have tipped over. If she hadn't sent Bovis home this morning he'd have taken one look at the mess and stomped off with his picking claw and a bin bag. The man hadn't taken a day off since last Christmas, even on high days and holidays when he was supposed to be at home doing whatever it was that a Bovis might do in his spare time. He'd always turn up and insist on staying at his post at the Big House.

Not having him glued to her side or skulking around the estate was an unexpected relief for Minty. The storm, she realised, had brought a moment's respite from her over-attentive staffer. She really would have to have a word with him come the New Year, encourage him into some kind of hobby, perhaps?

Her thoughts were interrupted by the sight of a blue tarpaulin that was supposed to be tied over one of the builder's skips flying past her window and up over the rooftop. It was getting dangerous out there. She pitied anyone still outside in this.

When Jowan got here she'd insist he stayed for supper and then the night. It was only right, and there was a put-up bed she could have made up in the ballroom for him by the fire.

It would be like the old days when soldiers were billeted here and the whole place was turned over to folding beds. Her grandfather used to talk about the men using the chapel's silver font and mirror for shaving. The prospect of Jowan bedding down at the Big House, unable to return to his home, sparked a Girl Guide sense of adventure and making do within her, but there was something else there too, something hopeful that told her if only she could get him away from his home with all its memories, if she could get him cosseted here with her overnight, there might be the tiniest chance of him forgetting how loyal he was to his Isolde. There might be the smallest chance of them talking honestly and openly to one another, something the old friends had never really attempted. Yet, just as she was imagining the possibilities that a night by the fire might conjure for them both, the memory of Isolda de Marisco snuffed out the little bit of hope she had. Jowan belonged only to Isolde, her old friend too, and nothing could make room in his heart for anyone else.

'Especially not you, silly Minty, lumbering old stick. Who'd want you? The last deb on the shelf,' she said to herself, echoing a voice from long ago, her mocking father, who never saw the harm in pointing out the truth.

'Sorry?' Izaak asked, glancing up.

'Nothing. I didn't say a thing,' she corrected him brusquely from above, making Izaak and Leonid exchange baffled glances.

'Come on, Jowan de Marisco, best foot forward, up the hill,' she urged under her breath, making sure nobody overheard this time.

Clove Lore was no place to be ranging about during a red weather warning. She tracked his climb until he was lost from view by the rooftops – her cue to scramble down the ladder.

'Take the rest of the day off, chaps,' she called, as she strode from the room. Izaak and Leonid hid their knowing smiles until she was heard tip-tapping down the staircase to haul the front doors open to wait for Jowan, eyes fixed on the footpath entrance to her estate and being blown about terribly.

'Any second… *now*,' she said. This was followed by disappointment. '*Now*,' she said again, more doggedly than before. 'Jowan de Marisco, I conjure you to appear before me *now*!' This was accompanied by a very small but very determined stamp of her foot and at that exact moment Jowan turned the corner, his neck bent against the downpour. She ran out to meet him with her father's ancient field umbrella which, like everything at the Big House, excepting perhaps Minty herself, had enjoyed better days.

They struggled back to the house, sharing its protection and it only blew itself inside out once, making Minty accidentally let out a scream like a teenager.

Jowan was attempting to tell her about meeting Magnús on the way here and she pretended that was news to her. She didn't want him to know she'd been spying.

'I told 'im Alex left half an hour ago at least, back to her boyfriend's. Ben, his name is. It's a bad business. Looked broken up and said he might as well go home.'

'Home? He's going to Iceland?' exclaimed Minty, leading the way across the threshold and into the echoing vestibule, now scattered with the damp brown winter leaves that followed them inside.

'That's what he said.' Jowan shrugged off his coat and Minty found a hanger for it in the cloakroom.

'Not in this storm, he's not. Nobody's going anywhere tonight,' she said, and Jowan cocked his head when he detected the strange tone in his old friend's voice, unusually shaky for Minty. It made some tiny vessel of his heart flicker with delight.

'Come along, there's some boiled ham and eggs in the kitchen with your name on it.' Aldous too looked hopeful.

'Not you, little friend,' she told him, as Jowan set the dog on the ground. 'I've made *you* a cheddar sandwich!'

Aldous's claws tap-danced on the floor as he turned circles around Minty gliding to the kitchen. Jowan followed behind, hands stuffed contentedly in his pockets, smiling fondly after Minty, forgetting the storm and his sorry-looking tenant at the bookshop, for now.

Chapter Twenty

The Voyager Returns Home

Magnús threw off his dripping waterproof coat and sat behind the old laptop at the shop counter.

She had gone with her boyfriend, Jowan had confirmed, and with her, she'd taken all the joy he'd found in running the shop yesterday. How could he have allowed himself to think for one minute that this stupid voyage to England was anything but a game? He'd been a phoney back home – kidding himself he could save his own bookstore – and he was nothing but a phoney here, too. Alex had told him she believed in him and that had been enough to have him grinning and sentimental, thinking himself a bookseller again. None of it had been real.

His thoughts spiralled. He'd grab the first flight out of here. Even if he left first thing tomorrow morning, he could still be back with his family in time for Christmas Eve dinner.

As the fans noisily whirred and the screen came to life, the shop's holiday ledger opened automatically onscreen, loading slowly line by line. Magnús impatiently jabbed at the exit button but the laptop didn't respond. It took all his willpower not to throw the thing to the ground, but he made himself fold his arms tightly and wait, eyes fixed on the ceiling until the computer had finished going through its slow start–up.

'Come on, come on,' he muttered, his jaw flexing hard.

When he looked again he saw his own name on the top line, marked out in green from all the others. He moved the cursor to close the page but was struck by the length of the list and instead scrolled through the list of bookings.

Sturluson, Iceland; Keeland, Vancouver; Forster, Belfast; Lǐ, Amsterdam; the list went on and on. All those dreamers were queued up, waiting to take their turn pretending to be a bookseller, and no doubt they'd take to it as though it were the very career for them.

They'd leave thinking themselves cut out for a life of stocktaking and till–ringing. How little they'd have seen of how hard it really was. They'd have all the success and none of the hard work, and no inkling whatsoever of the shame that accompanied failure.

He scanned the columns again. Almost all of the guests were set to travel here in pairs: friends, lovers, fathers and daughters, all kinds of happy combinations. Not one of them would feel quite so utterly alone as Magnús did, now that Alex had left.

He stabbed at the keys and this time the page closed. His fingers worked fast as he typed, murmuring, 'England to Iceland… leaving now.' It took a moment to find the carrier he needed.

He could be packed and out of here in half an hour if he was quick. 'There's no point in staying, standing around uselessly like an empty shell', he told himself.

Sure enough, there was a flight at eight o'clock tonight and even though he found he couldn't change his ticket, he could simply buy a new one. Expensive, but worth it.

All he had to do was get to Heathrow. How hard could that be?

Once home, he could take over some holiday shifts at the wine shop, let his colleagues off the hook. They'd thank him for it. He could work hard, put away some cash, and he'd go out at New Year with his brother and get good and drunk. It would be like old times, only easier, because he'd finally come to the realisation that he had to surrender his old dreams. Five days here had been enough to show him everything he'd got wrong.

Alex had said that night at Minty's that she refused to believe people couldn't get their dreams if they really went for them. 'Bullshit!' he told the screen as he typed in his details.

He sniffed a wry laugh as his thoughts churned. They may well have had fun running the shop and café yesterday, but that was no marker of his success as a book-seller. He was still the failure he'd always been, but he was going home an adult at last: fully aware of his limitations, dreamless, and utterly empty-chested and sore.

He'd learned he had to settle for the decisions life made for him. Some people didn't get their dreams. Some people ended up losing all their money and gaining a big chunk of debt in return for all of their studying and striving. That was just the way of the world.

Alex had talked about how important it was to be happy, but he'd come to understand that just wasn't an option for him, not if he carried on wanting the same things he always had. So he surrendered them now. He needed new smaller, easier dreams.

He wondered if Alex was happy now. He hoped so. Jowan had said as much when he told Magnús she was going home for Christmas with her loved ones. Maybe that was what he'd come here to learn? That in the big karmic balance of things there were natural winners and losers. If she could get the things she wanted; he'd accept that he couldn't have his.

More than anything, he hoped she'd win out over the demons that troubled her, whatever they were. He even hoped she was happy at home with that guy, if she truly did love him. He was willing to accept this distribution of contentment, even if it meant him being miserable for a while.

He hit the return key and watched the payment form he'd filled in disappear.

The Wi-Fi flaked out and the website buffered. 'Come on, come on!'

His ticket home was only seconds away and he still had to call an Uber and pack his stuff. The little blue circle span until Magnús swore with impatience. He had to get out of here now.

–

'How could you do that to me? And with Eve, of all people? How could you do that to her little boy?'

In the back seat, Alex hissed the words through gritted teeth while, beside her, Ben listened, now chastened after his heroic rescue.

Mr Thomas, navigating the winding single lane that led them away from Clove Lore turned up the music station on the car radio and discreetly pretended to hum along to 'Walking in a Winter Wonderland' while the tyres rolled slowly through spindly, gale-torn branches and the churning clusters of litter from wheelie bins blown over as far away as Appledore.

'I wasn't thinking,' Ben whispered, pleadingly. 'It lasted, like, a second and I felt awful the whole time, honestly. But that's not important now, is it?'

Alex turned fierce eyes upon him, exasperated.

'What I mean is, I regretted it straight away and I'll say sorry to you for the rest of my life if I have to, if you just give me a chance to fix things.'

Fix things? Alex searched his face. How was it possible to fix this?

'Look, let's just get through Christmas and we can talk afterwards. Come on, it's Christmas Eve tomorrow. You love Christmas at Mum and Dad's...'

'But...' Alex tried to interject, but Ben stilled her with his hands spread defensively in front of him.

'I promise you'll feel better when you're back in your own house.'

Alex didn't think she would feel better, alone at night in a house that had been left to go cold for near on two weeks, the way only English houses can lose all their warmth when owners leave town. 'I don't want to go home. I'm lonely there.'

Ben's eyes flashed with inspiration. 'Well, that's what I've been wanting to talk to you about. You always wanted us to move in together, remember?'

Alex barely hid the snort of derision. Of course she remembered.

Ben persisted. 'It didn't really make a lot of sense when I'd just found my own flat down the road from Mum and Dad's, but now I think it's time.' He tried to reach for her hand but she recoiled, folding her arms tightly across her body. 'I'm ready now,' he said in a whisper, casting a surreptitious glance at his father's eyes in the rear-view mirror.

'Ready for what?' Alex hissed.

'To move in with you of course, silly.'

The car, trundling along at twenty miles an hour, suddenly seemed to leave the road in a loop-the-loop. Alex clutched her stomach to quell the queasiness. 'What?' she cried, incredulous. '*Now* you want to move in with me, at my mum and dad's house?'

'It's *your* house, Alex. Think about it. You won't be rattling around there all on your own any more, and we can finally commit, you know?'

This was all Alex had wanted to hear a year or two ago. Now, the thought of her and Ben sharing the house her parents had set up together physically pained her. It would make a mockery of them and their devotion to one another if she were to pretend everything was fine with Ben now.

'I *was* committed,' she spat.

'Well now we can be together twenty-four/seven, except when you're out on the ferry of course. Maybe you could clear out your... *umm*, the spare room and I could have it as my home office? What do you say? Dad'll help us redecorate. He's already said he'll help, haven't you, Dad?'

Mr Thomas only nodded. Alex could tell even from the back of his head that he knew better than his son how badly this was going.

'And,' Ben lowered his voice again. 'It'll be different this time. The next step, yeah? And Eve's gone now, thank God, so she won't be hanging round, coming between us.'

The sadness circling her heart turned to a rising, burning fury once more. She glared piercingly at Ben who felt her ire right down to his boots but he was determined to plead his case.

'You have to admit, she was always there, causing trouble,' he said.

'*What?* How?' Alex had never thought of Eve as troublesome. She'd loved her, right up until the day they both betrayed her.

'You know,' Ben said, a vainglorious smile forming. 'She was always calling in when you were at work, making a nuisance of herself, flirting. And you must know what everyone thought of her back home.'

'No, what *did* they think of her?'

Ben edged closer to the cliff face, utterly unaware how precarious his footing was. 'You know? That she was a bit of a... well, a bit of a... slut.' Ben shrugged his shoulders as he said the word, as though it explained everything and now he was off the hook.

'A *slut*?' Alex echoed his tone, the word ringing louder than the storm building outside the vehicle. 'How dare you call her that?'

Ben's eyes bulged. 'What? It's true, isn't it?' He looked between his dad and Alex, appealingly. No support came.

'What does that even *mean*?' Alex turned her body to confront his. '*Slut?* She was a mess. She was lonely. She needed help.'

The words came to her as she pictured her friend in tears by the jetty after yet another argument with Maxwell, waiting for Alex to bring the ferry across the river again. She remembered holding her friend and comforting her. None of that was fake. Eve had been utterly lost, like a child.

'Maybe she's just a bit hopeless. Maybe she doesn't know how to help herself. Loads of people are like that.' Alex's eyes blazed. She was on a roll now and the words kept coming. She didn't admit she was thinking of more than Eve's situation as she spoke. 'Loads of people find themselves stuck somewhere they don't want to be, and with people who make them miserable. Maybe she didn't have the courage – or the means – to get out. And if you thought she was such a nuisance why were you kissing her in my living room? *Hmm?* Was she less of a nuisance at that point?'

Ben stared at the headrest, not quite realising he couldn't salvage this.

'Mr Thomas?' Alex said, getting no response. 'Dad, stop the car, please.' She said it softly at first. '*Please, stop the car!*' This time she yelled it.

She saw Ben's father's shoulders drop in defeat as he pumped the brakes. The car rolled slowly to a stop under the spreading branches of an oak tree growing from the hedgerow. Alex unclipped her seatbelt and grabbed the plastic bag containing her few belongings from the foot-well.

'Where are you going?' Ben yelped in horror, watching as she reached for the door handle.

'I'm not coming home with you. You have Christmas plans with your family, go and enjoy them.'

'No! No wait! What are you doing?' He grabbed ineffectually at her coat.

Alex thought of Magnús back at the shop that they'd planned to open together today. He'd have woken up and found her gone. Her hand swooped to her pocket. It was empty. No phone. It must still be in Jowan's spare room.

'I have plans of my own,' she replied.

'We'll drive her back,' said Mr Thomas, turning in his seat and addressed his son.

'But, Dad!' Ben whined.

'Let her go, son.'

Alex pulled the door open and slipped out. 'I'll walk.'

'In this weather?' Ben scrambled across the back seat after her. 'So, you *have* gone crazy! That's what everyone was saying at home, and I didn't believe them.'

She was surprised by the laugh this elicited from her. They could think she was mad and they could think that Eve was a slut. It didn't matter any more. She looked down at Ben sitting where she'd been trapped a moment ago. He was staring up at her at a loss for what to do now.

'It's not that far back down the valley, and we passed loads of bus stops. I'll get on the next bus that comes.'

The wind didn't feel all that bad in the momentary lull that had settled around them by the side of the car and in the shelter of the stone walls and ancient hedgerows. 'I'm walking.' Her voice was stony and resolute.

Alex extended her spine to her full height, looking at the road behind her and the dark sky and sea beyond. There was still a tiny patch of blue far out over the water. The storm might not come to much after all. Maybe it was already passing? She buttoned her coat as Mr Thomas forced the driver door open and stood before her, not minding that he was getting wet again.

'I'm sorry you had to come all this way,' she told him.

'I'm sorry it's ending this way, love.' He reached for her and she hugged him back. 'You are always welcome at our house. Remember that. We all love you very much, like our own daughter.'

When he pulled away, Alex could see in his eyes that he meant it, but she knew she couldn't call round any more. It really was over. She'd been desperately searching for a family and home comforts to the extent that she'd settled for any port in a storm. What she needed, she now knew, was a safe haven of her own making. Far better, she was coming to understand, to be her own anchor. She might not have all the answers – in fact, she barely had any – but she knew she'd seen a tiny glimpse of what was possible during the last few days down there, over the rain-sodden fields, in Clove Lore, and that was where she wanted to be right now.

'I'll pop in,' she lied. 'Once I decide what I'm doing with my life.'

'You really won't let us drive you back there?' Mr Thomas scanned the narrow road ahead for a turning place.

'No,' she insisted. 'I can't look at Ben…' The rest of her words tailed away.

Mr Thomas only nodded and delivered a kiss, on tiptoes, to her cheek. 'Bye for now, Alex. Just follow the road straight, it'll wind back down to the harbour car park behind the pub – twenty minutes' walk, I reckon.'

'I'll be fine,' she told him, and she believed it too. 'Tell Mu… tell Mrs Thomas I'm sorry I'm missing her Christmas lunch.' She couldn't call them mum and dad any longer.

This was her surrendering the Thomases, who she loved, to preserve herself, who she determined to love better. It was going to be far easier for the whole pack of Thomases to let her go than it was going to be for her to turn away from the only family she had, she realised with a stab at her heart, but she had no hope of a future of her own shaping if she went home with Ben now.

Turning away so Mr Thomas didn't see her tears, she took the first step towards Clove Lore – the first intentional step of her life.

Ben was out of the car, gaping and gesturing his disbelief. His father cautioned him to give it up and get in the passenger seat. They were leaving without her. 'She could at least put her boots on,' she heard him whine before he pulled the car door closed.

Alex's fluffy pink slippers pointed her in the direction where a piece of her heart lay, and she strode through the wind and rain, not knowing what tempests awaited but determined to get back in that warm spot by Magnús's side in his bookshop where she'd been so happy last night.

That would have to do, for now. When he left for Iceland in a week's time she'd have no regrets about wasting another minute of the hours afforded to them. She was going to have a happy Christmas with him and then, after that, even though she couldn't imagine how her future might look, she'd at least be steering her own course, and if it went wrong she would only have herself to blame. The determination and excitement drowned out so much of her old apprehension and grief, and she marched on.

Chapter Twenty-One

I Am Here For You

This had to be it: rock bottom. Magnús was officially abandoning his holiday mid-way through, walking away from a phoney bookshop he simply couldn't make a go of, and now he was crying in a rain storm in an empty car park on a dreary winter afternoon while hugging an increasingly damp woolly jumper to his body like a person with zero self-control and no pride whatsoever.

He could honestly say he missed his old pre-Alex self; the one who kept himself locked away safe and sound, taking no risks, doing nothing special. Even if he exasperated his family and his sullen nature drew some funny looks from people, it was far and away better than feeling like this, all exposed and vulnerable and incredibly, *incredibly* stupid.

He tried to picture himself on the flight, high above the North Atlantic, a vodka over ice in his glass, looking down through clouds at the tiny world below. He needed some height, he felt. From a distance this holiday might not look quite so humiliating. With miles between him and Clove Lore he might be able to think straight again.

Right now, all he could see was his failure, interspersed with intrusive flashes of Alex smiling in that way she did, all unsure of herself and so generous with her kindness at the same time.

The traitorous, loving little bit at the back of his brain wanted to cause him even more pain, and so it played on a loop a memory of the song Alex had sung, and in her sweet voice too, the song that she hadn't even been aware he could overhear, the one about the mermaid and the boy from the shore who she enticed into the sea and no doubt promptly drowned.

That was what had happened to Magnús. He'd been tempted out of his natural element (his safe dark box of brooding, regretful solitude) into a world of dreams and hopefulness, and no sooner was he up to his neck in it and thinking he might just float, Alex had swum off back to where she came from and here he was, a man half drowned in inconvenient, unwanted feelings. Yes, the quicker he was on that flight home, the better.

Yet, when the text notification buzzed on the phone in his pocket, he grabbed for it. There were two phones in there, one his own, and one Alex's. Jowan had given it to him, saying she'd left it behind in the hurry to get away. For a second, he thought it might be her trying to reach out to him through her mobile, but its screen was blank, so he checked his own and there it was. A siren call from Alex on some unknown number? He gazed at the words, his heart swelling.

I am here for you.

'Jesus, Alex!' He read it once more, trying to contain the pang of hope in his chest. He turned to look down the slope but it was impossible to see in this whipping wind and with his eyes somehow streaming. Was she Down-along waiting for him? He typed a reply, stumbling over the words, messing it up, but hitting send in seconds.

> You're back? I knew you would be! I've been frantic here. Listen, I don't just like you. I'm not some robot. I'm a man and I want you. I am crazy for you and I should have told you when I had the chance. Where are you? Don't go anywhere! I'll come to you.

How had she found him? They hadn't even swapped numbers, to his knowledge. All he knew was that he had to have her in his arms right away. The wait for a reply physically pained him, and he brought the phone close to his face and watched the rippling bubbles showing she was typing something back.

> This is Tony. Your Uber driver on the airport run. I'm here for you. At the visitor centre car park but the gate's locked.

'Oh Christ!' Magnús sank down onto his haunches and gripped his knees as the humiliation hit him with full force. 'Idiot!' Sure enough, at the other side of the car park, through the wide gate, was the glow of a car's head-lights.

Another message appeared and he cringed, looking at it in trepidation.

> You OK? Want the car or not?

Magnús typed his reply.

> Not.

Then thinking how this guy had probably left a warm home for him, and knowing how much English people loved to apologise, he sent another.

> Sorry.

Another message appeared. This guy was fast.

> Have to charge you, buddy. But the radio's saying flights are being grounded anyway. You're stuck here, mate. If you want my opinion, which you probably don't, I'm no expert, but if you like someone that much, tell them. Cheers, Tony

Magnús shoved the phone in his pocket as the car blinked its headlights and made a U-turn on the empty road.

Here he was, with a ticket to Iceland on his phone and an over-invested Uber driver on the edge of his seat, and he had no idea where Alex was now. Tell her how he felt? Impossible. Wasn't it? And yet, when he'd thought she was getting in touch hadn't his heart leapt, and then crashed when he'd found it wasn't her? That meant something.

Magnús stayed crouched in the rain, his brain whirring. Had he come this far only to accept failure now? Just because she'd left to be with those people for Christmas didn't mean that was what she wanted deep in her heart. She longed for family, craved it, he understood that, sure. She wanted peace and security, comfort and love, just like everybody else did. Why couldn't he be the one to give her that? Those men had laid claim to her, but the feeling bursting in his chest now wasn't going to be denied. If Tony the Uber driver could spark that kind of passionate hope in him, what could finding her and telling her how he felt do?

And then he was running, surprisingly slowly, down-hill, the wind pushing him back until he felt like if he leaned into it and raised his arms he might actually take flight, like all the litter and bits of moss and roof tile swirling in the air.

Where was she now? His brain fought for the inform-ation he needed. What was the place called? He'd heard her say it. Port? Port... Suddenly it came to him. Port Kerr-no. That was what it had sounded like when she'd said it, soft and lilting in her Cornish accent.

As he moved Down-along through the storm, he held on to the cottage garden railings, dragging himself, barely able to see. Another few metres and he'd be there.

He'd get into the shop, search online for her ferry company, get her number and he'd call her as soon as possible. He'd tell her everything that had raced through his head in the last hour and, crucially, he'd tell her that he wanted her.

When he reached the turning for the bookshop he threw himself into the shelter of the narrow passageway between the cottages and the wind sharply dropped away.

For a moment he leaned against the wall, panting hard and wiping the rain from his face. Would she want him? Well, that was the big ridiculous hopeful question, wasn't it? So far today, all evidence had pointed towards the obvious answer: Duh! She'd already left, hadn't she? And yet, the light Alex had ignited within him again after so long spent in the shade, still burned for her.

Turning his head towards the shop, all closed up and dark now, he had to blink and peer through wet lashes to be sure his eyes weren't playing tricks on him.

There, on the doorstep of the Borrow-A-Bookshop, was a woman with white hair hanging in sodden ropes down her back, slumped on the top step, her face hidden, sobbing over the note he'd left for Jowan only moments ago saying he was on his way to the airport.

'Alex!' he cried.

Magnús, unable to prevent the tender swelling in his heart at the sight of her, understood in that instant that he was in grave danger of falling very much in love this Christmas if she should only smile at him again.

He bounded through the passageway and across the square, the rain hitting him hard once more, and just as she lifted her head, exclaiming in bewildered amazement and relief that he was still here, Magnús pulled her to her feet.

She clawed strands of her wet hair from her face and tried to make herself presentable, impossible now she looked like she'd been dredged from the bottom of the sea, but Magnús was looking at her like she was a mermaid upon a starlit rock on a summer's night.

The only thing that occurred to him to say at that moment was to enquire if she wanted him to kiss her.

Her laugh warmed him right to his core. 'Of course I do,' she said. 'I ran all the way back here in a storm, ruining a perfectly good pair of slippers in the hope you'd kiss me again.'

Trying hard to hold back tears through his laughter as he glanced down at the muddy fur of her pink boots, Magnús's relief hit him hard and without thinking about anything other than the impulse building inside him, he kissed her against the bookshop door, not minding the storm at all, and she pulled him close against her as though telling him she'd never let go again.

The pair kissed on, utterly unaware that, as their lips met, all across Clove Lore the fairy lights on every Christmas tree, and every bulb lighting the mid-winter early-afternoon streets, flickered and buzzed before the power supply for the entire village cut out, plunging every home into darkness.

Chapter Twenty-Two

The Eye of the Storm

There is a point in the swell of a storm when all life holds its breath and hides its head. An innate animal instinct for self-preservation kicks in and while the wind and rain rage on, each creature settles itself, seeking comfort.

This moment befell all the inhabitants of Clove Lore at precisely two-fifteen on the afternoon of December the twenty-third, as the low-sinking sun in the west became obscured entirely by the thickest, darkest band of cloud to collect over the fragile, beautiful Devonshire coast in ten decades.

The clouds roiled and turned in upon themselves like black fire. Furious winds forced underneath the cloud formed a fierce corridor of air that blasted against the land and whipped up the waves.

When the lights went out, Clove Lore had been plunged into darkness, save for the Big House where the lights in the attics and kitchen, powered by their own noisy generator, glowed on.

After lunch, Minty and Jowan had drunk black coffees huddled by the old Aga. Aldous had lazily licked his lips and curled up asleep at his master's feet. They sat in companionable silence listening to the radio telling of the safe delivery of twelve Chinese sailors taken from the container ship now at anchor off the coast.

'Here's to them.' Jowan raised his mug, and Minty followed.

'Safe harbour,' she said, and both drank, sinking into silence again, waiting for the storm to pass.

Three floors up in the attics, Leonid read in his calmest voice to Izaak from his book about camellia cultivation, stroking Izaak's brow as he listened, both crushed together on the big armchair.

They'd carefully unpacked the poppy seed cake – a Christmas gift from Izaak's mother in Krasnik, with a note signed in defiance of the prejudices that had driven him to England in the first place: 'For my two sons, from your loving Matka'.

They were trying hard to ignore the storm outside and the inevitable thoughts of Leonid's parents' abject silence this winter. They had remained unmoved by Leonid's many messages asking them to try to be happy for their son and his groom.

Leonid kissed Izaak's temple and they each took bites of the cake as Leonid turned another page, both of them visualising camellias coming into fat green bud in the spring sunshine and red poppies bobbing their heads in peaceful summer fields.

Out in his little house on the main road that led away from Clove Lore, Bovis did not yet know the electricity had shorted. In a bubble bath neck-deep, by candlelight, he feverishly turned the pages of a book he'd meant as a gift, now desperate to discover which of the Miss Bennets' stories would end happily and which in regret. This is how readers are born.

A little farther along the main road, when thrown into sudden darkness, Elliot and Jude had scrabbled for the torch from Elliot's vet bag. At least their gas stove still worked in the power cut, so they cooked together in the dim kitchen, their LED star lights shining in the steamy windows.

Elliot found himself wishing he'd remembered to buy candles as he thumbed the small velvet box in his pocket, deciding to defer the question he'd been meaning to ask Jude this evening until some other peaceful night in front of the TV. Jude couldn't help glancing at him in concern. 'Are you OK?' she asked gently.

'I...' he hesitated. 'I'm just thinking of the animals at the practice. They'll be frightened by the sounds of the storm.'

Jude smiled at her soft-hearted Elliot, turned off the heat and abandoned the stir fry, reaching for him.

'They'll be all right, they're safe. Anjali's there with them, right?' Seeing that this might not in fact be the thing making Elliot fret, she added, 'And we're safe here. All is well, OK?'

He nodded with a smile and let her kiss him.

Gently, he lifted her and set her onto the kitchen counter so they could be closer, and she laughed at this, like she always did.

'You're right,' he told her, before taking a deep breath and slowly lowering himself to kneel at her feet. He presented her with his gift.

'Jude Crawley.' He gazed up at her with soft eyes as she brought her hands to her face. He opened the box to reveal the fiery orange stone in its silver setting. 'Will you have me, forever, as your husband?'

His face fell when Jude hopped down from the counter telling him to wait there. He stood again, unsure what to do. Was it too soon? Had he blown it?

She was back a moment later with a wrapped box from under the Christmas tree. 'Only if you'll have me as your wife,' she told him, and his amazement turned to happy tears as he tore the paper away to reveal a gleaming band of his own.

The rest of their evening slipped away by torchlight beneath the covers as easily as those rings had slipped onto their fingers.

Down in the village, not all of Clove Lore's inhabitants were quite so comfortable.

Mrs Crocombe sat alone in her ice-cream parlour weeping, not so much at the thought of the freezers losing power but more because, in rare moments like this, she felt very much alone in the world.

She pulled the notebook from her pocket and leafed through the names of old pals and people who'd passed through; those she thought would stick around, and those who'd left for good. She was one woman trying to build a village on love. Not an easy task.

She knew what some of the locals called her. She was a busybody, a gossip, a pain in the neck. But she'd seen the village in its prime, when there was no such thing as holiday houses left vacant all winter then rented out all summer to people who brought in their own food and left nothing but litter.

She remembered the names of every one of the villagers going back generations whose little white cottages clung to the rocks Down-along.

She knew what the school run sounded like when old Mr Caffey would ring his bell in the playground and thirty kids of all ages would open cottage doors all at once and snake their way up to the little school on the promontory, all boisterous laughter and high jinks.

There were no children living in the village now; too inconvenient without access for cars. Her own grandchildren lived out on the promontory in a new build where they had a nice level garden – not a postage stamp on a slant – and two parking spaces.

So many of Clove Lore's cottages were falling into disrepair now or had been gutted and fitted out with all mod cons. There were five planning permission applications in at the council at the moment for vertical extensions so that dear old wonky roofs could be ripped off and further storeys added, as if her parents and grandparents hadn't tried to preserve the old way of living for these younger ones. It was all wrong, to her mind.

She wept for all this, and for her own hard work starting up the ice-cream parlour thirty years ago, helped by her three brothers, all fishermen, none married and now all gone, keeping her late husband company some place where there were no such things as storms, she hoped.

Love. That was what Clove Lore needed if it was going to survive into the next century. And happy homes. Not those fancy 'lifestyle units' going up inside the gutted shell of the Big House that no locals could afford anyway. Even Elliot and Jude, her biggest matchmaking success – after the Burntislands with their three pre-school age offspring – had settled down way out of the village on the main road.

She blew her nose and told herself she'd been through worse than a bit of rain and a touch of the winter blues.

She should pull herself together and have a bit of mint choc chip.

At the sound of thunder and another hard blast of wind, the walls of her little cottage shook and she clasped at her chest, feeling very sorry for herself indeed and, not for the first time, terribly lonesome.

Down at the Siren's Tail, the doors were bolted shut for the first December afternoon since that period during the war when the barrels had run dry. Bella's granddad had told her all about it. She considered putting masking tape in crosses over the windows like he'd described, only not to stop bombs sending smashed glass everywhere, but a storm that sounded at that moment, out on their vulnerable spot by the sea, far louder than bombs.

Bella remarked to her husband that she was glad their guests had cleared out on the nineteenth when they'd had the chance. She felt sorry for the Austens, hiding away in their suite upstairs. 'Some Christmas this is going to be for them, stuck indoors with a baby.'

They sat in their little den just off the bar. Finan topped up their gin glasses after a long morning poring sorrowfully over their accounts.

This had been their make or break winter. Bella's wet cheeks told her husband she was broken.

Tomorrow they'd ring the brewery and, come January, the 'for sale' sign would go up and the Siren's Tail would run the risk of becoming just like all those other boarded-up pubs all across the country with beer towels over dry taps. Who bought a pub these days? You'd have to be mad.

Finan stroked the back of his wife's hand and told her they'd had a good run. 'Twelve years is better than most country publicans manage, especially ones depending on tourists!'

He'd tried to cheer her up by talking about how they could get a nice little place just outside of Launceston near their nieces and nephews and although the thought of moving away from the home she'd always known caused her pain, they'd both smiled bravely and tried to convince themselves a fresh start would be good for them.

In their father's fisherman's cottage at the top of the slope, Tom and Monty Bickleigh sat by the fire. They'd listened to the clatter of decorative nets, buoys and lobster pots that had, until this morning, been arranged artfully around their front door, scattering themselves across the visitor centre car park fifty yards farther up the slope.

Monty turned a piece of toast on a fork near the flames in relative contentment while Tom, eight minutes his junior and always the more agitated, stared at the flames and brooded about how he'd really thought he'd had a chance with the girl from the ferry.

Their cottage was so close to the entrance to the Clove Lore estate they could hear the donkeys in their stalls braying every time the wind rattled the doors. The stable master, Mr Moke, had been recalled from Christmas at his brother's in Barnstaple by a flustered Minty. At that moment he was trying to get some sleep on the bales next to his charges. This was not the holiday he'd planned at all.

Nobody stirred abroad. The village was pitch black. The curtains at every window were drawn and barely a fire-glow escaped them as the storm did its worst.

Whilst the clouds rumbled with sounds of rapidly approaching thunder, and jagged electric shards forked across the horizon, Magnús and Alex stood frozen before one another and asked themselves what on earth they were supposed to do now.

Chapter Twenty-Three

By Candlelight at the Borrow-A-Bookshop

'Bath?' Magnús said, staring at Alex taking off her sodden slippers on the shop doormat.

'What?' She dragged her tired body upright, shaking raindrops from her coat.

'I said, I should make you a hot bath.'

Alex pushed her hair from her face, bewildered. 'Should we talk about what happened?'

'Did you almost leave, then come back here in a hurry, even in the storm?'

'Uh, well, that's the long and the short of it, yes.' She shrugged. 'I came back because I wasn't finished spending time with you.'

'I see,' he said, eyes growing softer by the second.

'Can I please stay?'

'OK.'

'OK? That's it? You don't mind?'

Magnús didn't mind one bit, but when he realised how much Alex was shivering he found that all he minded was getting her warm again. 'Quick,' he told her, 'bathroom,' and by the light from his phone he bounded up the spiral staircase to run the hot tap until the last drop of warm water was gone. Alex dragged herself after him, exhausted and elated all at once.

Someone, no doubt Jowan, had had the foresight to furnish the bookshop with enough Price's white candles to last an entire winter without electricity. Magnús clustered them five at a time in coffee mugs, lit them with long cook's matches and set them all around the foot of the bath as well as on every table in the bookshop so the whole place glowed a soft orange.

Alex had waited until he'd gone downstairs before undressing and lowering herself into the steaming bath and she listened as he swept out the fire and set it again with kindling. She heard him striking matches and the eventual crackles of the hearth coming to life, then there was the sound of running water in the tiny kitchen at the back of the shop and, a few minutes later, the whistling sound of an old-fashioned kettle boiling on a gas ring.

When he came back upstairs he knocked at the bathroom door. 'I've made hot chocolate. I'll leave yours here for you.'

Alex laughed at the sight of his hand reaching round the door and Magnús trying to set the mug down on the sink without looking. This shyness between them was new. She supposed running through the rain to be with him again had taken their relationship – could she even call it that? – to a new emotional level, and it was awkward trying to figure out what that meant, especially as they only had another week together.

She had no idea Magnús was bursting with words he wanted to say to her, but was holding off, not wanting to overwhelm her after whatever it was that had happened between her and her family this morning.

'Just come in,' she told him.

'Should I?' he said, still behind the door.

'Come on!'

Candlelight and a deep bath was a totally different thing compared to last night by the fire. It had been magical of course, but somehow this all felt much more intimate.

The glow of the flames hid the pink in Magnús's cheeks. He glanced at Alex, her hair washed and sleek over her shoulders, the ends fanning out across the surface of the water.

'You can get in,' she told him.

'*Hm?*' He tried to look casual and not at all alarmed at the suggestion.

'The electricity's gone for the whole village, it looks like. Who knows when we'll next have hot water? Get in. I won't look.' To encourage him, she slapped a hand over her eyes above a wicked grin.

His shyness was all the reminder she needed that she didn't yet know him all that well, in spite of everything that had happened. They needed to go back to baby steps again, feeling their way around each other, and that included sharing the things she'd been reluctant to share before.

She knew Magnús was grinning too as he threw his clothes to the floor and clambered into the tub, because she peeped through the gap in her fingers. The glimpse of his broad shoulders and flexing delts as he lowered himself into the water made her want to bite her lip and turn her eyes bashfully to the ceiling. His skin glistened in the candlelight as he scooped water into his hands and rubbed it over his face, making his lashes spike and turning Alex's insides soft and wanting. All the while, the rain pattered icily in near horizontal sheets at the steamy bathroom window.

'It's a bit of a squeeze,' she told him, lifting her hand from her eyes at the sensation of their bare skin touching and their long limbs tangling underwater.

Something in Magnús's demeanour told her he had to get words out of the way before he could truly relax in here with her.

'The men at the beach,' he said after a moment's pause. 'Jowan told me they were your family?'

Without hesitating, Alex unburdened herself of the whole story, taking quick sips of hot chocolate every now and then. She found she couldn't hide her sadness from Magnús at losing the family she'd been so content with, and she choked up when talking about Eve, but there was nowhere near the same pain when she explained how her three-and-a-half-year relationship with Ben had ended.

'I'm not surprised he cheated, actually. Things haven't been right for a long time. He knew that long before I'd figured it out. It wasn't fair to stay with him when we weren't happy. So,' she shrugged, making the water ripple in waves over her breastbone and shoulders, 'it's over, and for the first time in a long time, there's just me.'

'Well, here's to just you.' Magnús held out his mug and they clanked their hot chocolates together and drank.

'So, what have you done all day?' she asked. 'Did you open the shop?'

'Open the shop? First of all, nobody's shopping in a storm. Second, you'd left without saying goodbye. I didn't know what to think, but I knew, deep in here,' he touched his hand to his chest, 'you didn't belong with those people and… I wanted you back. When you didn't come, I tried to leave, but something stopped me. I—'

The buzz of his phone on the bathroom floor stopped him, and he reached down to read the message.

How'd it go? Did you find her? My missus wants to know. Hope you did, mate. Merry Christmas. Uber Tony.

Magnús sniffed a laugh at the screen.

'Who's that?' Alex asked.

'Our fan club,' he told her, still smiling to himself. 'Doesn't matter.' He waved the interruption away, but Alex was already moving their conversation on.

'They kind of flustered me into leaving with them, and a big part of me wanted to go, in a way, but then I woke up. I can't explain it any other way. I woke up and knew I had to get back here.'

Magnús listened carefully.

'I realised something when I was walking back here,' she added.

'What's that?'

'I'm not fixed yet.'

'Are you supposed to be fixed?' said Magnús.

'I don't know,' she shrugged. 'I need something of my own, something that's mine that I can be proud of. Not something external that other people can give to me. Even you.' She added these last words, unable to meet Magnús's eyes. 'We can spend this week together, and that's great – beautiful, even – but I still need a life of my own. I need to fix myself up.'

Magnús was nodding. He understood. 'I feel the same.'

'You do?'

'I was so happy yesterday,' he told her, his eyes glazing a little at the memory. 'I thought I had it all. But all it took was you leaving this morning and it all just came crashing back over me. I can't recover from how sad I am to have lost my bookshop. I know it sounds pathetic, you could say egotistical. Like, why should I be any different from all the other people losing their businesses? But I need something else too.' He seemed to think hard then added, 'Something bigger than being happy. I need something bigger even than making you laugh, even though that feels amazing, something bigger than making you…' His words faltered again and he looked away.

'Go on.'

'Making you orgasm.'

'Hah!' Alex laughed and brought her hands to her cheeks to hide the blush.

Magnús pressed on, caught up in his thoughts. 'Even though these are things I want. There's more inside of me that needs to be fixed, and I still don't know how to do it.'

'Well, that's OK,' Alex soothed. 'I don't have a clue what I need either. How am I supposed to make up for all my lost years, doing nothing with my life? How am I meant to move on from being so sad when I was so young? We both need to figure out what our bigger pictures look like. Right?'

'Right,' Magnús nodded slowly, still thinking. 'I guess as a book nerd I should know the story isn't over until everybody's happy.'

Alex smiled back. 'Getting really properly happy might take a long time, but I think that's OK. At least I made a good start today.'

Magnús laid his empty mug on the side of the bath then reached for Alex's and placed them together. 'I want to know… you came back for your own sake, *já*? But did you also possibly… want me, a little? And not just for this week?'

Alex grinned again and, with some difficulty, lifted herself onto her knees so she could lean towards him. The sight of her rising from the water, wet hair clinging to her curves and the candlelight iridescent on her skin like glistening mermaid's scales sent a jolt of desire through Magnús's core like a bolt of lightning. This was a vision he would never forget for the rest of his life.

Leaning over him so she could reach his lips, Alex said, still smiling, 'I want you.'

When she covered his mouth with hers, Magnús's entire nervous system responded in a wave of wanting, and he pulled her wet body down onto his, water sloshing onto the floor, Alex sighing against his lips, kissing him deeply until she suddenly pulled away, awkwardly disentangling herself. There seemed to be knees and elbows and hard surfaces everywhere.

'You can't be comfy in this little tub,' she said.

'Nei, and the water's going cold,' Magnús agreed, and they were out of the bath somehow and wrapped in the same towel in seconds, kissing against the bathroom door, then kissing all the way down the spiral steps, neither of them using their eyes to find their way, until they made it back to the heat of the fireside again.

This time, their feelings were all on the surface. No secrets or silences held them back. They had one more week together. This was their time – to hell with the storm. They were going to extract every last breathless, desirous second of pleasure and comfort from it.

Chapter Twenty-Four

Granny Clove-Congreve's Chapel

While some in Clove Lore forgot all about Storm Nora, Minty didn't have that luxury.

'I've never seen rain as heavy as this in all my life,' she told Jowan, peering out the kitchen window.

'You can't see it now, neither,' Jowan joked. Beyond the glass, the night was completely dark, and no stars or moon visible.

Minty paused at this. 'Back in a minute,' she said and strode out of the room. Aldous dutifully followed her in the hopes of another cheese sandwich.

Jowan sat by the Aga, pouring a fresh mug of tea from a chipped pot. He noticed the gloom outside the window lifting. Minty was switching on every light in the house, even in the empty rooms she'd turned over to the developers. Soon Jowan could make out illuminated sheets of rain immediately outside and for a few metres into the grounds.

Thunder rumbled nearby and Jowan pinched at the bridge of his nose.

'Everything all right?' Minty asked, barrelling back into the kitchen and making sure Aldous was safely in the room before closing the door behind her.

'It's this air pressure, givin' me a headache, it is. It'll go once the thunderclouds break.'

Minty searched in a drawer, finding everything but painkillers. 'Would a brandy help?'

'It'd make it worse, if anything. Come, sit down.'

Another loud rumble came from the clouds above them, so violent it seemed to stop the rain for a second.

'I can't sit still,' Minty confessed, pacing to the dresser and pulling out drawers, rummaging for paracetamol she was almost sure she didn't have.

'You've lit all the lights, then?' Jowan rose and carried a china cup and saucer to her; Minty always told him tea didn't taste the same in a mug.

'The whole house,' she said, taking the tea with a distracted smile. 'We're supposed to be a beacon, aren't we? We landowners?' Minty's voice was cynical and Jowan sniffed a laugh.

'You certainly light up Clove Lore, Mint.'

Now Minty laughed. She gave up her search and slid the drawer shut.

'Papa was never all that feudal, he left the villagers to get on with things, but Grandfather would host the entire village every Christmas, back when it was thriving. The whole place smelled of mulled cider and roast partridge. He'd present each of the estate's men and all the dairy girls with a gift – very formal, I remember. They didn't quite curtsy and bow but it wasn't far off that kind of thing. Grandfather felt he owned a share in the whole village's fortunes, and he was right, of course; he certainly owned all the land and cottages. Unfortunately, our family took the village down with them. Still, there's a part of *me* that feels guilty. One rather wishes to repair some of the damage wreaked by Papa.'

Minty walked back to the aged Aga and stood with her back to it, gripping its metal rail with her free hand. Jowan followed her and took his seat again.

'You do all you can to keep the Big House going, and the estate gardens too. Everyone sees it.'

'And pretty soon they're all going to see me fail. I'm no better than my old man.'

'Hey,' Jowan sprang up, reaching for her hand. 'It's far easier to squander a fortune than to make one, Mint, remember that. Raising money isn't easy. Especially these days.'

At his touch, Minty's teacup rattled in the saucer so loudly she had to put it down, but Jowan didn't release her hand. In fact, seeing his effect on her made him bolder.

The first crack of lightning over their heads only served to heighten the electric tension suddenly passing between them.

'You are the finest woman in all of Devonshire, and there's no way I'd let you believe you've let any of us down. You *are* a beacon, Mint. Look how everyone here moves around you like you're the sun itself. We rely on you.'

Minty cast her eyes low and shook her head.

'Who oversees the Christmas lights?' he continued. 'Who makes sure we have daffodil teas in the spring and strawberry teas in the summer, eh? You make so many things happen here.' With these last words he unconsciously raised his hand to his heart, and Minty's eyes followed it.

Realising what he'd done, he snapped his arm to his side once more and released Minty's hand, but he didn't step away. A tear rolled down Minty's cheek and he had to ball his tattooed fist to stop himself wiping it away.

She pulled a handkerchief from her pocket. 'Goodness, look at me. What a state to get in.' She waved the hankie as though dismissing her sadness as a silly thing, before loudly blowing her nose. Jowan smiled tenderly at the sight of her being vulnerable.

'You're allowed to be sad, and you're allowed to let other people know your worries. Let us help you more. Let *me* help you.'

'Jowan?' Minty pushed the hankie back into her pocket and met his eyes. 'You're my oldest friend. You already do so much for me. Asking for more would be taking advantage.'

At this, the two stood in silence, neither wanting to cross the delicate line that separated their treasured friendship and the uncharted waters of a romance, and yet they'd both been inching closer to the boundary these last few days.

Jowan, who'd been so bold a moment ago, gulped and faltered as he tried to find the words that would bring them closer.

'I feel I've had a… a revelation of a kind, this week. I feel that having young Alex in the house and giving over…' Jowan swallowed hard. 'Giving over my Isolde's belongings, and letting the girl sleep in that room where I nursed my wife…' Jowan's voice shook, and Minty pressed her hand to the spot where his heart was aching. 'I feel I've allowed some… movement, after all these years of being afraid of losing touch with her, keeping her room just as she left it.' Tears fell fast down his cheeks. 'I feel now that I could… I could—'

The tumultuous air above the Big House bellowed a sudden thunderous cry as the sky released a flash of lightning so bright they both jumped closer. Jowan was surprised to find it was Minty who held *him* protectively.

'Jowan,' she whispered low, as more thunderbolts split the sky, seeming to pierce the ground all over the estate. 'I can't lose your friendship, I couldn't bear it.'

Jowan pulled back. The sincerity was etched across Minty's face and it unnerved him, but before he could torment himself any longer with his fears and reservations, Minty pressed a kiss to his lips.

They held still like that for a moment, neither daring to move, as the rain poured and the lightning flashed, until Jowan took her in his arms and kissed her properly, the way he'd wanted to for a long time, longer than he'd wanted to admit.

For the first time in years Jowan's mind was quiet. He wasn't poor old Jowan de Marisco, the bookseller who'd given it all up to nurse his wife. He wasn't the grieving husband haunted by the gaping mouth of the grave where he'd dropped a red camellia bloom on an awful winter's morning. He was just a man remembering what it felt like to kiss a woman.

For them, there was no more thunder or rain, no sounds at all. There was only the two of them together, not thinking any further than their lips touching.

And yet no kiss, not even one this good, was going to hold it all back for long.

It was Minty who broke away first, blinking and astonished, looking for all the world like a girl of twenty, her eyes great pools of innocence and surprise. 'Jowan?' she breathed.

Hearing his name brought him back to the kitchen of the Big House with the harsh unshaded bulb too bright above them. The thunder and lightning was right above their heads now.

He stared back, unsure what to do. His mouth worked, knowing he should say something but no words came. He was frozen to the spot as everything he'd pushed to the back of his mind while they kissed came flooding back to him.

'Jowan? Jowan, don't,' Minty said, somewhere between pleading and warning.

He took a step backwards, then another, as Minty's eyes widened.

'Don't you dare, Jowan de Marisco!' Minty's voice quaked as it dawned on her. He was going to run.

That was when the loudest thunderclap rent the sky and the whole of Clove Lore was lit from above by shooting fingers of blinding fire bolts accompanied by the sound of stone blasting apart and bricks flying somewhere at the back of the estate.

Minty picked up her feet. She ran all the way through the house, bursting through the doors onto the parterre patio and out into the lashing rain.

Jowan followed behind her, leaving Aldous to cower under the kitchen table.

Down the stone steps and across the lawn, now so waterlogged Minty struggled to keep up her pace. Down the dark rhododendron valley lit only at intervals by the flashes in the sky.

Minty only understood what had happened when she stumbled over the first of the masonry blocks blown clean off the chapel roof by the lightning strike. Still, she picked her way towards the chapel, her hands extended in front of her, expecting at any second to make contact with the wall but meeting only airy nothingness.

Jowan finally caught up to her, calling her name. 'Stay back,' he cried, but she couldn't hear him.

The thunder clouds, blowing fast, now passing over the main road, heading inland, gifted them one last bright burst that confirmed all Minty's fears. The chapel was gone.

She stepped up onto the great pile of slate shards, rubble, shattered glass and splintered wood. It was as though an incendiary device had detonated inside the place.

'Minty!' Jowan called again. 'Come away, get back inside.'

The lights from the Big House began to penetrate the gloom a little as their vision adjusted.

'It's ruined,' she said, barely audible. Minty turned blank eyes upon him as she staggered out of the destruction. 'You,' she said, rain drenching her hair and soaking through her layers of clothing to her blouse, her skin prickling with cold. 'You kissed me, and you regretted it.'

'Mint, I...' Jowan tried to protest but gave up, seeing the tears shine in her eyes. 'Mint, this is the camellia grove where I proposed to my Isolde. This is the village where she lived and breathed... and you... you loved her too, I know you did. No woman could have a better friend, but I... I am her husband still, even though I'm a widower. I...'

Minty's face turned hard like flint and she pushed past him. She didn't look back when she spoke. 'There's a bed made up for you in the ballroom.'

Making her way back to the house like a woman in a trance, Minty's muddy feet carried her to the small bedroom she called her own at the back of the kitchens.

She brushed her wet hair back and changed into a night-gown, letting her sopping clothes fall in a heap on the bare floorboards. Her body rattled with shock and cold until she was under the covers in the dark.

That night she cried herself to sleep while the storm blew itself out over the hills and towns inland, its anger calming as Christmas Eve dawned in Clove Lore.

Chapter Twenty-Five

The Stowaway

Magnús had kept the fire burning all night. The shop was warm, even if there was no electricity to light the place. In the middle of the night he'd climbed the stairs looking for blankets and they'd made a makeshift bed by the hearth.

Alex stirred first. 'Happy Christmas Eve,' she told him, placing a kiss on his chest where she lay wrapped in his arms.

Magnús smiled lazily and slid down the sheets so he could kiss her mouth. 'Good morning.'

'Do you hear that?' said Alex. 'The wind's dropped. I think the storm's over.'

Rain pattered softly on the cobbles outside, nothing like the torrents of last night, like a kitten following in the footsteps of a lion. Distracted by the need to kiss him again, she let herself ease into his arms, reaching for his mouth.

When they pulled apart, Magnús let his eyes rove over her face like he was seeing her for the first time.

'You're the most beautiful woman I have ever met,' he said, all the air leaving his lungs with the force of feeling behind his words. 'This thing between us,' he told her, pressing kisses to her mouth as he spoke. 'Do you feel it too?'

'I feel it,' she told him.

'I've never had this before,' he confessed.

'Me neither, but I like it.'

Everything was so easy between them. All he had to do was rake his fingertips softly over her back and she would melt into his body. She needed only to smile and he could forgot his own name.

Neither of them spoke again about what would happen at the end of next week. It was too soon for all that, so they stayed together, kissing by the hearth until the watery winter sun came up.

Eventually, Alex told him with a grin that she had something for him. 'For Christmas Eve.'

A few moments later Magnús was standing before her, modelling Alex's oversized 'Crocombe's Ices' T-shirt and nothing else.

'New clothes. To keep the Yule Cat away, remember?' she said.

Magnús looked down at the ice-cream sundae in pastel colours across his chest. 'Do I look good? I think I look good.' His face was serious, even as he turned his hips from side to side, posing like this was a photo shoot.

Alex's laughter filled the shop and Magnús ended up on his knees by her side once more. She thought again how the light shone from him, incandescent on the inside.

After making coffee on the gas ring and sharing a breakfast of bread and the last of the café's cheddar, Alex surprised Magnús by announcing she was nipping out for a while.

He held onto her arm, burrowing his face into her neck and kissing her on the spot which, he'd learned last night, made her close her eyes and her breathing accelerate. 'Stay,' he whispered, kissing a low trail across her jaw towards her lips.

'I'll only be ten minutes,' she told him, kissing him back but extracting herself from their spot by the fire. 'Shouldn't you phone the power company or something?'

When she pulled on her jeans and jumper, he knew she was serious.

'What are you doing with that?' he asked as she folded her ferryman's coat into a neat bundle.

'I'm giving it back to the boat,' she said, and he seemed to understand in an instant.

'You want me to come with you?'

'No, I'm going to do it on my own. Wait for me here.'

He waved her off from the shop doorway. The last he saw of her, she was blowing a kiss and turning for Down-along, wearing Magnús's jacket and pulling on her pink beanie and her gloves.

Magnús set about tidying the shop, wondering if he could sell books by candlelight today.

—

Clove Lore had resisted the storm as best it could, but as Alex picked her way Down-along, its impact was evident everywhere.

Gate posts and trellises, birdfeeders, festive wreathes and bin bags were strewn everywhere, and the winter detritus of rotting leaf piles and the browning remnants of summer bedding plants that had accumulated in each little garden since autumn were now thrown messily across her path.

Looking up, through the drizzle, she saw that strands of Minty's tasteful white Christmas bulbs that had been strung between the lampposts were here and there loosened and looping down over doorways or blown up over rooftops.

She stopped to right the antique bicycle that had come unfixed from Jowan's front garden railings. Its wheels were twisted and its basket smashed like it had collided with a car. His cottage appeared dark and empty. Maybe he was walking Aldous?

She'd call in on her way back Up-along, just to let him know she was back and to ask if it was OK if she stayed at the bookshop until Magnús checked out on January the second – a date she knew she'd begin to dread the closer it got. Still, she wasn't going to let that spoil today.

There'd be a big tidy-up effort this afternoon. No doubt Minty had it all in hand. She was probably assembling her staff and issuing orders from behind her clipboard at this very moment. Even the idea of sweeping cobbles and litter-picking was appealing, if she was doing it with Magnús. For now, though, she had a different job to do.

Still clutching the coat bundled in her arms, she made her way down onto the harbour wall.

The water was slate-grey and turbulent, and the swell surged as if it had forgotten all about retreating for morning low tide.

Huge white clouds lined with grey and looking heavy with yet more rain gathered out on the horizon.

'Better get this over with quick,' she told herself, making for the *Dagalien*, which yesterday had seemed safe from further harm on Tom Bickleigh's trailer far up the beach but this morning now looked fragile and precarious as the waves reached all the way up to the trailer's back tyres. She walked over the pebbles towards it.

'Poor thing,' she said, lifting a hand to touch its prow. 'What a way to end up, eh? After all those years of hard work. Up on a trailer in a strange harbour.'

The tarpaulin that the men had fixed over it yesterday had come loose and was lifting gently in the dying wind.

Alex pressed her forehead to the gunwale and closed her eyes. Aside from the surging surf and the noise of trickling water running in rivulets down every slope and channel to the sea, there was not a sound.

Not a gull shifted on the shore – they were still sheltering. The harbour was deserted; she was the only person braving the chilly drizzle this morning and she was glad of it. She wanted to be alone to say goodbye to the life she'd lived for eight years.

'Dad,' she said. 'I've come to tell you I've decided to sell your *Dagalien*, once she's repaired.' Alex ran her gloved hand down the boat's curved hull, crouching to look under the keel. 'She needs a lot of work, but... so do I.' She smiled sadly. 'I don't really know what I'm going to do yet, but I know it's not this. This was your life. For the first time ever, I feel like I've something else waiting for me. I don't know what, but I'll find it. Maybe I'll open my own tea room somewhere... not Port Kernou, though. I don't want to go home at all. I...' Alex shivered as she found the words. 'I know I could definitely do with finding someone to talk to – a professional, I mean. A grief counsellor. I didn't even know I needed one until yesterday, can you believe that? It was me and Magnús talking about how there are no quick fixes that did it. You can't fast-track healing, even if you're happy and right in the middle of falling in love.'

She paused, smiling at the sudden knowledge that this was exactly what was happening to her. She was falling in love. It seemed so miraculous she wanted to laugh and cry at the same time. The realisation strengthened her resolve. 'And I… I want to sell the house too, I think. Get it on the market, along with the *Dagalien* and… move on. What do you think?'

She lifted her eyes to the sky and watched as if for a sign that she'd been heard but, like all the times before, there was nothing. Only for once, there was a little blossoming sense of peace within her. She'd brought that about, along with the help of storms Minnie and Nora. She wondered at how so many seemingly unconnected factors had combined to get her to where she was now. She'd run off not knowing she needed to get away, not just from Ben, but from everything, and she'd shipwrecked her boat thinking the whole time fate was giving her a raw deal and taking away her livelihood when in fact this harbour had given her so much.

With a deep breath, she took the coat from under her arm. 'This belongs to you,' she said, addressing the spot where the boat's name plate had once been fixed. 'It never fitted me. I was drowning in the thing. It belongs on board.' She kissed its waxy surface and stepped up onto the trailer's metal axle so she could lay the coat safely inside.

Now that she was here actually making the break she felt lighter than she could ever remember being, even with her future so uncertain.

Alex ran through her plan, such as it was.

Ben's dad had told her that arrangements had already been made to take the boat to Bideford for repair. While it was in Tom's friend's boatshed being tended to, she'd get the advertisements posted. She wouldn't see the *Dagalien* again and that was OK.

Now the moment had come, it wasn't as hard as she'd imagined. She was turning a page, wondering what the first words of her next chapter would say.

One thing was for sure; she'd have to repair the straps on the ripped tarpaulin this instant before she headed back to the bookshop. The boat would end up filled with rain at this rate.

As she reached for the heavy plastic sheeting, trying to haul it over the open deck, she said her last farewell, thinking of Magnús waiting for her and wanting to get back as soon as possible. That was when she caught a glimpse of the huddled figure through the steamed porthole in the cockpit door.

'Who's there?' she yelped.

Was someone sheltering from the storm? Were they hurt? Or homeless? Should she shout for help? What the hell was going on?

The cockpit door opened slowly and a pale, pinched face peered out. Alex lost her footing, staggering backwards onto the pebbles, unable to believe what she was seeing.

'Eve?'

Chapter Twenty-Six

Fallen Mistletoe

Alex had been right about the clean-up already being underway up at the Big House, but Minty was nowhere to be seen.

'She's still in bed?' Leonid quizzed Izaak as they dragged the huge mistletoe boughs into the ballroom.

'I knocked on her bedroom door; she told me she wasn't to be disturbed.'

Leonid shrugged. 'That is not like her at all.'

'So where am I putting these?' Izaak asked, lifting his two spheres of mistletoe. They'd found them scattered all across the lawns this morning, blown from the estate's oaks.

'They're festive, yes?' said Leonid. 'Minty will want them to be saved, for decoration.'

Izaak agreed she probably would. 'You know it's for kissing under?' he asked his husband as they hung the boughs off the rusty sconces along the ballroom walls.

Izaak held one over his head and Leonid obliged him with a slow kiss to the side of his smiling mouth.

'It's supposed to be good luck if you hang it over your bed on your wedding night,' Izaak told him. 'I know we're not newlyweds now, but should I keep one for us?'

Leonid looked at the white berries on their fragile bracts, tangled like a green chandelier. 'You know they are poisonous?'

Izaak looked at the berries. 'You're sure?'

'And they're parasitic. They love a dying tree most of all. They thrive while it slowly decays.'

'That's not romantic at all,' said Izaak.

'Let's have one anyway,' Leonid told him. 'Here, this one is good. Hang it over our bed.' This time Leonid held aloft the ball of greenery, pulling his husband closer.

Their kiss was interrupted by the sound of Jowan stirring on the put-up bed by the fireplace at the deepest end of the room. The Christmas tree near his feet sparkled brightly in contrast to the dull look in his tired eyes.

Aldous lifted his head lazily from the covers and immediately decided he deserved a longer lie-in after the rough night they'd had.

'Jowan? We thought you'd left already,' Izaak said, stepping apart from his husband.

Jowan was on his feet, glancing around the room, piecing together his memories of the night before. 'Where's Minty?'

'Not to be disturbed,' Leonid told him. '*She vants to be alone,*' he added wickedly in his best Greta Garbo voice.

Only Izaak chuckled. Jowan seemed stricken.

'I'll get you some coffee,' Leonid offered, but Jowan refused and gestured to the mistletoe.

'Windfalls?' he asked. 'Is the estate as bad as I think it is?'

'Worse. The whole chapel has crumbled,' Leonid replied. 'I've left messages for Bovis to gather his men, get it cleared as much as we can, before Minty sees it.'

'She's already seen it,' Jowan told him, his eyes cast down.

Leonid and Izaak exchanged glances.

'You should get home, check your cottage roof is all right,' said Izaak.

'I'll stay, if you don't mind. Put me to work,' replied Jowan, his dry eyes turning watery. 'Please. I need to work today, and I promised Minty I'd help her with the estate more, so that's what I'll do.'

The husbands led Jowan outside to where the wheelbarrows and shovels were already lined up. Jowan cast an eye over the untidy lawns. 'To the chapel, then?'

'To the chapel,' Izaak replied, and the men pushed their barrows in silence along the path that led to the unsalvageable ruin behind the House. The gentle seascape was strangely altered in the chapel's absence. Where yesterday there had been a vaulted roof peeping out through the rhododendrons, there was now only grey winter sky.

Arriving at the spot where Minty had stood horrified last night, Jowan set his barrow down and pushed up his coat sleeves. 'Let's fix this mess as best we can,' he said.

The chapel walls and roof were beyond saving but, with effort, the tiled floor might be preserved, possibly the altar too. Perhaps even a few pews could be repaired but, Jowan brooded, his place in Minty's affections looked far less salvageable than the sorry scene before him. Broken bricks and slates were one thing, but the ruins of his friendship with Minty was something else entirely. Where would he even begin fixing the mess he'd made of things?

Minty had been right. He had kissed her and regretted it. She'd told him she was afraid of losing his friendship and he hadn't listened. He'd wanted to kiss her with a desperation that had shocked him, and yet the guilt that had hit him in the moments afterwards had shaken him even more. Now Minty wouldn't get out of bed. Unheard of, especially when there was work to do and people waiting for their orders. He'd really blown it.

With a heavy heart, he bent his back and set to work.

Chapter Twenty-Seven

Eve

'What are you doing here?' Alex stood by the *Dagalien* looking up at Eve framed inside the cabin beneath the tarp. 'I don't want any trouble!'

Alex couldn't bear confrontation, far preferring the run-from-your-problems technique that had served her so terribly up to this point.

'Word was, you were here,' Eve told her, her whole body shaking. 'I didn't have an address but I figured I'd find the boat before I found you, and here I am.'

Alex's heart hardened at the thought of how quickly the news would have spread back home but the state Eve was in had her concerned too. 'You've been in there all night? You're freezing,' she said, unsure what was expected of her. 'Look, just get back inside the cockpit.'

Eve retreated once more and Alex clambered inside after her. There was still the little gas stove, and fresh water and cocoa powder in there. She could warm Eve up, shut down any nonsense she wanted to tell her about how bad she felt, and send her on her way.

Instructing Eve to take the captain's seat, Alex set about making the hot chocolate. Just one cup – she didn't want to share anything else with Eve.

The familiar routine of lighting the gas flame and heating up the enamel pot gave Alex pause. She'd miss this, she knew. The quick pang of sadness mixed horribly with the awkwardness of Eve's presence.

Eve always wanted to talk things over, getting to the bottom of everything. Alex couldn't be more different – well, until she'd got to know Magnús. Telling *him* things about herself was a relief and a joy, and the careful, solemn way he listened to her made it all the easier. Eve was no Magnús.

'Let's get this over with,' said Alex, keeping her back to her friend who was sniffing tearfully in the cockpit, still dark even in daylight with its window covered over with tarp. 'There really was no need for you to come here. It's Christmas Eve. Shouldn't you be with Stevie?'

Eve's eyes dropped at her little boy's name. 'He's at his gran's for Christmas, with Maxwell. I'm letting them have some time away from me, the best Christmas present I could give them, eh?' She tried to smile but her mouth contorted horribly and a little strangled sound escaped. Tears followed.

'Stevie wants to be with you,' Alex replied. 'Take it from me, no child wants to be away from a parent at Christmas. You should get going soon.'

The water bubbled. Alex turned down the heat and opened the jar of powder, glad she had something to do while Eve said whatever she'd come to say.

She heard Eve inhale and blow out a long breath before she said, 'Maxwell's left me. For good. He's living at his mum's. I'll go back to Port Kernou and Stevie's coming to live with me after Christmas. We didn't have time to tell the landlord we were leaving, so the house isn't let yet.'

More tears followed, and Eve tried hard to stem them. 'Sorry, it's not me who should be crying.'

Handing her the steaming mug, Alex leaned against the galley counter. 'Careful, it's hot.'

Eve thanked her with a watery smile and Alex stared back, saying nothing.

'I haven't come to talk about Ben.'

'Good.' Alex heard the spite in her voice and immediately recoiled. She wasn't like this. She loved a quiet life without drama. She'd had so much drama as a kid she only ever wanted to avoid it. Yet these last two weeks, drama had followed her everywhere she went.

'I came to talk about us.'

At this, Alex's eyes snapped to Eve's and the pain she saw there set off an ache in her chest.

'I betrayed you after everything you did for me. If I could go back I'd never have—'

Alex couldn't keep quiet at this. She interrupted, bitterness in her voice. 'If you could go back to *when*? What point would you go back to? Ben said you were always around him, flirting and causing trouble, visiting him when I wasn't there.'

'Ah!' Eve nodded. 'I guess he would say that.'

'It's not true?'

'You'll have to decide what you believe. It won't matter much what I say, but I *never* chased him. I never wanted him. That day... it was a moment of madness and I regret it.' Eve gripped the mug, her shoulders dropping. 'I shouldn't have come. We're not going to retrieve this, are we?'

'Retrieve what?'

'Us. You and me. We were good friends.'

Alex froze. If this was a movie she'd have thrown her head back and laughed, but the ache in her chest was growing, choking her up. Eve was right. They had been good friends.

'I told you all about Mum and Dad,' Alex heard herself saying, her voice shaking. 'I never tell anyone about that stuff.'

'You did,' Eve replied, staring guiltily at the cup in her hands.

'You knew me, and I knew you,' Alex continued. 'And I know for a fact you didn't want Ben. So why did you do it?'

It took Eve a long time to answer. When she did, her voice wavered uncontrollably. 'Because I was sad, and lonely. And Maxwell didn't want me.'

Alex tipped her head to one side, waiting for Eve to say more. It was going to take more than this to move her.

'You know Maxwell never came out to the pub with us, never did anything with us, in fact. Turns out, he had some other woman in Port Kernou. I always told you I was suspicious, didn't I?'

Alex had to agree. They'd talked about it often, but Eve had never had any proof and when she would confront him he'd laugh it off, saying she was crazy.

'I overheard customers whispering about it in the post office on the morning of the day you left. One of them was a mum at Stevie's pre-school. Been going on for a few months, according to her.'

'What?' Alex slumped onto the swivel stool fixed into the floor beside Eve's. It felt like they were right back at the quayside and Eve had come aboard between sailings to tell her the latest instalment in her crumbling marriage story.

'I confronted him. He loves her, apparently.'

'Oh.' Alex absorbed the news. How could she be feeling pity for the woman who'd capsized her life?

'He *always* loves them.' Eve arched a brow, before her face fell again. 'He's done it before. Loads of times.'

'You never said.'

'The marriage counsellor bloke we were going to in Truro said that if we wanted to stay together I had to stop punishing him and try to move on. Part of that was never criticising him in public. Not holding anything against him. That included telling people about the affairs.'

'That's crazy. He made you so unhappy.'

Alex thought of all the times Eve had wandered over to the riverside to find her, and of how reluctant she was to head home on Fridays after the pub quiz; how she'd try to keep Alex talking till past midnight standing in the street outside her house. She never wanted to go home.

'I tried to keep us together. We were doing all right for the first few months after we moved to Port Kernou. I had the post office job, Maxwell was in charge of school runs and… well, not a lot else – watching daytime telly, mainly.'

Alex allowed herself a small laugh of sympathy. Hearing it, Eve's eyes welled again.

'I knew weeks ago that he was at it again, I knew in my gut, you know? Something really wasn't right.'

'And you tried to ignore it,' Alex added.

'For Stevie's sake.'

'But then…?' Alex urged, knowing how the story ended, only not understanding the stages in between. 'What made you decide to cheat with Ben?'

Eve recoiled, a sickened look spreading across her face. 'I didn't decide to. I was just… miserable, and that day, when I came round to drop your Christmas presents off, Ben invited me in. I knew what he was thinking, as soon as I got inside. He was looking at his phone, checking the time. We chatted for a bit, and he moved over beside me, wanted to know how things were with Maxwell and I couldn't help crying. Apparently Ben had seen Maxwell with the woman that morning, going into a house off the market square, so that confirmed it. I knew we didn't have any friends living round there so it definitely had to be her. I was sobbing and embarrassed and hurting, and Ben was right there, and suddenly he kissed me.'

'Ugh, no, please. Don't tell me.' Alex wrapped her arms around her stomach.

'I never had any intention of doing anything with Ben. But…'

'But he paid you attention when you were low, and he had the opportunity to cheat, so he took it.' Alex stood again, all her feelings churning. Hurt, anger, annoyance. What good was this doing her? This hadn't helped at all. 'You didn't have to come here to tell me all this.'

'I did, because I don't regret losing Maxwell, and to be honest, Ben didn't deserve you, so I can't really regret that you're not together any more.'

Alex's eyes blazed but Eve pressed on. 'I've always known he was no good. The way he always kept you hanging, never doing anything nice for you, never listening… but I didn't ever want to say anything, and then, well, I went and proved he's rotten, didn't I?' Eve drew a fist to her stomach as if she held a dagger and would pierce her flesh. 'I *know* I'm as bad as him – and Maxwell, for that matter – but the regret I'm left with… my only regret is losing you. You were literally the best thing that's happened in my life since Stevie, and I hurt you so much.' Eve broke down as she spoke. 'I love you, Alex, and I know I'm a terrible person, and you're right to hate me... only I don't think you do hate me.'

Alex watched Eve bent double and crying hard. She'd never seen her friend like this before.

Eve talked on through sobs. 'I wish we could go back to Port Kernou and just live on in our homes, without the men around, and Stevie there with me all the time, and we could just be friends again. We could just be happy. I would make it up to you.' With this, Eve hung her head and wept inconsolably. 'I know I can't get you back in my life, but I had to tell you that I won't forgive myself for hurting you.'

'I think you hurt yourself more,' said Alex, and Eve stilled, lifting her head slowly to meet Alex's eyes.

'You don't have to cry. You're right, Ben isn't worth all this...' Alex raised her hands, gesturing to the scene in the boat. She wanted to say he wasn't worth all the theatrics. 'He really isn't. Losing Ben hasn't hurt me as much as you think. I was more afraid of losing my spot at his mum's dinner table. Coming here showed me that.'

Eve's eyes grew wide.

'I don't miss Ben, it turns out. We barely spoke towards the end there, and we certainly didn't... you know, not for ages.'

Eve clamped her lips and nodded in understanding.

'You're right about one thing. You did me a favour, Eve. Only you hurt yourself in the process. You don't have to feel bad about me.'

Eve listened, astonished.

'You and me, we were both lonely and stuck with blokes who didn't make us happy, and we didn't make them happy, and life was just passing us by.' Alex sighed, her eyes glazing. 'Do you remember when I came to Stevie's pre-school sports day? Back in the summer?'

'Of course, I do.' A hint of a smile formed at Eve's lips.

'And we did the parents' three-legged race?'

'Because Maxwell refused to come, said he was busy?' Eve added.

'Yeah, busy watching *Bargain Hunt*. And we were losing until we both tripped and fell over the finish line.'

Eve's mouth widened into a sad smile, and the sight of her old friend unable to be happy after all her difficulties turned Alex's heart inside out.

'I'm not coming back to Port Kernou,' Alex told her quickly.

'Because of me?'

'No, because of me. I'm selling the boat and the house and I'm going to do something new. For me.'

Eve wept afresh, only these were happy tears and she really was smiling now. 'You were never happy ferrying.'

'I told you that?' Alex said with amazement.

'Never with words.'

'It was that obvious?'

Eve only crumpled her lips in a sympathetic smile and nodded.

Alex thought back to the last months before she ran away. Dragging herself out of bed and down to the quayside every day had felt like moving through treacle. The thought of the long winter ahead with its sailings and sparse takings had chilled her to the bone. Yet she'd kept it to herself, not wanting to admit to anyone how badly off course she'd steered her life.

'What are *you* going to do now?' Alex asked.

Eve shrugged. 'Go home, face the music. Let the talkers talk. Be Stevie's mum. They haven't advertised my job at the post office yet – not that I was much good at it. I only took it because Maxwell wanted me to.' A shudder shook Eve's body.

'Still cold?'

'Freezing.'

'Here, try this.' Alex placed the bundled ferryman's coat in her hands. Eve looked warily at it, knowing exactly what it meant to Alex.

'Go on,' she urged, 'it's not mine.'

Eve stood and pulled the coat on. It skimmed the ground at her feet.

'Better?' Alex asked.

'I will be… if you think we could salvage something? Of us, I mean.'

Alex didn't hesitate. 'Maybe. If we started all over again, as ourselves, and not keeping things bottled up, and just trying to laugh a bit more. We were good at laughing, in between the fed-up bits and the waiting-around-for-two-crap-men-to-notice-us bits.'

Eve laughed now, and moved as though to hug her friend, but stopped herself. Alex didn't hold back, and stepped towards her, pulling her into her arms. She'd take her up to the bookshop now and introduce her to Magnús. Maybe the electricity would be back on and they could have some lunch.

'Come on, let's go,' Alex said, lifting the little gas stove. It would come in handy for someone in the village if there was still no power. She took one last look around the cabin, and then clasped Eve's hand. 'No regrets.'

Eve seemed younger and less careworn than Alex had ever seen her.

They made their way towards the prow, checking locks and securing the tarps and canopies as they went.

Only when they were in the fresh air ready to clamber onto the beach did Alex realise there was no beach.

Instead, there was mud-brown water at least two foot deep and concealing the entire trailer the boat was raised upon, and that water was flowing, gushing hard in fact, under the *Dagalien* in the direction of the ocean.

'What's happening?' Eve asked, glancing all around them.

'Look!' Alex lifted a finger to the slope where a river of water was careering Down-along, past the door of Jowan's cottage, past the lifeboat building. The same brown water poured off the cliffs all along the headland.

'Run-off,' Alex said darkly.

'What?'

'Run-off, from the storm. The whole village must be flooding with water running off the land. And there's only one place it can go.'

The women screamed as the beach pebbles shifted and the *Dagalien* juddered and moved upon the trailer.

'We have to get off! Jump!' Alex shrieked, but it was too late. The ferry had come loose from the trailer with the force of the water and was turning like a toy in a bath tub, swirling and bucking. It was being forced out to sea.

Chapter Twenty-Eight

The Flood

The most frightening thing about floods is the sound.

That's what Minty's mother had told her when she was little, and she should know; she'd been in Valencia in nineteen fifty-seven when the Turia burst its banks and so many lives had been lost. Minty hadn't understood it at the time. How could the sound be the worst part? Soon she would know that her mother had been right.

It was the noise that had wakened her, late on Christmas Eve morning, when she sprang suddenly from her bed at the ruckus, thinking the earth was splitting apart, immediately trying to get to Jowan in the ballroom, hoping he was still there.

Even though Minty had seen floods on television reports and everyone in these parts knew what it meant when waters massed in sudden violent torrents and swept down a steep valley, she still didn't make the connection. It had happened in gentle, wooded Lynmouth. It had happened in historic Polperro. It had happened in beautiful Boscastle, but not here.

Only when she stepped into the foyer and saw through the grand doors the wide river, only a few metres away, of dirty, debris-filled water flowing over the far lawns in bubbling, gurgling gushes at least three foot deep, did she understand what was happening.

The house itself was raised up just high enough on its mighty stone plinth to avoid the water but to the west of the building and all down the rhododendron valley and over the lawns towards the visitor centre car park, the water took the quickest route downwards and into the village.

When her brain registered what was happening she ran straight for the ballroom, heaving the doors apart only to find the place empty and Jowan's bed folded away neatly in the corner.

The flash flood had begun miles inland where thousands of hectares of waterlogged fields had reached saturation point, rivers had risen and burst their banks, tarmacked roads ran like canals, and metal covers had been lifted from drains and sewers, all overwhelmed by last night's deluge. Every drainage channel, well, gutter and stream had filled to bursting and overflowed.

All of these sources had combined with the four inches of rain that had fallen during last night's electrical storm and were now gushing into unsuspecting Clove Lore.

To Minty, standing breathless in her Big House, the water sounded very much like jets flying past, mixed with underground thunder.

She paused only for a blank, terrified moment before she ran for her mobile, dialling the number while dashing up two flights of stairs into Leonid and Izaak's rooms. They weren't there either. Where was everybody?

'Coastguard, ambulance, police, fire, send everyone to Clove Lore!' she shouted as soon as the call connected.

Holding the phone between cheek and shoulder, she heaved herself up the ladder to the porthole window and saw it: the wall of water washing violently into the village.

'Launch all lifeboats, and helicopters too,' she screamed. 'Please, hurry!'

–

There was little time to think. As soon as Magnús saw the square outside the bookshop filling with water like a paddling pool, he knew he had to investigate. Down the little side street where the bookshop stood, the water level rose gently, but when he reached the turning for Down-along he immediately grasped its severity.

The water gushed at great speed and almost high enough to claim each of the cottages' raised front gardens.

He'd stood close enough to an erupting volcano before to recognise the sound of the earth in chaos. Now he knew *both* fire and water have the power to shake the earth beneath a person's feet like an inferno.

Fresh mud and gasoline scented the damp air. Magnús was too alarmed to register much more than that. All he knew was that Alex was nowhere to be seen.

She'd said she'd be gone for ten minutes. That was almost an hour ago.

A sled carried past him on the tumbling water's surface, then kindling and hewn logs from someone's winter store, all racing downhill and mixed with plastic and trash, even cobbles wrenched loose from the path.

Over the noise, he heard himself yelling Alex's name.

A few people, the handful of Clove Lore residents still left in the village over Christmas, stood at their open doors and watched the scene with stunned, disbelieving faces.

Some filmed the deluge on phones held out of bedroom windows.

None of them dared step out into the flow. Magnús too knew he'd be swept clean off his feet and carried down to the harbour if he dared – that is, if he didn't meet with a wall or lamppost first. Either way, he'd be broken and drowned in moments.

Instead, he did the only thing he could think of to get Down-along where he believed Alex to be. He climbed over the railing into the little raised garden beside him – it, too, was under water but only by a few inches. Then from there he clambered over a low hedge into the next garden and so on, until he was halfway Down-along.

An elderly man called to him from his doorway opposite. 'Stay put, lad. Never put foot in flood water!'

Magnús ignored him and called for Alex all the harder.

The water gushed and the rain drizzled and Magnús's heart thumped hard.

He couldn't lose her now. He'd only just found her. Surely she'd be at Jowan's, taking shelter? He'd find her there and later they'd laugh at his panic. It would be all right. It had to be.

Only, as he drew closer to Jowan's cottage on the opposite side of the flood water he knew for sure there was no way he could cross its path. So he screamed for her.

Nothing. No movement at all. The door was closed and curtains drawn. If Alex was in there, she'd be standing in the doorway or at the window, like the others were. She'd hear him shouting over the tumult. She'd come to him.

From his spot in a stranger's garden almost at the foot of Down-along but not quite at the turning point into the harbour, he could make out one corner of the Siren's Tail where, in an upper window, Bella and Finan peered out, waving, with the Austens behind them. They were calling to him.

He squinted and cupped his ears, only to find they were bellowing the same words at the same time, desperate to make themselves heard. 'Get back!'

They threw their arms as if they could force him to stay where he was, frantically trying to prevent him making an attempt for the harbour.

He raised a hand to them, telling them he couldn't go any further anyway. It was useless. His path was blocked. There were no more gardens to climb over.

He tried to scramble onto the roof of the stone storehouse before him. From up there he might be able to get on top of the lifeboat house and then the old lime kiln and get a good view of the *Dagalien* on the beach, but there was no way to climb up, nothing to use as a foothold. He couldn't get to Alex.

If he'd had the benefit of Bella and Finan's vantage point he'd know already that the entire beach was lost under the brown swell. The *Dagalien*, along with the harbour's Christmas tree, all the pub benches and every net and lobster pot that had been stored along the sea wall, had been swept away in the sudden surge of water, right out of the harbour mouth and into the rough Atlantic.

When, seconds later, the helicopter flew low over the village and hovered over the harbour, surveying the scene, ready to drop ladders and airlift souls in need, Magnús knew he'd failed.

He'd have screamed himself hoarse for Alex if it hadn't been for the woman's voice calling for help somewhere Up-along.

He turned and vaulted back over the garden railings and fences, his trousers growing heavier and clinging horribly as they soaked up icy water, until he came to the howling woman.

Mrs Crocombe's front door was open and she stood helplessly inside, her slippers submerged in filthy ankle-deep water behind the stone threshold.

'My shop,' she cried. 'It's under water.' She flapped her hands helplessly and shivered so much Magnús knew he had to walk her back inside. There was no safe way up or down the slope; they'd have to wait for rescue.

With blankets over their shoulders they watched the rescuers from Mrs C.'s bedroom window. Three more helicopters had arrived within seconds of the first and the airlifts began.

All they could do was watch the village transformed by the surge. This was what helplessness felt like.

When it was their turn to be lifted from the slope, Mrs C. refused to put her arms inside the harness, but Magnús told her firmly that she'd be all right, he'd be next and they'd fly out of there together. Eventually, she agreed and was winched up into the sky from the casement, crying piteously while the men and women worked heroically to evacuate the stranded.

Left alone for the five minutes it took the coastguard to drop down his winch for him, Magnús stood stiff and wide-eyed, telling himself it would be over soon, that they'd find her. She'd be waiting for him at the gathering point when he arrived and the very first thing he'd tell her was that he was in love with her and he wasn't ever going to let anything bad happen to her ever again. He climbed out onto the windowsill, his legs dangling in the air, his body buffeted by the down draught, and the man strapped him into the harness, shouting instructions and reassurance and all Magnús could do was holler back over the rotor noise, 'Alex Robinson? Have you found her?'

Switchboards across the area were jammed with 999 calls. RAF Chivenor saw all rescue units scrambled while RAF Kinloss was on standby to fly at any moment. The coastguard helicopter crews worked tirelessly over the village while three lifeboats patrolled the coast.

News rooms listened in to emergency frequencies and reported live, interrupting Christmas programming, to tell the whole country that two publicans from the Siren's Tail, a family with a newborn, one elderly woman shop owner, a male holidaymaker, along with three other residents in their seventies and eighties, had all been airlifted out of the way of danger.

Then followed reports of a man in his sixties conveyed to safety by a coastguard rescue unit after being found caught in the currents, wading across the edge of the estate towards Clove Lore's Big House, struggling against the swell and with a shivering little dog zipped inside his jacket.

News vans arrived quickly on the scene and drone footage, that immediately went viral online, showed a local vet and his fiancée assisting the RSPCA in evacuating a stable yard. Shaky, bird's eye images showed one especially stubborn old donkey refusing to walk in convoy through the receding waters on the bridle path, now a slippery, muddy mess.

Viewers, glued to their screens, watched as the creature was secured in a harness and airlifted twenty feet into the air and over the grounds of the manor house where it was unclipped and dragged up the grand front steps by a stoic-looking blonde-haired woman in a green bodywarmer and wellies.

In all, it took forty minutes to evacuate Clove Lore.

Rescuers being interviewed on camera soon afterwards said they dreaded to think how much harder it would have been if seasonal tourists hadn't been kept away by the bad weather of the past week.

One by one, village residents arrived at the Big House to be counted, and to drink tea made by Izaak and Leonid – who, in their quick thinking, had dashed to the flooding cellars and rescued as much of the House's store of fire-wood as possible, and the few folding beds, chairs and tables the house owned, as well as the vast tea urn Minty kept for big events in the garden. They'd be required tonight, they knew.

Thinking again, Leonid had rushed back down the stone steps in the dark, just as the water table became over-whelmed and the dampness seeped in through the found-ations, slowly flooding the basement with filthy water. He grabbed the crate containing Minty's family photo albums including the folio of pictures capturing the now devast-ated chapel and camellia grove in Clove Lore's halcyon days. At the last second he'd rescued the very last case of Minty's mother's vintage Madeira brought home from her travels in the late seventies. Everything else in the cellar was now under water, but the house itself was safe.

By lunch time on Christmas Eve the whole world had seen images of the flash flood that had swept through the sleepy Devonshire village leaving material devastation in its wake.

'No lives lost,' the reporters repeated all morning. 'Only one person yet unaccounted for.'

Chapter Twenty-Nine

Afterwards

The power was still out across the region, except up at the Big House where the fire was lit and the Christmas tree lights sparkled absurdly in bizarre contrast to the mood of shock and disbelief.

Mrs Crocombe was crying into her daughter's shoulder with all her grandchildren gathered around her. The Bickleighs, who had climbed onto the roof of the lean-to at the back of their property and had been accompanied by fire crews from there onto the Big House lawns, were ashen-faced and cracking weak jokes to comfort each other.

The older residents from Down-along passed Minty's mobile around in the hopes of reaching relatives, but nobody was having much luck getting a signal.

Bella and Finan held onto each other for dear life, just as they had when they'd been lifted together from the roof of the pub. The Austens stuck close by them and baby Serena napped on as if nothing had happened.

Family groups, friends and neighbours settled themselves on the folding beds and deckchairs that Izaak and Leonid were quickly setting out around the ballroom.

The vicar had arrived only moments ago and had already been berated by Minty for not thinking to bring any biscuits. He had been positioned behind the tea urn with instructions to keep the hot drinks coming.

Magnús dashed between the groups. 'Have you seen Alex Robinson?' he asked each person, realising he didn't have so much as a snap of her on his phone to show those who hadn't met her yet. 'Blonde and tall, with blue eyes... like a sort of amazing mermaid, really,' he'd told one woman, who looked back at him with concern. He'd wanted to cry when he found that not one person had laid eyes on her all day.

Leaving the bustle of the Big House just as Jude was taking instructions from Minty to get baking in the kitchens – there were hungry mouths to feed – Magnús ran through the mud left in the flood's wake.

'No access to the village,' a police officer told him, her hands outspread like she'd rugby tackle him if he tried to get through. 'Residents can't return to their properties until morning at the earliest.'

A 'No Entry' sign behind her, right at the top of the slope, reinforced her orders. 'Too dangerous,' she told him. 'We don't know the state of the path or any of the retaining walls, and there's a lot of standing water inside properties. Can't let you pass until they've all been checked.'

An Environment Agency van pulled up beside them and the officer left her post to talk with the men in hard hats stepping out and rubbing their faces as they surveyed the state of the place.

Magnús was about to run for it down the slope when he heard the sound.

'*Psst!*' It was Jowan at the turning to the estate and Aldous by his feet.

Magnús approached him.

'You're goin' to search for our Alex?'

Magnús nodded, glancing over at the police officer still talking with the men.

'You can get down to the harbour if you take the cut-throughs down the back of the cottages. Only locals use 'em, with good reason; they're narrow and like a maze.' Jowan pointed a finger to a gap between two posts in the hedge behind them. 'Keep headin' down and you'll come out at the car park behind the Siren. It'll be a mess, mind. The flood washed down those gullies and into the backyards like a waterfall, lot o' debris. Mind your step.'

Magnús thanked him sincerely. As he was about to pass through the gap, Jowan reminded him to keep his phone switched on.

'No signal,' Magnús told him, pulling out his useless phone and checking it once more. He'd already tried ringing Alex at least twenty times. No one yet knew how all the phone companies were busy trying to reconnect the area but it would be hours before they could successfully get everyone talking again.

'Want me to come with?' Jowan asked, but Magnús thought Jowan was probably still in shock, judging by his worryingly grey pallor. He looked like he hadn't slept at all through last night's storm.

'Get warm at the Big House. The fire's burning and there's tea.'

He didn't stay to witness Jowan's indecision, instead racing off down the back ways to the harbour.

What Magnús saw as he picked his way down past the cottages' backyards turned his anxious heart to a jumping, frenzied pulp. Every cottage he glimpsed inside was flooded. Every back garden was lost under a layer of brown silt and stones. Gates hung off their hinges and whole fence panels were gone. At least the rain had stopped, making visibility better.

He called for Alex with every few steps he took, trying at once not to draw attention to himself from any police officers nearby, but wanting to rouse Alex if she was somehow sheltering in the steep confusion of narrow, twisty paths carrying him down to the Siren's Tail.

Not a bird sang or dog barked. Even the sea was subdued and the waves at last receded with low tide.

Magnús didn't realise he was crying – no, he was howling – until he stood on the harbour wall and saw not only the *Dagalien* gone but most of the beach pebbles too. Instead of shining stones rounded from years of water-wear there was dirt and branches – whole trees, in fact – and masonry, bricks and splintered planks everywhere, and no sign of Alex.

She'd said she was nipping down to the boat. She'd said she'd be ten minutes. Even before the waters came, she'd been gone at least an hour.

Had she taken a walk along the harbour wall and been swept away? It was worth looking, he felt. Magnús ran its length, criss-crossing back and forth to inspect the, now shallow, waters on each side. There were no ledges or rocks down there where she could be stranded, nothing but churned up silty water. He stopped at the end of the sea wall where the big glass lantern stood, useless without electricity. She wasn't here.

He scanned the horizon for boats. Nothing. Only a great container transporter like a blue dot miles out at sea.

Turning, he ran his hands over his head. 'Alex!' he shouted into the stilling air.

Where were the helicopters now? Why weren't they looking for her? Frantic, he clutched his stomach. The hungry need inside him was back, only now it was mixed with sickening fear.

In the distance, way along the cliffs, he spotted a group in neon vests walking in a line, advancing slowly. They were the search and rescue team, all in hard hats, one with a dog in a yellow jacket with the words 'recovery dog' along its side, it's snout to the ground.

Magnús ran back along the sea wall, jumping the plastic crates that had somehow escaped the pub's store room and scattered themselves everywhere. He leapt from the lifeboat ramp and onto the beach, wondering dimly where the pebbles were, out at sea or buried under this cloying brown clay beneath his feet? The whole strand was eerily transformed and unreal, like something from a disaster movie.

He'd join the search, lie if he had to, and say he was from the environment agency, like he'd seen written on that van. He had to help find her.

They were still a way off yet, along the bay. He could see their faces were lifted to the cliffs as though sizing up the state of the rocks when they should be looking all around for Alex.

Magnús walked close enough to the cliffs to be able to see inside all the little caves and crevices but repeatedly turned to scan the shoreline too.

Broken boat parts scattered the beach, none of them brown and white like the *Dagalien*.

'Alex,' he called, over and over.

Each time he thought he saw a glimpse of white hair he found his eyes were playing cruel tricks; it was torn plastic or stone or nets.

As the search line grew closer he heard their radios crackling. 'Still nothing,' a man told a command centre somewhere.

Magnús didn't know he was cold, and he couldn't feel his hunger now. He searched on, crying out for Alex, until he heard the radios again. This time the message was incoming.

'*Female found on an unnamed boat off Lundy. Repeat. One female retrieved from the sea. On route to District Hospital.*'

Magnús's feet moved faster than his brain and he reached the line, shouting all the time. 'They found Alex? Is she all right?'

The rescuer with the dog frowned at the sight of him, and told him he shouldn't be on the beach, the cliffs overhead weren't safe; there could easily be a serious rock fall.

'She's alive?' Magnús shouted, utterly desperate. 'Tell me!'

Before anyone could answer the radios crackled once more. 'Search for Alexandra Robinson to resume. The airlifted woman is a Mrs Eve Holsworthy. No injuries. Repeat, the search for Alexandra Robinson must continue.'

Magnús didn't understand. Reeling, he turned away from the rescuers, all of whom were telling him to get back up to the Big House.

He couldn't hear them.

'*Nei, nei,*' he shook his head, his hands on the back of his neck. '*Nei!*'

Looking out to sea as if Alex would emerge from the waves, Magnús stumbled onto the sand, then he was back up on his feet and running, his knee sending out pain signals where it had twisted. He didn't care. She was somewhere out there needing him.

'Stay away from the cliffs!' one of the party bellowed as Magnús ran past them along the beach. 'Requesting police presence; there's a civilian impeding search efforts on the beach,' they told their radio.

Magnús wasn't aware of any of that.

They hadn't searched the line below the dripping cliffs. They'd kept to the middle of the beach. Now that he knew he wasn't looking for a boat, he'd look for a body. He prayed for a living one, a breathing Alex, somewhere here amongst the fallen rocks and mud.

'Alex!' This time his voice was so loud he feared the cliffs might come down upon him.

He froze, listening to the reverberation. Police radios in the distance told him he was going to be dragged away.

'Listen, Magnús,' he told himself.

There was the sound of water dropping onto rocks. Like music. He followed the sound blindly, staggering over stones and wood, getting closer to the waterfall that had flowed down over the cliffs and onto Clove Lore beach for the last thousand years – never heavier than today. Its crystal-clear fresh water trickle had been replaced by the heavy brown flow of the run-off. The air smelled of earth and wet stone.

All the ferns that had clung to the rocks around the waterfall had been torn free and were strewn along the beach in newly formed sand channels leading to the sea. Magnús drew closer to the black rock face and the brown waterfall, and all the time he listened to the watery music. In his desperate state it sounded for all the world like someone singing.

Words seemed to reach him and he cursed his frantic brain for conjuring up a siren's song, the same one Alex had sung in the café as she baked that day when they'd both been so happy.

He sang back, weeping too, knowing he was losing his mind as well as the woman he loved, and knowing the police officer's boots were thumping over the wet beach behind him and they'd soon have their hands on him.

'*Soft, hear the merfolk, sing I,*' Magnús sang, his voice barely audible and broken with tears. '*I call to thee, boy of the shore. My pretty one, my pretty one, hear me sing my water song.*'

He staggered the last few paces to the waterfall, his breath catching at the sight of the pale white hand and arm limp across a rock behind the curtain of falling water, and hair, white and wet, spread over the stones, and over the sound of the waterfall, a voice echoed his own, singing weakly, barely audible, only a whisper, '*I call to thee, boy of the shore. How I love you, my boy of the shore.*'

'Alex!'

Magnús forced his way under the wall of water, getting instantly drenched. There, in the darkness of the shallow black cave behind the waterfall, lay the woman he loved.

He didn't dare move her. Her hair clung to her face and her clothes were filthy with mud. She didn't look as though she'd fallen, thankfully, more like she had slept on the rocks all morning.

Her lips moved as she mouthed her song and her flesh shivered.

'Alex, you're alive. I knew you were alive. I heard you singing to me!' He turned and called for help, just as the out-of-breath police officer reached them and put in a call on her radio.

Magnús knelt by Alex's side, cradling her head and kissing her cheek. 'You're safe,' he told her. 'It's over.'

Her eyelids lifted and he saw recognition there.

'I love you,' he told her, and finding the words so good to say out loud, he said them again. 'I am *seriously* in love with you.'

She smiled weakly and sang on, audible only to Magnús with his face pressed to her cold cheek.

'*How I love you, my boy of the shore,*' she breathed.

Chapter Thirty

Gathering

Minty loved it really; the being needed.

She'd marched around telling everyone what to do, even instructing one of the men from Environmental Health that she'd had it on good authority there were eleven perfectly good Christmas turkeys locked in the Siren's Tail's freezers, probably nicely defrosted by now, and he was to recover them immediately or they'd spoil.

He'd shaken his head and said, 'Now look, lady—' but she'd only had to fix him with sharp eyes and repeat the word, '*Immediately!*' and he'd lost confidence and ordered his team down at the pub to search the kitchens. Within the hour, the turkeys were conveyed by stretcher up the back paths to the Big House.

Jude worked in the kitchen all day, having chased away a fussing Mrs Crocombe and Bella intent on helping, saying they needed to rest, while everyone else milled around the ballroom drinking tea and sharing their stories of what they'd seen. Some stood in more subdued groups in the reception hall (where in one corner Elliot and Mr Moke watched the donkeys settling on hastily scattered hay) saying on repeat that they just couldn't believe it, and how it was 'just so horrendous' and 'unreal', as if reiterating those same words was helping everyone process the shock.

Nobody was allowed to leave the Big House until morning, the rescue teams said, even those, like Mrs Crocombe's family and the Burntislands, who lived up on the promontory and had dry homes to go to. The roads into Clove Lore were needed for bringing in the diggers overnight.

As darkness fell around three o'clock the roads rumbled with heavy machinery and orange lights flashed. Down-along was taped off and work started on making emergency power lines.

Jowan set up an old TV in the ballroom and let the news programmes run endlessly until it was announced that the woman airlifted from a washed-up ferry was staying in hospital for observation but was uninjured.

That was when Magnús woke Alex, who was lying on a camp bed by the ballroom fire, to ask her how it had happened. How Eve could have been in the boat and not Alex?

After being monitored in the back of the ambulance at the top of the village, Alex had been given the all-clear to head to the Big House with all the others and told she simply had to stay warm, hydrated and get plenty sleep, the very same diagnosis Doctor Morrison had given her a week ago when she'd been found washed up the first time, only this time she wasn't burdened with a heavy heart any more.

She was, however, exhausted from jumping from the *Dagalien* and clinging to mooring chains while the water gushed around her. She told Magnús how she'd held on, thinking of him, and just when her strength was leaving her she'd felt the flood waters weaken and she'd waded up the beach with trembling legs of jelly. She'd fallen through a wall of water, found a spot on the rocks and must have passed out with the tiredness and relief.

Eve hadn't been quick enough to jump free and Alex hadn't even seen the *Dagalien* swept from the harbour mouth in frothing brown water as the little boat was lifted and turned in circles like a waltzer car at a fair.

The room grew quieter as everyone watched the news but when the special extended report was about to play again Minty decided they'd all had quite enough of the images of their homes under water. She changed the channel to *The Snowman* and everyone, without exception, sat on their bunks and folding chairs and watched it with glassy eyes, some singing along with the music, others mouthing the words for the sake of Mrs C.'s grandkids and the Burntisland boys, even if they couldn't sing all that well for the lumps in their throats.

Tom Bickleigh had befriended a reporter from the local paper who had arrived two hours ago only to find she couldn't now leave. The pair were talking in hushed tones about how his fishing boat was thankfully still afloat and moored in the harbour. He'd find out what state it was in tomorrow morning. The reporter offered to go with him – for the sake of her story, she'd quickly put in with a shy smile – and Tom's eyes lit up.

Seeing his brother getting on with the reporter, Monty had taken a stroll in the dark to where the police officer was once more stationed at her post. He carried with him two cups of tea and some of the excellent gingerbread men Jude had made in Minty's kitchen while they waited for the ovens to come to temperature for two of the turkeys. He'd been gone for so long it was safe to assume the officer was glad of a friendly person to talk to as she marshalled the traffic and kept the place clear of rubberneckers from the nearby villages – all of whom had fared far better than Clove Lore where all the region's run-off had converged.

'We'll have Christmas dinner in two hours!' Minty had told everyone through an old loudhailer kept for the estate's fox and field day announcements in the summer. The loudhailer really wasn't necessary but this had still been met by a cheer and she'd retreated to help the vicar with the tea urn.

It all helped keep her mind off Jowan who was sitting by the fire cradling Aldous with a sorry frown and not speaking to anyone. Minty had barely glanced his way since she'd seen him brought inside by the rescue team. She'd watched as Leonid took him away to get changed out of his wet clothes and said nothing when he returned half an hour later smelling of her lodgers' shampoos and shower gels, wearing something baggy and soft of Izaak's apparently called 'lounge pants' and a hoodie in khaki and cream over a white cotton T-shirt, also oversized and soft, with a thick pair of Leonid's woollen welly socks. He'd have looked ten years younger if it weren't for the repentant wistfulness etched across his face. Still, Minty couldn't help feeling tormented by the scent and proximity of him as she delivered up his share of the coffee and gingerbread biscuits by the fire.

'Mint?' he'd attempted, but she'd only said a flustered, 'Busy, busy,' in response and hurried away leaving him to sit dejected by the fire, sharing his gingerbread with Aldous who felt all his doggie birthdays were coming at once: a spot by the fire, gingerbread men to eat *and* the promising smell of turkey roasting!

Alex had eventually got a signal and spoken to Mrs Thomas in Port Kernou.

'I really am all right. I'm glad they both got home safely too. New Year? No idea, to be honest. I'm not thinking that far ahead, I'm just glad to be alive.'

She lay flat across a camp bed with squeaky metal springs and Magnús sat crossed-legged on the floor by her side, stroking her cheek with his thumb. She'd made a second call to the hospital and been told Eve had already been discharged and was heading home to spend Christmas with her little boy.

When she hung up the call, Magnús lowered his face to hers and they talked in whispers punctuated by discreet kisses.

At four o'clock the postman was shown into the ball-room by someone in a hard hat and incredibly muddy waterproofs. Bovis too slipped in, his hat in his hands, complaining that he'd been behind a police cordon for hours and they'd only let him through when he saw the postie being allowed in and complained that he worked here, so if anyone was allowed in, it ought to be him. The inhabitants of the ballroom welcomed them like heroes.

The postman quickly had a crowd around him and he thoroughly enjoyed telling everyone how he hadn't been let through at first. 'But I'd a van full of your parcels. Told 'em I couldn't very well take 'em back to the depot, could I? Not when they might 'ave some Christmas cheer inside for you all.'

The postie called out names and Minty emerged from the kitchen to comment that it was like 'letters day' at boarding school. Nobody in the room had the experience to concur that it was indeed just like that, but they all stepped forward to collect the bundles of Christmas cards and packages that on any normal Christmas Eve would have been brought to their doors hours ago.

Some struck it lucky: Bella and Finan unwrapped boxes of chocolates from family members far afield; one of the old men held up a bottle of whisky from his brother in Torrington. That received a rowdy cheer. Others were less fortunate. Poor Monty received an outdoor clothing catalogue while Monica Burntisland opened, of all things, a water bill.

'One 'ere for Magnús Sturluson? Care of the Borrow-A-Bookshop?' the postman called.

Magnús hadn't paid much attention until this point; he'd been too busy telling Alex soft things in her ear and letting her whisper back words that made him blush and bite his lip. Now he was amazed to find he was the recipient of a parcel passed from group to group across the ballroom.

'For me?' he asked the package once it was in his hands. 'Ah! It's Mamma's writing.'

Alex sat up and watched as he tore the wrapping away and turned over a book, a copy of the *Vinland Sagas* in Icelandic, in case he was at risk of forgetting where he came from. He took a deep sniff between the pages before realising what he was doing. Alex laughed brightly and told him it was nothing to be ashamed of.

Inside the flyleaf was an inscription written in English, his mum's idea of a good joke for her son living the life of an English bookseller. He read her message a few times with a light coming on inside him and glowing brighter as his eyes re-scanned the words. Then he held it out for Alex to read.

Son, you will have your Christmas book
flood, even in England. We are proud of
you. Please enjoy your bookshop and
come home happy again. Love, Mamma.

'Christmas book flood?' Alex asked.

'*Já*, the *jólabókaflóð*. Everyone gets a book on Christmas
Eve in Iceland. It's tradition. And we read all evening. It's
the best part…' Magnús's mouth snapped into a straight
line. He was thinking.

Then he was up on his feet.

Everyone watched as his eyes darted from Alex's to
Jowan's.

It had taken only a few minutes to formulate the plan
and the whole ballroom had waved goodbye to Magnús
and Elliot (roped in because of his strength and fitness),
as well as the man in the hard hat (who worked for the
council, it turned out, who'd said he'd accompany them
on their way down to the middle of the slope), and of
course, Mushy Peas, the best donkey for the task, as they
went on their mission to the Borrow-A-Bookshop to
retrieve gift books for all the villagers.

Alex sent Magnús on his way with a proud kiss pressed
to his forehead. 'That one's from your mum,' she told him.

After they'd left, Minty had informed the postal worker
that he was staying the night even though he'd objected,
saying he could sleep in his van. Of course, he'd been
powerless against her insistence and was immediately
tasked with helping to push the tables together for the
turkey dinner that was imminent.

The most wonderful aroma of thyme, lemon and onion
along with Jude's homemade bread rolls was filling the

ballroom, already scented with gingerbread, pine needles and log fire. Everyone's thoughts turned to their stomachs so Bella passed around the chocolates.

'Right!' Minty told the room, brushing her hands over her apron. 'There are donkeys in my vestibule, at least twenty campers in my ballroom, three foot of muddy water in my cellars, and umpteen spare turkeys squeezed into the fridge. What else!' She turned for the kitchens again.

'*Ahem!*' The sound of a throat being cleared behind her stopped Minty in her tracks.

Turning, she was met by the sight of an earnest, gulping Bovis. He was grasping a ball of mistletoe from one of the sconces.

'Araminta Clove-Congreve, uh... Minty,' he said, grandly, before swallowing hard and adding, 'Mistress.'

'Bovis?' Minty's brows creased.

The whole room watched on in silence, eyes alight with fascination. Mrs Crocombe was on her feet and listening, open-mouthed. What on earth was happening?

'My... *um*... my feelings will not be repressed,' Bovis told Minty bravely, his chest swollen like a pigeon.

'Goodness, Bovis, are you quite all right?' Minty glanced immediately to Jowan who could see exactly what was coming and was shrinking for his old friend in her embarrassment.

Bovis had clearly rehearsed this. He wasn't going to be put off. 'You must allow me to tell you how ardently I admire and...' another gulp, '...love you.'

A gasp of wonder spread across the room. Someone definitely stifled a laugh.

'Have you had a blow to the head, man?' Minty said, warning him with her eyes not to continue. 'Can someone check him for concussion? Elliot knows about these things, oh he's gone, hasn't he?' Her shoulders slumped a little but she met Bovis's ardent expression courageously.

Nobody moved a muscle, except the devoted estate's man, who, forgetting his lines, drew the novel from his pocket and read. Reassured, he intended to press on.

Seeing his copy of *Pride and Prejudice*, its covers folded back on Mr Darcy's proposal scene, Minty muttered, 'Dear Lord!' and turned her eyes heavenward.

'In declaring myself thus I'm fully aware that I will be going expressly against the wishes of my family, my friends, and, I hardly need add, my own better judgement... oh no, I was meant to skip that bit, 'old on.'

'Bovis,' she called in an exaggeratedly loud voice, even for her. 'You're not well, my man.'

Bovis was surprised to find Minty's arm around his shoulder and he was led away towards the kitchens. 'It's the flood you see, making everyone giddy. What you need is a stiff drink. Come along. We'll have you right as rain in a jiffy.'

As she guided her groundsman away, Minty scanned the room, stamping out any sniggering coming from Tom Bickleigh's corner. Poor Bovis may never be able to forget his misjudged passion but the look in Minty's eye warned everyone present that they'd better wipe their memories of it quick sharp.

Having disarmed him of his Jane Austen and his mistletoe, Minty discreetly slipped away, leaving Bovis with Jude in the kitchen to sip his brandy and cool his ardour.

When she closed the door behind her, exhaling sharply and shaking her head, she found Jowan there to meet her.

'Everything all right?' he asked.

'Yes, yes, fine, thank you. You'd better sit at the table. We need someone to carve.'

This wasn't what he'd wanted to hear but he did as he was told and set about sharpening the carving knife.

By the time the tables, all different heights, were arranged in a row before the fire and chairs and stools of all sizes had been dragged around it, and mismatched glasses and mugs located for the Madeira and orange squash, everyone was saying how they were half starved.

Minty was passing around the cutlery when a cold draught swept in from the vestibule along with the smell of mud and donkey.

In clopped Mushy Peas with four pillow cases tied together across his back filled with books. Elliot untied them and led the donkey away for his reward – a carrot from the kitchen presented lovingly by Jude who had at last finished cooking.

Jowan abandoned his spot at the head of the table to welcome Magnús back.

'What was it like? The bookshop?'

Magnús didn't like to say, only baring his teeth and inhaling. 'It could look better.'

'Mornin's soon enough to see the place, I s'pose,' Jowan said sadly, slapping Magnús's shoulder and telling him he'd done a 'grand job'.

Monty Bickleigh arrived from the dark afternoon along with the police officer, drawn by the good smell of food, and that made up the whole of the Christmas Eve party.

The books were quickly distributed amongst the campers, some glancing across the table for an exchange, finally arriving at something they liked, and they gazed at the covers as they shuffled chairs, tucking themselves in, while Jowan carved the turkey which had been carried through accompanied by a fanfare tootled through Finan's cupped hands.

It was all unexpectedly jolly. Even when everyone's nerves were rattled and their futures uncertain, there was still laughter, if a little hysterical, heightened by gratitude and the knowledge that things could have been far different.

Minty and Jude had rustled up some stuffing and cranberry sauce and a lot of giblet gravy. There were nowhere near enough sprouts and carrots to go around (Minty had only planned on a quiet lunch tomorrow for herself and her tenants) but nobody minded as there were some roast potatoes and the softest, freshest bread rolls they'd ever tasted. The case of wine went a long way to cheering everyone's spirits too, and as they ate, everyone turned over their new books in their hands.

Magnús and Alex had been separated across the table but were smiling at one another. The wistfulness in Magnús's eyes told Alex all she needed to know about the state of the bookshop, but as Magnús had proven there were many dry books – enough to select from the newest stock and bring everyone a gift.

'To the *Jólabókaflóð*,' Magnús proposed, holding up his glass, and everyone echoed, mangling the pronunciation and laughing as they drank.

'And to Minty,' Izaak added, and everyone cheered even louder, except for Bovis who sat chastened and quiet by his mistress's side, and Jowan who raised his glass in silence to her.

Minty looked pleased with her Barbara Cartland, and Mrs Crocombe with her love poems. Reverend Morgan was delighted with his *Murder at the Vicarage*. Baby Serena had *The Velveteen Rabbit*, which her parents thought looked expensive and wouldn't allow her to hold, and a cloth copy of *The Very Hungry Caterpillar*, which Serena soon discovered was very good as a teething chew. The older children had Mr Men books, Julia Donaldsons and Judith Kerrs, and their grown-ups read to them between mouthfuls to keep them quiet through the feast.

Watching the children at her table, Minty wished aloud that they had some Christmas crackers to pull and everyone had told her not to be silly, they had more than enough of everything they needed, then Tom obliged by telling terrible jokes about how Darth Vader knew what Luke got him for Christmas having 'felt his presents', and explaining how, if you ate Christmas decorations, you'd get 'tinsellitis'. Everyone groaned and laughed and a few wistful tears were wiped away and replaced with smiles.

The flames in the grand fireplace crackled and sparked, the wine flowed, everyone wanted seconds or even thirds of the turkey, the tree lights glinted and it felt very much like Christmas.

'Hold on! What's that?' Mrs Crocombe asked sharply, spreading her hands over the table in front of her to silence everyone. She had her beady eye fixed on Jude's ring finger.

'Oh, yes, we *um*, we're engaged,' Jude confirmed, and the noise that went up in the ballroom almost lifted the roof.

Jude was made to do a lap of the table showing everyone her ring, and Elliot shook hands and grinned dopily from all the attention.

'I *told* you there would be a wedding at Clove Lore before long!' Mrs C. said, sighing happily.

'You should get married here,' Izaak put in, making Mrs C. wink at him. He'd always been a supporter of her matchmaking. Nobody paid any heed to Jude and Elliot shaking their heads and saying they weren't planning on rushing anything; this pinpoint of light in Clove Lore's future was too irresistible not to conspire about.

'Get married where? We've no chapel now, remember?' Minty tolled.

'Well, when you think of something, there'll be the pub for your guests to stay in,' Bella put in.

Finan asked his wife if that meant they were staying put and she'd told everyone assembled that the Siren's Tail was staying open come hell or high water and there'd been more cheers and tears at that.

'Glad to hear it,' Finan told his wife, leaning in to kiss her.

It wasn't the Christmas anybody had planned – it had come a day too soon for starters – but it still felt like Christmas around that table, enough for everyone to forget, just for a few minutes, what their world must look like out there.

Tomorrow would be a different matter entirely. Cold hard reality would have to be faced. For now, it was Christmas Eve and there was food and books and company.

Minty held on to the spark of pride burning inside her, hoping it would be enough to burn away the other feelings she wanted to shut out. The feeling of having lost a friend, of having been kissed and then not wanted – feelings far worse than standing in the ruins of her family's destroyed chapel.

Yet she wouldn't look at Jowan across the table; it hurt far too much. Better to treat him with civility and keep him at arm's length. Of course he wanted to talk about it, but what could he say? He loved Isolde and no one could replace her in his heart. She'd been a fool to think she could.

When it was time, she helped clear the dishes and shouted over the happy rabble, 'Charades, anyone? Anyone? No? Righty-o then,' and Monica Burntisland and Mrs Crocombe's daughter had remembered they were teachers and gathered everyone for stories from the children's gift books.

Minty couldn't avoid him, though. In a quiet moment between stacking clean dishes away in her dresser and cutting the Christmas cake she'd been saving for a far different kind of Christmas, Jowan made his way to her side in the kitchen, the spot where they'd kissed only hours before.

'Mint, shouldn't we talk?'

'We've spoken every day for the past twenty years. Can't we take one day off? Or a week, even? In fact, Jowan,' she set the knife down and forced the platter of sliced cake into his hands. 'Unless you have anything to say to me that isn't about your beloved Isolde, I don't have ears to listen.'

Jowan's lips stretched thin and apologetic.

'Well then,' Minty concluded. 'Let us not speak for some time, eh? In the morning you can get back to the cottage. There'll be a great deal to do, as there is here. A bit of a break from seeing one another might do us both some good.'

Had he protested, it would have sounded weak, so he said nothing and carried the cake into the ballroom where the candles in their sconces glowed orange and the children were settling on makeshift beds and turning pages in their books.

Minty was right, he brooded. They needed to stay away from one another. Then maybe these feelings of guilt and regret would pass. He settled in a chair by the fire once more and absently scratched at Aldous's head.

Everyone was quiet and still, full of food, and putting off thoughts of their flooded homes with storytelling and illustrations. Only Jowan's mind circulated with unquiet thoughts as turbulent as the storm that had caused so much mischief, only there'd be no recovering from this mess. He feared that, once hurt and betrayed, Minty would protect herself from him forever. They would never be close again.

Chapter Thirty-One

Christmas Morning at the Bookshop

'I'm dreading this,' Jude said over Jowan's shoulder as he turned the key in the lock.

Magnús stood back at the foot of the steps, holding Alex's hand. He'd seen it all last night and it had been bad. That was by torch light. In the harsh light of Christmas Day it would be an even sorrier sight.

'Just remember,' Magnús said, 'it can all be repaired, OK?'

Jowan pushed his way inside without a word and his heart cracked in his chest.

Most of the water had seeped away through the floor-boards of the Borrow-A-Bookshop but it had left behind a layer of silt, mud and Jowan dared not think what, which was deposited everywhere like a sludgy blanket.

Jude took Jowan's arm as they shuffled further inside. The rugs bubbled and squelched when stood on.

'Ah,' Jowan exhaled hard, before pinching his lips tight to stop them trembling. His eyes streamed with silent tears.

Everything at ground level had drunk deeply of the flood waters. Every book on the lowest shelves was spoiled. The feet of every piece of furniture were discoloured and blown with the wetness. The smell of damp

279

and cold had already set in to the shop and would, Jowan knew, grow far worse as the December days passed. With no light from the fire and the bulbs dead in their sockets, what had been cosy reading nooks and a browser's paradise was a dark palette of greys.

Nobody spoke as they took it all in. Jude picked up her grandfather's cookbooks from the counter and held them to her in a bundle.

Alex stepped slowly through the morass to lift a blanket from the armchair. She folded and smoothed it in her hands, looking despairingly at the spot by her feet where the logs and ashes from the fire had washed out onto the carpet and mixed with the slime.

'OK, don't panic,' Magnús said, spreading his hands out as if he could soothe everyone's fractured emotions. 'You heard Minty this morning. Her planning committee are putting in orders for shovels and skips. They'll be here soon. We'll get all this gunk out of here in days.'

Even Magnús didn't believe that. It would be weeks of work. Weeks he didn't have left in England to assist.

'Yeah,' Alex said, her eyes on Magnús, wanting to shore up Jowan with her confidence that things would be all right eventually. 'And that guy from the council said there were dehumidifiers and fans and portable heaters on their way. As soon as the electric's restored they'll get to work drying the place.'

'Those'll take days to arrive at this time of year,' Jowan replied sadly, still looking all around him in disbelief. 'While we're waitin', all this sopping wet filth will spread itself into every fibre in the building, even the bed upstairs will absorb the damp. The window frames'll warp and stick, the curtains'll mildew, all this plaster is going to blow apart and the ceilings'll weaken. This isn't going to be a clean-up. It needs gutting and startin' all over again.'

Too wearied to stand, Jowan perched on the display table by the door, shoving aside the home décor books the last guests had left. He shook his head slowly. 'What am I supposed to do now?'

'Will Borrow-A-Bookshop shut down?' Jude asked in a small voice.

Jowan looked all around him as if to say that was more than likely.

'I couldn't bear that,' Jude cried. 'And just have no bookshop in Clove Lore? No bookshop holidays?'

'Think of the work this place'll need to get it cleaned up,' he said sadly. 'I have my own cottage to dry out and fix.' He'd put off going home, wanting to see the bookshop first.

'You can't just put it up for sale,' Jude said. 'It belongs to the community.'

'It belongs to me,' Jowan retorted. 'As does all the responsibility for its upkeep.'

'But the charity, the holiday lets. There's a three-year waiting list. We can't cancel their breaks, not all of them.' Jude looked around, knowing full well she was being unrealistic. 'Can't we just postpone them? Until the shop's fixed up?'

'Jude, even Magnús can't finish his holiday.'

Alex squeezed Magnús's hand. 'That's true. What are you going to do?' she asked.

Magnús said he didn't have a clue, but he knew he didn't want to leave. 'I'm staying. I can do a lot in a week.'

Jowan laughed bitterly. 'I like your gusto, but it's hopeless.'

Jude wasn't having any of it. 'No it's not. I'll be here, and Elliot! We can get the place up and running.'

Jowan cut her off. 'It's hard enough being a bookseller these days. Do you know how many bookshops are closing down all over the country each week?'

'How many?' Jude was close to tears now.

'I dunno; a lot. See it every time I open a trade paper. It's the rents doing it, and the landlords, and the whole world being skint, 'cept a handful of millionaires.'

'Not the booksellers themselves?' Magnús shifted his feet, tipping his head in interest.

'How could it be their fault?' Jowan wanted to know, his eyes narrowing.

'Not being good enough? Having the wrong stock? Bad service?' Magnús could have gone on, listing all the things he'd blamed himself for when Ash and the Crash folded.

Jowan gave a crumpled smile, making his beard bristle beneath his lips, and the sides of his eyes crinkle. 'No, and it's not the readers, neither. Folks want books more than ever. Think how desperate everyone was to hold a book when we couldn't get outside or do much else? Even with all this demand, it's a hard game, bookselling. Do you hear me, Magnús?'

The way Jowan pinned him with his eyes set off a shift in Magnús's chest and he knew he was in danger of crying.

'Small bookshops go under all the time, even with the best staff in the world.'

Magnús inhaled shakily, his mind working.

Jowan kept his eyes fixed on him as he spoke. 'People think bookselling's easy. In reality it's a lot o' hard work for not a lot of money, and that was before the big book behemoths came along and ate up so many little stores just like this one. Do you understand?'

Magnús nodded, his eyes flitting around at nothing, like it was finally sinking in.

'You don't know what I've seen, over the years. The changes. Isolde and I, we were young and idealistic, couple of hippies my pa called us.' Jowan said this with a faraway look and a laugh. 'We made this place in a time when if you wanted a book you had to go looking for it. Your bookseller would order it for you, or you'd send away for it. Yes, really!' He looked now at Alex. 'Borrow-A-Bookshop's kept going with takings from the café and the holiday lets. I think you saw that, all of you?'

Jude, Magnús and Alex couldn't help but agree. They looked at the ground, not wanting to vocalise it. Magnús thought of the tiny profits of the last week. Not even enough to cover the electric and gas they'd used up, he guessed.

Jowan was waxing warm now, his hands clamped together and his eyes barely seeing the mess in the shop. 'Booksellers are a rare breed. They're born with a love of books so strong they can't do nothin' but get into the book trade. I should know, I was one of 'em, and so was my Isolde. We did well for years, we were lucky. Down to the tourists, it was. But starting again now? That's a different story. I'm not the man for resurrectin' the place. I'm, I'm...'

Jowan wanted to say that he was tired. He'd given up the bookshop, then he'd given up the B&B. He wanted retirement and peace and most of all he wanted companionship and something easy and quiet. 'I don't want to be redesignin' and refittin' and restockin' a shop. I've no appetite for seeing this place stripped out and changed beyond recognition into something my Isolde wouldn't know as her own.'

'What if *you* didn't do the work?' Alex interjected, her feet shuffling, and her finger raised. 'And what if the shop could look the same, only better?' She glanced back and forth between Jowan and Magnús. 'What if *we* did it all?' Alex said, her eyes shining. 'What if we stuck around and fixed the shop for you?'

Magnús's face lit up. He too looked imploringly at Jowan. '*Já*, Jowan, what if?'

Jowan only listened, his face stretching long.

Jude joined in now. 'Maybe this is the bookshop's chance to move into this century?'

'You have to admit it needs new heating?' Alex said.

Magnús added, 'Needs rewiring too. Can't do that without replastering anyway.'

'True,' Jowan said eventually. 'But how will you live? *Where* will you live?'

'No idea!' Alex told him, grinning.

'It's the worst idea I've ever heard,' Jowan told her.

'*Ó, já!* Me too, totally the worst,' Magnús had to agree. 'But still, I want to do it. If Alex does. We can stay upstairs once the place is dry and watertight again. Live and work on site. And we will do a full restock. These books are curling already!' Magnús plucked a book from a shoulder-height shelf. It was soft with damp. '*Já*, we'll restock.' He replaced the book and wiped his hand down his thigh.

'And re-open the café as soon as we can,' Alex bounced upon her heels. 'All the workers coming into the village will need somewhere to grab a coffee and a bite to eat. I can do that side of things too.'

'Is that what you want?' Magnús asked, turning to her. 'Truly?'

Alex nodded vigorously. 'Yes. Don't you?'

They were grinning at one another now as if they weren't standing in the ruins of Magnús's holiday and Jowan's life's work.

'Don't you have real jobs?' Jowan asked. 'Elsewhere?'

'Not any more,' Alex said, as if this was a good thing. 'The *Dagalien*'s over on Lundy right now. If she can be reclaimed, I'll be selling her. I am *seriously* out of work.'

Now it was Magnús's turn. 'The wine shop can find a new evening shift guy. I am meant to be in a bookshop. I'm one of those crazy booksellers you described. I couldn't fix Ash and the Crash but I can help here. Then I will return it to you repaired and ready to trade again.'

'Why would you do that?' Jowan asked.

'I don't know,' Magnús shrugged. 'To prove I can? To show myself I may have failed once but I can resurrect a lost business? Not mine, but still, I can do it for you and the village, and the bookshop charity, and all those other people on the waiting list dreaming about being booksellers.'

'They haven't a clue how hard it is,' Jowan said.

'*Nei*, they don't. *We* do. We know what it's really like to have a bookshop and to love it and to want it to survive – no, not just survive, to *flourish* – and we know what it's like to see it go wrong. Who better to fix the place?'

'What will you live off? There's not a lot of money in the charity accounts,' Jude asked sensibly.

'Again, no clue!' Magnús said, shrugging like it didn't matter.

'I have an idea,' Alex said, her finger raised. 'And a little ready money too. I'd already decided I was selling the house and the boat, now I know what I'll be doing with some of the cash. And the shop's insured, right?'

Jowan nodded.

'Then I'll get my investment back. Until then we'll manage. Maybe Minty could put us up in her ballroom until we work something else out.'

'You're crazy,' Jowan said.

'So, will you let us stay and help?' Alex could barely contain the hope within her.

Jowan watched the pair of them, thinking how like his younger self and his Isolde she and Magnús were. Idealistic, tough and tenacious, risk-taking. 'OK,' he said.

Magnús and Alex were in each other's arms already while Jude clapped excitedly.

'Please stay,' Jowan said, his eyes watery. 'Stay and save Borrow-A-Bookshop. But I don't want it all shinin' white and plastic in here.'

'Neither do we,' Alex assured him.

'I remember the day Isolde made those signs,' said Jowan, looking about him again. 'The care she took choosing everything. I remember how we first painted the door sky-blue, her choice of colour, of course. We'd scour the house sales for stock, no matter how far away they were. The shelves were filled to burstin' on opening day. I swear there's books we acquired that first year still on these shelves somewhere.'

'Yeah, that's not a great business model. You should really have shifted those by now,' Magnús said.

Jowan's laughter was so unexpected and so badly needed. It dislodged something in his heart that had been a sore sticking point for so long. 'You'll keep Isolde's signs?'

'Nothing leaves the shop without your say so,' Alex told him.

'Takes a brave person to move on with their life and try again when they lost it all once before,' said Jowan, getting a little lost in his train of thought.

The three of them withdrew a little, letting Jowan ruminate.

Jowan knew he couldn't hold on to the past any longer. Only, change was so unsettling. It required so much courage. It meant risking losing it all and getting hurt all over again and yet, if things didn't take a great leap forward now, how would they ever get any better?

Jowan's back straightened like a lightning bolt had struck at his feet. 'I have to go,' he announced. 'I have to talk to Minty.'

'Maybe get changed first,' Jude said, as gently as she could.

Jowan looked down his body at Izaak's oversized outfit. 'Oh, right enough!' he said, before his face fell into a determined straight-browed eagerness.

He walked right out the shop and Down-along, barely seeing all the detritus from the storm, dodging the diggers and council pick-ups parked along the slope, saying 'mornin' to members of the clean-up crew giving up Christmas with their families to help with the disaster effort.

He strode past the ice-cream parlour where Mrs C. was being let inside by an official in a hard hat, all of her family around her. She was pale and afraid, but she followed the man inside. Jowan caught the sounds of her crying and her daughter comforting her, before pacing on. So many people would be facing the toughest morning of their lives.

He knew his own cottage would have borne the brunt of the waters, being at the end of the slope and at its turning point. The water would have welled there before being forced in a sweep to the right and down into the harbour.

Whatever was waiting for him he'd just have to accept it; smashed windows, filthy carpets, the kitchen all spoiled. It didn't matter. He'd accept it.

He'd have to move with the times, fill a skip and buy a replacement everything. It was just stuff, he knew now.

All of that could be faced later. Right now, what mattered most was making himself presentable for Minty and getting back up to the Big House to tell her that he really, *really* wanted to ruin their friendship.

As he drew closer to his old B&B, head down, thinking only of how quickly he could get changed and how on earth he was going to wash, he didn't notice that the front door of his home had been forced open by the water and was now gaping. He didn't notice the armchairs lifted into the corner of the living room and deposited in a sludgy pile along with Isolde's cushions and rugs and all the accoutrements of his old life. He didn't notice the tidemark around the walls five foot high, or the way the wallpaper was washed clean away in parts and peeling and blistered in others.

Jowan saw only Hunter wellies, then sensible slacks, a green bodywarmer and a silk scarf tied in a smart knot across a slender throat and blonde hair framing a bold, beautiful face.

'Mint?'

She stood bolt upright in the spot where, until yesterday, the cottage's low hedge and metal fence posts had been.

'I didn't want you going in there on your own,' she told him in her familiar way, reserved and imperious, but kind.

She wasn't angry with him any more, at least.

Minty's eyes belied her anxious state, even though the way she held herself was the picture of poise and calm.

Neither of them made any move towards the cottage. She stared entreatingly at her old friend. Jowan knew he would have to be the one to fix this, and it had to be now.

'Mint…'

Her mouth tightened and she turned her face a little to one side, as though that could stop her having to listen to any more painful excuses about how Isolde would always be the one for Jowan.

'Mint, you are my oldest friend, and I promised you I would always be there for you.'

Minty closed her eyes, readying herself for another bout of rejection.

'No, Minty, no, it's not like that, come here.' He reached for her hand and she let him hold it, barely daring to look in his eyes. 'The promises I made to you in friendship, I want to make all over again as your… as your—'

Now he had Minty's full attention and her eyes threatened to overflow with tears. Her brow crinkled in a way that made Jowan's heart soften even more.

'Go on.' She wasn't going to let him off the hook that easily.

'As your lover.' As soon as the words were out, Jowan gulped and clamped his lips closed. He and Minty stared hard at one another.

'I mean, as… your partner? Your best friend. Your most important person.'

Minty's laughter rang out as she brought a hand to her mouth. 'My most important person?'

Jowan blushed and tried to find more words but there were none. 'Yes, my most important person,' he shrugged.

'Right then, well… Good.' Minty nodded sharply, accepting the new arrangement, and Jowan's smile burst across his face.

Ever so slowly, he stepped closer, taking her other hand in his, then bringing his fingertips in a slow trail all the way up over her arm and across the knot of silk at her throat.

Seeing her gulp and her lips soften – she was barely breathing, it seemed – he let his hand settle along her jaw, sweeping his thumb across her cheek and the edge of her lips, his eyes sinking to her mouth before he closed the last of the distance between them in a soft kiss the likes of which could only happen between best friends well on their way to becoming lovers.

Chapter Thirty-Two

Always Look for the Helpers

The news cameras left Clove Lore soon after Christmas, and the tourists stayed away, but the thing about a place like Clove Lore is, it lives on in people's memories.

Those who had spent happy childhood holidays, or honeymoons, or Christmases in the village and remembered it fondly certainly didn't forget the images on their screens of the place in peril, and while the diggers and bricklayers, glaziers and plasterers moved in and every cottage ran dehumidifiers night and day and skips arrived to take away everyone's wrecked furniture and spoiled possessions, the envelopes began to arrive.

Almost all of them were addressed 'Care of the Clove Lore Estate', which meant Minty had the pleasure of opening them. Some contained cash, others cheques, all sent in sympathy and solidarity to the people of Clove Lore to help them rebuild their lives.

A delegation was formed, headed by Minty, of course, aided by her right-hand man and most important person, Jowan. The money was to be split between residents and businesses Down-along and there was to be no delay in divvying it up.

Still the envelopes arrived all through the winter, prompting Minty to ask around the village if there wasn't an easier way of doing all this.

Alex had been the one to suggest the donations website and as soon as it was up and running (and Minty had given yet another of her rousing, stoical interviews to the press – she was becoming quite the poster girl for the entire project), the money poured in from across the world, and everyone in Clove Lore wiped away happy tears and remarked with wonder about the astounding generosity of strangers.

The Siren's Tail, just like the bookshop and Mrs C.'s ice-cream shop, needed a complete refit of its ground floor. The stable got underfloor heating, much to Moira, Bon Jovi and Mushy Peas' eternal delight. The cellars of the Big House had to be dredged and relined and Mrs Crocombe had to claim for two hundred litres of spoiled ice cream on her insurance policy.

On one very solemn Sunday the site where the chapel had once stood was cleared away entirely, leaving only the tiled floor, the font and the front pews. Leonid replanted the whole area with camellias with the intention of extending the once-famed camellia grove all the way up to the back of the Big House. The whole operation was undertaken with the plodding slowness that local red tape and petty bureaucracy brought with it but there were signs of progress everywhere.

The works would take many more months to complete, but when the first hint of summer reached Clove Lore, the village's mood and fortunes had improved enough for a very special event to take place.

Elliot was the first down the aisle, handsomer than ever in his dark suit, and nervously sweeping back his long, sleek hair.

Leonid and Izaak, with matching frothy blooms in their lapels, and Mrs Crocombe with Bovis by her side, filled the front pews.

Bella and Finan stood behind them, a little flustered after all the work that had gone into readying their inn for its first paying guests in months. The freshly decorated bridal suite was ready and waiting for the happy couple, and the wedding breakfast all prepared and waiting for the whole party.

Tom Bickleigh took his spot at the back with the newspaper reporter, Lou, who'd become a familiar face around Clove Lore in the days after the disaster and even more so now the pair were officially dating.

His brother Monty stood alone beside them, uncomfortable in his suit. Weddings weren't for him. He'd far rather be back in his chef's whites down at the pub's gleaming new chrome kitchen, where he had everything to a professional standard and shipshape. Yet, he still had the look of a man wishing he had a date by his side.

All of the builders and engineers, landscapers and decorators arrived (Minty had persuaded them to down tools for the afternoon in return for the buffet at the Siren's Tail) and the whole party stood in their rows looking up in wonder at the clear blue sky.

'Quietest Clove Lore's been in months,' someone said, and another agreed that without the noise of the machinery you could really hear the birds singing.

It really was a fine June day. The waves shushed gently against the sea wall far below the estate gardens, and the music of the shore mixed in the cool early-summer breeze with the music of the violin quartet stationed on the parterre above the camellia grove.

Magnús and Alex arrived last, having waited as long as they could for the first delivery of stock to arrive at the bookshop and, concluding the driver must be stuck on some narrow B-road above the village, they'd set off running in their smartest clothes, not easy for Alex in her high heels – the sight of which had made Magnús want to take her straight to bed and miss the wedding altogether.

The freshly stripped and varnished shelves stood ready to be stocked down at the Borrow-A-Bookshop, almost the last stage in the refurbishment, and the signal that it was coming close to the time for the pair to leave the bookshop they'd lovingly restored. They took their positions at the back of the crowd, Alex holding Magnús's hand tightly and leaning in to kiss him.

The vicar made his way down the aisle towards Elliot, giving him a friendly nod. 'They're on their way down now,' he said, clutching his order of service.

Everyone fell silent and listened to the music, the whole congregation taking a deep breath of summer and thinking how it seemed like forever since they'd last stood still with the sun on their faces with nothing whatsoever to do for a whole day but celebrate and unwind.

Emerging from the open doors and onto the parterre came Jude in a long floaty dress in sweet shades of peach. Even from this distance Elliot's heart swelled at the sight of the woman he loved. Jude had been so frantically busy all of the previous day putting the finishing touches to the wedding cake, but that was forgotten now. The fiancés smiled and waved to one another across the gardens.

Jowan was the next to step out of the house and into the sunshine. Mrs Crocombe, turning in her pew, told everyone, 'Here's the groom now!'

All heads turned to watch Jowan walk across the lawns, groomed and tailored into the very vision of a handsome husband. At his feet skipped Aldous in a bowtie to match his master's, only just having forgiven him for this morning's bath and brush because of the Double Gloucester chunks Elliot had fed to him throughout his ordeal. Elliot had taken his duties as best man very seriously indeed.

The two men shook hands at the altar and turned to face the Big House with expectant eyes. Aldous watched for his mistress too, his tail whipping against the old tiled floor.

Jowan was already smiling, his heart full, when Minty stepped carefully out over the threshold ready to receive her bouquet from Jude, her maid of honour.

Everyone heard Jowan's shaky breath as the quartet struck up a breezy wedding march and the congregation turned to watch.

Even though the chapel walls and roof were gone, it didn't matter. What better ceiling than a blue sky, and for stained glass, the glittering blue Atlantic?

Mrs Crocombe was already weeping. She had been tasked with inventing a new ice cream especially for the wedding breakfast and she'd found a willing taste tester in Bovis, who had helped her perfect her clotted cream confetti sorbet. He snuffled a little now too at the sight of his mistress advancing towards them. Mrs C. handed him a handkerchief which he took with a brave smile.

Minty swept down through the rhododendron valley, now alive with honey bees and hoverflies, and onto the gentle lawns bordered with sparse young camellias, short and waxy, putting down strong roots in fresh soil and promising a heavenly first bloom next spring.

Minty's vintage silk gown (her mother's) and strings of antique pearls (her grandmother's) looked utterly perfect against the backdrop of her beloved Big House.

Jowan's heart sang along with the music at the sight of her. Jude and Izaak had convinced Minty it was time to bring in another kind of renovations expert and that morning she'd said goodbye to her brassy blonde bob and embraced a wavy thirties style in softest platinum.

Her bouquet was all Leonid's work: simple greenery from the estate grounds, including fresh mistletoe right at its heart. Everyone admired his work as the bride arrived at the entrance to the open-air chapel.

The music ceased. Jowan reached out his hand and Minty swept towards him in a sudden rush. They met with a kiss, clasping each other tightly.

Aldous turned in circles at his master's feet, yapping and dancing, and the whole party applauded and dabbed at their eyes while the vicar raised his hands up into the blue and gathered the wedding party to speak their vows.

Chapter Thirty-Three

August in Reykjavík

Magnús's mum and dad peered around Alex as she gave them the tour.

'And this is where the bedroom will be, en suite. Um, what's that in Icelandic? You know, the bathroom will be through there too.' She kept forgetting they were fluent English-speakers, like everyone else here.

'And over here they will have a place to sit and read at night,' Magnús added enthusiastically.

'Very impressive,' said Mr Sturluson, his hands behind his back, eyes alight.

'There's even space above us to keep extra stock,' Magnús added, pointing to the loft door over their heads. Alex slipped under his arm before he brought it back down around her and pressed a proud kiss to her cheek.

They'd only taken possession of the keys that morning, though this wasn't their first time inside the little shop right in the centre of Laugavegur, Reykjavík's main street and shopping district. The family made their way back down the stairs into the empty shop.

Magnús and Alex had cooked up the plan weeks ago, when it dawned on them it was time to leave Clove Lore. They'd done all they could there.

Magnús had helped Alex oversee the sale of her house during the spring and there'd been a tussle over insurance money on the boat, but it had all come good in the end. Alex had wanted to buy the Laugavegur property outright as soon as they found it online, but Magnús had sensibly insisted they fly out to see it and Alex had been introduced to so many Sturlusons her head had swum with hard-to-pronounce names.

She'd been happy though, staying in Magnús's old bedroom, trying all the lovely food, and riding the red tourist bus all over Reykjavík while Magnús commentated on the sights.

It hadn't felt at all like home to Alex. It felt better; like an adventure. Like a new life entirely opening up to her beneath a summer sky where the sun barely dipped below the horizon in August. She couldn't wait to see what this place would be like in the winter either.

Now that they had a new flat on the street opposite their business venture, where there was always some member of Magnús's family calling in on their way past, Alex was feeling for the first time in her life the warm, grown-up assurance of standing on her own two feet, and it was wonderful – even if there were no guarantees that it was all going to work out in the long run. It didn't matter; the trying was what was important.

'Ah, the sign painter's here!' Magnús called. He bounded over the painted floorboards to the door. 'Klara! Come in!'

Magnús's parents glanced at each other, still amazed at the transformation in their son. He'd arrived from the airport like this that first day when they wanted to look at shop properties, so alive and enthusiastic, like they'd never seen him before.

They knew Alex was partly responsible, but there had been healing too. He wasn't ashamed or troubled any more. Here was their boy starting from scratch, having learned that he couldn't live his life live afraid of failing, at last understanding that there was nothing that couldn't be rebuilt in time with effort and courage.

'You've got the ideas we sent you?' he asked, and the artist put down her bag of paints and brushes and reached for her mock-up.

'Something like this? *Já?*' she asked, smoothing the paper across her lifted knee to show everyone.

'Dagalien Books, Bed and Breakfast?' Magnús's mother read aloud.

'*Dagalien?* What is that?' Magnús's father asked, and the owners of Iceland's first live-in bookshop for vacationers grinned back.

'Do you like it?' the painter asked.

'Very much!' Magnús told her and they all piled outside into the fresh, clean Icelandic summer air to watch her set up her ladders and get to work.

The sight of the new owners outside their shop attracted a good crowd of well-wishers, and Magnús had introduced Alex to scores of old friends all that afternoon.

There was still plenty of work to do, but they'd done it all before in Clove Lore, leaving for Magnús's home town only when they were satisfied with every aspect of the renovation and when Jowan and Minty had declared the place even better than before.

They'd even taken care to arrange the table display by the door with their choice of books ready for the next set of bookshop holidaymakers. They had selected books with 'flood' in their titles by Atwood and Rankin, and there was even a Noah's Ark picture book. The new booksellers couldn't fail to understand the significance of those, but some others would be a little harder to decipher, including a new paperback of the *Vinland Sagas*, translated into English, nestling beside an old, well-thumbed copy of *Mermaid Myths of Devon and Cornwall*. There were clean, second-hand copies of *Treasure Island*, and *Pride and Prejudice*, and lastly, a special copy of Mary Norton's *The Borrowers*.

When they'd finished setting them out, they'd handed Jowan his keys and cried all the way to the visitor centre car park where Tony was waiting with his Uber and effusive hugs. He'd even insisted on taking a selfie with them both when they'd arrived at the airport.

It all seemed like a lovely, slightly crazy dream now, looking back at their six months spent rescuing the Borrow-A-Bookshop, as well as rescuing themselves at the same time.

'So, what is it?' Jón asked when he dropped by to cover the story for the local paper where he worked, and Magnús and Alex excitedly filled him in on their business plan.

'People from anywhere in the world can come and work here?' Jón asked. 'Just like the English place you went to?'

'Exactly,' Magnús told him. 'Only we'll work here too. We'll oversee the whole thing and help sell the books and make the coffees and Cornish pasties and crispy cakes, that kind of thing.'

'And there'll be sofas in the windows so shoppers can sit and eat and read,' Alex told Jón, watching him take down pencil notes in Icelandic.

'But you're gonna work yourself to death again?' Jón asked, letting the pencil stop on the page.

'*Nei!* Now we'll have the holidaymaker booksellers to help. Alex and I will leave after the lunch rush and do our own thing.'

'And we've got trips planned all over Iceland!' Alex didn't feel the need to tell him that there was also the matter of her bereavement therapy, now taking place weekly online, alongside her Icelandic lessons, which were proving very slow going but she wanted to be able to talk to the locals in their own language, if they ever let her. She'd found that as soon as anyone realised where she was from they switched to perfect English, and that made her feel utterly inadequate and desperate for her next lesson. Speaking the language certainly helped with her cooking lessons at the culinary school too, and she was learning Icelandic recipes to add to her repertoire of Cornish café classics. She had her own life here in Reykjavík and that would take her away from the bookshop holiday business sometimes, and that was exactly how she and Magnús wanted it.

'*Já!* We won't be here *all* the time,' Magnús promised his brother.

He had been careful to plan things for himself as well, setting up a reading group for locals to share their love of Icelandic authors and their books. He was looking forward to that only slightly less than all the trips he had planned with Alex in the autumn.

That wasn't all he'd planned, and the sight of his mother emerging from the shop with the white confectioner's box, followed closely by his father with the champagne bottle and paper cups reminded him it was time.

Alex was already looking at him suspiciously. 'What's this?'

The burst of song from Magnús and his family confirmed her fears. She didn't know the Icelandic words they were singing but she knew the tune, and when Magnús's mother lifted the lid to reveal a cake with her name on it, she knew for sure this was a birthday ambush.

Her protest that it wasn't her birthday for another week was met by the sound of Magnús's dad popping the cork and everyone applauding.

'Yeah, well, get used to it,' Magnús told her as he unstacked the paper cups. 'You've years of missed birthday celebrations to catch up on. This is only the first; next week, we'll do it all again at our apartment-warming party. OK?'

'Who wants cake?' called out Mrs Sturluson, wielding a knife, and the little group gathered round for a slice. As they were being handed round in napkins, Jón carried on with his interview for the paper.

'And if things go wrong this time?' he asked, gently.

Magnús knew why Jón was asking. So did Alex. 'They might,' Magnús said, shrugging. 'With this business model and in this district, I can't see that happening, but still they might. And that's OK.'

'Things we can't plan for will still happen,' Alex added, before accepting her slice of cake with a practised '*takk fyrir*'. 'And they'll hurt too, no doubt, but the going wrong is never the end. There's always the chance of starting again, if you're brave enough.' She squeezed her arm around Magnús's back. 'It's only the end of the story when everyone's happy.'

'OK,' Jón said, smiling, before hugging his brother and his remarkable new English girlfriend, and they all turned to watch the sign artist climb down her ladder. Above the shop doorway, resplendent in gold script, were blazoned the words: '*Dagalien Books, Bed and Breakfast,*' and below it in bold black lettering: 'Lestu, borðaðu, elskaðu, dreymdu.'

'Read, Eat, Love, Dream,' Alex said, smiling up at their new premises, her head leaning against Magnús's as Jón raised his camera and captured the scene for his paper's front page.

Epilogue

Two and a half thousand kilometres south of Reykjavík, a sweet, summer-warmed breeze blew Downalong, making the sails on the little girl's windmill spin fast upon its pin.

'Careful!' her mother warned. 'Nobody told me it would be this steep.'

Excited tourists tramped past them, gripping the fence posts and exclaiming to one another what a lovely day it was. Some trundled cases behind them, heading for the Siren's Tail and a few nights' dinner, bed and breakfast by the Atlantic, others carried crabbing nets and buckets, looking forward to dropping bait over the sea wall all afternoon.

'Can we get an ice cream, Mum? Please!' the child asked in an urgent tone, having spotted the bright flag of Mrs Crocombe's Ice Cream Parlour lifting gently against a blue sky.

There was a decent queue outside. That meant the ice cream must be good. But her mother was looking at the GPS on her phone and turning this way and that.

'Let me concentrate, it must be here somewhere.'

'There's only up or down, Mum,' the girl reminded her. 'Is this it?'

'Hah! I suppose it must be.'

Between two dazzlingly white, freshly painted cottages there was a sharp turning to the right. The sounds of drilling and hammering resounded within the buildings on either side as they passed between them. Evidently the work of restoring Clove Lore continued even eight months after the world-famous flood.

The young woman dragged the case along behind them and the child shouldered her rucksack – which was stuffed to bursting with her treasures – as though she was used to carrying her life on her back.

They made their way through the passage, past the old sleds leaning against the painted masonry on either side of them. Entering the little square, the girl stumbled on the cobbles, which were freshly laid out in swirling patterns like a mermaid's scales set in sandy-coloured concrete.

The paint smell, which was strong throughout the whole village, was especially strong here and it mixed with the scent of cut grass and warm soil and something good cooking way down at the pub on the harbour wall.

The woman set down her case and took in the squat little bookshop from its stone steps to its conical roof, squint like a wizard's hat.

'Bookshop! Bookshop!' the child cried, running around the palm tree in its big terracotta planter standing at the centre of the square with its cracks visibly repaired with silvery mortar.

The child dodged in and out of the new tables and chairs of sky-blue metal (which matched the sky-blue shop door perfectly), set out in little clusters all over the cobbles as though the owners meant this to be an outdoor café or some kind of meeting place.

Overhead were strung white bulbs criss-crossing the square, and even higher above circled the gulls watching the latest arrivals in Clove Lore and laughing on the wing.

The woman tried not to think too much about how lovely it would be to sit there on a late summer evening and drink cold wine. She'd be far too busy for that.

'Mind the paint, I think the door's wet,' she told the girl as she found the key in the jacket of her preppy blazer, pushed up her glasses, then slipped the key into the lock.

'First thing we'll do is install the code lock, do away with the need for keys,' she said to herself as the door swung open.

The little girl shoved past her mum's legs to get inside first.

'Woah!' Her windmill was immediately discarded on the freshly sanded and varnished floorboards.

The woman cast her eyes around the bookshop. Empty shelves stood like sentries along the walls, interspersed here and there with brightly coloured vintage armchairs and little reading nooks. Dotted about were old vases filled with dried summer flowers in faded pastels. At the head of each shelf stack was a sign with words painted in curling gold script.

'Bi-ology, gen-rul fiction, children's books!' The girl squealed in delight at discovering what would soon be the children's corner below the curling staircase of gleaming black iron, also from its glossy sheen, the mum guessed, freshly painted.

Throwing herself across two patchwork beanbags the girl shrieked, kicking happily, before lifting the lid off one of the many cardboard crates shoved under the stairs – matching the others piled all around the shop – and found to her glee it was filled to the very top with picture books and board books and chapter books, all bright and inviting.

'Gently, they're not for us. They're for the customers.'

'What customers?' The girl walked her feet all the way round to the other side of the beanbag so her back was turned upon her mum and she huddled over a pop-up *Beauty and the Beast*.

With brogues clacking on the shiny floor, her mother dodged yet more boxes to peer through a low door into a white café with lace curtains at the windows and red-and-white checked tablecloths and red tomato-shaped squeezy bottles on each of the tables. Framed on the wall by the counter was a handwritten recipe for 'Mum's Deluxe Chocolate Crispy Squares'.

Turning for the shop once more, she stepped towards the table by the door which was set out with a display of books, the only unboxed books in the whole place. There was a handwritten note.

It read, 'Dear Joy, the village's first Digital Nomad! Welcome to Borrow-A-Bookshop. Everything is ready for your stay. The paint is (just) dry so you don't have to worry about smudges. Good luck installing all the new shop tech and cataloguing the stock! Who knows, maybe you'll enjoy a bit of bookselling too! Happy (working) holiday. Love, Magnús and Alex, the last Borrowers. x'

She had the feeling digital nomads were a new concept at Clove Lore and hoped she wasn't going to attract much excitement or attention from the local volunteers who she'd heard about from Jude Crawley, the woman who'd sorted out her contract.

She must be the first visitor actually being *paid* to stay here, she realised. She'd soon bring the place into the new century with a decent sales point and comms devices and then she'd get out of here and onto her next job, which, she recalled, was in Lisbon, then the next one was... London? Or was it the Southampton job after that? Not to worry, her diary had all the details and flight information. These jobs all just blurred into one another after so long on the road as an itinerant IT expert.

She looked again at the note. God, she certainly hoped nobody expected her to actually sell any of these books!

Joy took a deep breath and looked over the titles on the table. She instantly understood the relevance of some of them; books referencing floods. The flood was the reason she was here, after all. The reason she was being paid to stay here for two weeks and install the new tills, entry system, security cameras, and all the rest of it. The village were paying her wages out of their recovery fund. Jowan de Marisco Clove-Congreve had said as much in his email back when she asked for more information about the job.

The other books in the display she couldn't account for quite so easily. Something called the *Vinland Sagas*, books about mermaid myths, *Treasure Island*, she supposed because they were by the sea. Her eye fell upon the copy of *The Borrowers* with its intriguing cover showing tiny human-like people peering through a mouse hole at a giant world beyond the wainscoting. There was a note card on top of the book which read, 'This one is a gift from Borrow-A-Bookshop to our littlest Borrower yet. For Radia Pearl, happy holidays!'

Joy turned with the book in her hand. 'They've left a gift for you. That's a first!'

Radia raced towards her and without even checking to see what kind of story it was, clutched the book to her chest. 'I told you this one was going to be different! Like a real holiday!'

'No Rads, it's just work.'

'But we'll read books together and we'll go to the beach?'

'Of course we will.'

'And we'll have ice cream every day for breakfast.'

'*Hmm*, not sure about that one.'

'And maybe we can stay longer this time?' She already knew what her mother was going to say before she heard the words.

'Just a couple of weeks then we move on, OK? Just like all the other jobs.'

Radia Pearl, however, already sensed what her wayfaring mother was too world weary and restless to grasp: that Clove Lore really was different to all the other places they'd stopped at.

A whole summer of adventure and possibilities were waiting for the pair of them, only they'd have to cram it into two short weeks.

Soon they'd know the magic Clove Lore can do, but for now they set about unpacking, looking wistfully at yet another strange bed in yet another strange place, Radia wondering if her mother would ever be happy enough in any of the corners of the world her work dragged them to, to stay put for a bit.

Meanwhile, all over Clove Lore, the hard work of clearing away all signs of the one-hundred-year storm continued, a storm that could have taken so much from the Devonshire harbour village, but which had, in fact, opened up new possibilities and new futures as yet not fully realised by the people lucky enough to live here.

A letter from Kiley Dunbar

Hello, lovely readers,

This is the bit where I thank you for picking up my book and I ask you to please think about writing a review online, especially if you enjoyed it! Reviews help readers find my books and make a huge difference to me as a relatively new author.

This is my seventh book and I *loved* writing it, probably more than any I've written so far. I asked myself why that was and can only account for it by looking at the world around us.

Things are desperately worrying and frightening out there for so many people. There's a lot to be said for escaping into comforting stories, and that's exactly what I did over the winter of 21/22 when writing *Christmas at the Borrow a Bookshop*. That's why you'll find there's so much comfort food being consumed (pasties, posh milkshakes and chocolate cereal squares, anyone?) and so many Christmas lights shining and hearth fires crackling in this tale. Get cosy, grab something nice to eat and enjoy the break from real life, just for a while.

All my books end with Happy Ever Afters, but in this story I wanted to write a romance where the protagonists like each other from the beginning. I simply did not have it in me to set these two people against each other, warring and bickering, and decided instead to have Magnús and

Alex find each other completely delightful from day one. The story centres upon them teaming up early on and facing their problems together.

We've all learned a lot recently about how much we need the support of others to get through stormy times. I hope Magnús and Alex's gentle storyline is soothing and uplifting. If you've read book one, *The Borrow a Bookshop Holiday* (Hera Canelo, 2021), you'll want to know how Elliot and Jude are getting on and you'll be pleased to see they're as adorable as ever. I hope you like finding out how Minty's faring as her fortunes decline. Luckily she has someone special in her corner too. Of course, there's plenty of drama, especially when my favourite bookshop comes under threat!

I was mindful when writing this story of the many, many people across the world who have lived through flash floods in recent years, and I was especially cognisant of the feelings of residents of Boscastle who saw a flood very much like Clove Lore's rip through their homes and businesses in 2004. I'm always struck by the persistence of hope and the desire to help others that accompanies devastation. After Boscastle flooded the residents were inundated with generous donations and offers of help, and I borrowed that kindness for Clove Lore's storyline. Ultimately, this is a book about finding the strength to carry on and holding on to hope for a brighter future.

If you're looking for Clove Lore or the Devonshire bookshop you can borrow I have to let you know it's all made up, but the steep street, harbour and waterfall of my fictional village do look a wee bit like beautiful Clovelly. If you're lucky enough to visit there any time soon, do be sure to tag me in your holiday snaps! I miss the place so much. There is a real and historic donkey stables in Clovelly too (though my quirky Clove Lore donkey sanctuary is *not a bit* like the real place), which you can support with online donations and donkey adoptions.

Now for the Thank Yous.

I have my own wee support network here around my writing desk. Nic, Robin, Iris, and Mouse, thank you for loving me. You keep me going. I love you so, so much.

Keshini Naidoo, my brilliant editor, is always the first person to read these stories and I'm so grateful for her wisdom, talent and collaboration. Jennie Ayres too, carefully edited this book, and Vicki McKay proof read it and spotted some right clangers! Danielle O'Brien works so hard behind the scenes at Hera too. Thank you, all!

An especial thank you goes to the generous and knowledgeable Freyzi who helped correct my Icelandic. Any mistakes that remain are my own fault entirely.

Vicky and Lisa give me daily doses of strength and encouragement, as do all my writing friends met online and in the Romantic Novelists' Association.

Thank you to YOU, amazing readers, for all of your support and kindness. I love receiving your letters and messages, especially when something in my stories has given you a bit of encouragement or comfort and you write to let me know. That means the world to me.

Book bloggers and reviewers make the book world go round and are a vital part of my author story. Thank you so much for taking the time to read my work and spreading the book love. I appreciate you!

You can find me on The Kiley Dunbar Author Facebook Page. I also have a quarterly newsletter full of bookish gossip, exclusive content and giveaways. You can sign up on my website at www.kileydunbar.co.uk.

I'll keep on writing, always trying to do my best with your support.

See you all in spring 2023 for the third instalment in the *Borrow a Bookshop* series.

Love, Kiley x